FATAL CUT

A Selection of Recent Titles by Christine Green

Featuring Kate Kinsella

FATAL CUT

Christine Green

This first world edition published in Great Britain 1999 by
SEVERN HOUSE PUBLISHERS LTD of
9–15 High Street, Sutton, Surrey SM1 1DF.
This title first published in the U.S.A. 1999 by
SEVERN HOUSE PUBLISHERS INC of
595 Madison Avenue, New York, N.Y. 10022.

British Library Cataloguing in Publication Data

Green, Christine, 1944-
  Fatal cut
  1. Detective and mystery stories
  I. Title
  823.9'14 [F]

  ISBN 0 7278 5438 0

Typeset by Palimpsest Book Production Ltd
Polmont, Stirlingshire, Scotland.
Printed and bound in Great Britain by
MPG Books Ltd, Bodmin, Cornwall.

One

The couple, firmly entwined around each other, moved as one up the garden towards the front door. Only moonlight guided their way and on arriving at the front porch, they wedged themselves into a corner as if trying to escape from the moon's view.

"This is bloody ridiculous, Jan. Why do we have to put up with it?"

Jan was about to answer sharply but Mike had already started kissing her. Just lately, they argued often. Jan tried to blame herself but it wasn't really anyone's fault – it was merely circumstances.

Mike's hands were on her breasts now but not in an interested way, they were simply placed there, like feet on a footrest.

"How much longer, Jan?" he asked.

Jan kissed his lips and murmured, "You can't blame Denise for everything."

"If the bitch wasn't around, we could be together."

"We will one day, I promise," she whispered in his ear. Then, just as she added, "I love you," a light snapped on above their heads.

"I swear to God that woman's a witch – she's got ultra-sensitive hearing," said Mike loudly.

"Sh . . .ush," murmured Jan. "She'll hear you."

"I don't give a toss. You know that."

"I'd better go in."

Mike lifted her chin with one finger and stared into her soft hazel eyes. "We've got to do something, sweetheart. We can't let your sister ruin our lives."

"We can't talk about it now, Mike." She tried to look away but he held her gently by the back of her hair, forcing her to hold his gaze.

"There never is a right time for you, is there? The old crone puts her poison in and you swallow it."

"That's not true Mike, I don't listen half the time. She goes on and on but I switch off."

Mike moved away, stepped outside of the porch and gazed up at the leaded window from where the shaft of light came. He was positive he saw the curtain twitch.

"There's got to be a way," he said quietly, as though thinking aloud.

Jan fumbled in her pocket for her keys. As usual after an evening with Mike, she felt a sense of desolation when they parted, but she tried not to show it. "Goodnight Mike," she whispered.

He kissed her cool cheek. "See you soon, sweetheart."

Jan opened the front door and watched as Mike drove away, then she called out to her sister, "I'm home, Denise."

Denise stood at the top of the stairs wearing a navy blue towelling robe and matching slippers. Her curly permed hair looked black in the dim light and her thin face was in shadows, her eyes seeming sunken behind heavy dark brows.

"Has he gone?" she asked.

"Of course he's gone – you heard him drive away." Jan hung her coat on the hook by the door and Denise descended the stairs saying, "I'll make us a hot drink, then."

In the tiny kitchen, Jan sat down and watched her sister make cocoa – not the instant sort, but proper cocoa. Being

2

'proper' was one of Denise's main preoccupations and her ideas on being 'proper' ranged from marriage to using tea-leaves instead of tea bags. Denise had fixed ideas on most things, ideas planted while their mother lived, and fully propagated since her death six months previously. Occasionally, Jan thought her own sister had somehow transmuted into their mother. She knew it was fanciful, but Denise had always shared their mother's traits. It was only now that Jan was beginning to notice the way Denise had changed, and the physical differences between the sisters as they grew older seemed more marked. Janine's colouring was fairer, her face rounder. Age seemed to have hardened Denise's face, whereas Jan felt more attractive now than she had in her twenties. Mike thought she was very pretty; he said her full lips and long eyelashes were her best features.

"I was thinking," said Denise, as she handed Jan a mug of cocoa. Jan waited, hoping that changes to the cottage were being considered. They had argued for some time about the need to make improvements, but Denise had resisted all suggestions. "I was thinking," repeated Denise, "about Mother's room."

"I'm so glad," said Jan swiftly. "It's been on my mind. We do need to clear it."

Denise scowled, her dark brows almost knitting together like warring caterpillars. "I wasn't thinking of clearing it. I was planning to make it my room."

"Whatever for?"

"It's larger, for one thing. For another, I think Mother would have liked me to take over her room."

Jan's hand trembled slightly and a little of the cocoa split on the white tablecloth, the brown stain spreading rapidly.

"Now look what you've done! That was clean on today."

"It's only a Formica table. Do we really need a table-cloth?"

Denise, snatching up the mugs, yanked the tablecloth off. "I do wish you wouldn't argue with me."

"I'm not arguing."

Denise stared at her for a moment. "Now Mother's gone and I'm the eldest, I feel responsible for you."

"What's that got to do with having a tablecloth?"

Denise almost smiled but not quite, her thin lips merely twitched slightly. "You seem to resent the fact that I want to keep things as they are."

Jan leant over and touched her sister's arm. "Mother's gone. We can do as we please."

"Oh yes. You want to please yourself. Mother wasn't even cold in her grave and you'd taken up with . . . him."

"His name is Mike. I wish you'd call him that."

"I heard something at work today," said Denise.

Jan felt a spidery touch of dread flicker across the back of her neck. She knew, only too well, that this was her sister's prelude to some nasty piece of office gossip or, even worse, something personal. "Did you?" asked Jan, trying to feign a calm she didn't feel.

Denise's dark eyes shone brightly as though spite itself excited her. "Someone saw your beloved boyfriend leaving his wife's house yesterday morning."

"Ex-wife, Denise. He's been divorced for four years."

Denise leant forward across the narrow table, close enough for Jan to see the crow's feet around her eyes and the fine lines around her downturned lips. She looked older than her forty-two years. "Not in the eyes of God, Janine," she said. " 'Till death do us part,' as it says in the marriage service."

"I don't believe in God, as you well know, and I knew about that visit. He's having trouble with the Child Support Agency."

Denise banged her mug on the table. "When are you going to see sense? The man's a loser. You deserve better than him. You're quite pretty, you've got a good figure. You could have anyone."

"I don't want anyone. I want Mike. I love him, and one day we'll be together."

"You won't, you know. He'll go back to his wife. I know he's told people he still thinks she's a lovely woman."

"You're a liar, Denise. There's as much chance of Mike returning to his wife as there is of our father walking through the door now."

Denise's mouth tightened into a thin, angry line, her shoulders stiffened and her fingers grasped at her towelling robe as if she were squeezing flesh itself. "Don't you dare mention him," she said. "You know how much it upsets me."

Of course Jan knew that, and it was one way of getting her own back. Any mention of their father created an angry, sometimes tearful, response in Denise. Jan hardly remembered him at all. She'd been five years old when he left, Denise had been fifteen. There were no photos of him in the house, but occasionally Jan had seen men in the street who seemed to awaken long lost memories and she followed them to get a better look. Usually they were the wrong age-group, or quite simply didn't match up to the vague, shadowy impression she had of him. Of one thing Jan was certain, he must have been a saint to put up with her mother, Maggie. Denise, however, hated him with a passion, even more so since Maggie had died. It was almost as if Denise felt she was the abandoned wife.

"Anyway, we were talking about your used-car salesman," continued Denise. "He's just as bad as our so-called father."

Jan struggled to keep her temper. "Mike's a decent man,

whatever you say about him. He loves his children, and the fact that he and his wife got divorced wasn't his fault alone. They simply got married too young."

"Huh! No doubt she was pregnant at the time. There'll be no babies for you, of course. You'll never be able to afford them."

The words hit Jan like a blow to the stomach, her eyes filled with tears and for a moment she felt unable to breathe. This was the first time Denise had mentioned babies and at thirty-two, Jan longed for a baby, for Mike's baby. And for once, what Denise had said was probably true. Mike already had three children to support, and since his wife had lost her job, she'd been forced to go on Income Support and therefore the CSA had become involved. Mike lived in a tiny flat above the car showrooms and his basic salary was pitiful.

"I don't want to upset you Janine, but you have to face facts. Neither of us is getting any younger and I can see you're only going to get hurt, just as I did."

Jan bit her lip in an effort not to say something really spiteful. Years back, her sister had been quite attractive, but her boyfriends had never lasted longer than two or three weeks and Jan doubted she had ever been in love. Denise had been far closer to Maggie and Jan suspected they'd shared secrets. But Jan's boyfriends weren't secrets. She'd brought them home, and subsequently their jobs, characters, looks, politics and religious inclinations were so critically analysed that it wasn't surprising Denise found each one of them lacking. Jan had learnt by hearing Maggie and Denise shredding personalities never to bring friends home, male or female.

"I'm going to bed," said Jan abruptly.

"All right dear," Denise smiled. "I've put a hot-water bottle in your bed and the fire's on."

Jan walked into the dimly lit hall with its faded green

walls that had been that colour ever since she'd been at school, up the stairs that creaked, for some reason, on alternate footsteps, and into her bedroom. There, in her room, the smell of damp was the strongest. And she loved that smell. What she didn't enjoy was the chill that surrounded her. The cottage may have been picture-book material on a summer's day with roses around the porch and a dove perched on the thatched roof, but the small windows caused a dim interior and the winter cold seemed to permeate the walls. The two-bar electric fire lit the room rather than heated it, and Jan shivered as she undressed. She stepped into fleecy-lined jogging bottoms and a tee-shirt and quickly got into bed. Once she'd warmed up she'd clean her teeth, she decided, and she wanted to avoid Denise on her way to the bathroom. Tonight's confrontation had upset her, confirming that the relationship with her sister was worsening and if it wasn't for Mike, she would be making plans to leave Fowchester.

She wiggled the hot-water bottle between her toes and stared at the room she'd decorated many years before. She'd been particularly proud of the wallpaper with its forget-me-nots and cornflowers. Now it was as faded as the rest of the house and she knew she had to escape again. Only Denise was holding her back.

Two

Mike glanced at his watch as he drove towards the town. It was eleven p.m. He felt utterly depressed. He dreaded going back to his empty flat and yet he couldn't call in again on Lyn and the kids – could he?

As he neared the town he decided that if the lights were still on, he'd 'pop in'. He'd been doing that a lot recently. Strange how in some ways, since the divorce, he'd felt more at home there. Lyn seemed more confident now, less needy and, he had to admit, more attractive. Even his children seemed less of a burden, more of a treasure.

The lights were on, and somehow it seemed completely natural to call in as he passed.

"Twice this week," said Lyn as she let him in. "You'll have the neighbours talking." She was wearing a white mohair sweater and a skirt well above her knees, her short blond hair was slightly tousled and her mascara had smudged.

"You look great," he said, and meant it.

"One of the kids is ill," she said, inclining her head stairwards.

"Which one?"

"Guess."

"Daniel."

Daniel, who'd just started school, managed to catch every cold, virus, stomach infection, throat infection and fungal infection going.

"What's he got this time?"

"It's a nasty cough."

As if on cue, Daniel began to cough. The sound trailing downstairs signalled a dry, rasping cough that really alarmed Mike. "I'll go up and see him," he said, rushing upstairs two at a time and feeling an anxiety that was akin to being stabbed in his own chest.

In the bedroom, lit by the light from the hall, he saw his son, sitting upright, wide-eyed and anxious. Mike flicked on the light and could see the signs that Daniel had a raging temperature. His face was flushed, sweat beaded his forehead and his frightened blue eyes, dulled with tiredness and fever, registered no sense of knowing Mike was there in the room.

"Lyn!" Mike yelled. "Come up here."

"I'm coming. Don't panic," she called back.

The sound of her footsteps on the stairs reassured Mike a little and Daniel, as if sensing something, struggled to push his Postman Pat duvet from his chest as another spasm of coughing started. His small face grimaced, his chubby chest now showing a straining rib cage, still unaware that his father stood watching.

At the sight of his mother, Daniel wailed, "Mum . . . eee!" and stretched out his arms towards her.

"Mike, put the kettle on."

"This is no time for tea," snapped Mike.

Lyn sat on the bed, threw back the duvet completely and cradled her son. "He's got croup," she explained. "The steam eases his chest so we need to keep the kettle boiling in here. I'll stay with him."

"I think he needs a doctor," said Mike evenly, trying to remain calm when every nerve felt taut as elastic.

"He's on antibiotics. He needs steam. He's been like this before."

9

Mike felt a pang of guilt. He hadn't known, and Lyn obviously carried that burden alone.

Three hours later and several kettles kept on the boil, the room was Turkish bath damp, and although Daniel was still coughing, the dry, rasping, exhausting nature of it had changed. He lay back on his pillow, his face pink now, damp hair stuck to his forehead but sleeping peacefully.

Mike and Lyn, exhausted but relieved and satisfied with their efforts, fell asleep on the sofa. At six-thirty Mike woke abruptly and rushed upstairs to check on Daniel. A wave of pure relief swept over him as he watched his son now sleeping peacefully. He kissed him, brushed the damp hair from his forehead and then went downstairs to watch, for a few moments, Lyn's sleeping form, curled up on the sofa as peacefully as their son. He left the house resolving never again to forsake his children.

As he started the car, he noticed a curtain twitch next door. He smiled, not caring. He was sure Janine would understand if she found out. If she didn't understand, Mike couldn't decide whether it mattered or not.

Three

O n Saturday morning, Denise woke early. It was barely five-thirty, still dark and the room felt, she thought, as cold as a tomb. It had been her first night in her mother's room. It was larger and some would say gloomier, but it made Denise feel closer to her mother, and that was all that mattered to her at the moment.

Of course Janine could never understand. She'd not spent all her life in this cottage, hadn't worried and fretted about Maggie, but had gallivanted off to London periodically, only coming back when she was bored or when the money ran out or when some man had dumped her.

As for Mike, Denise had seen him from a distance a few times and thought he looked shifty, with his black greasy hair and slightly rounded shoulders. And, of course, she knew he was a liar and a cheat.

She lay in the warmth of her mother's bed, covered her face slightly with the eiderdown to avoid the cold air, and thought about how she could either expose Mike for the liar he was, or persuade Janine that only misery could result from their relationship. Her sister could be stubborn and Denise realised she would have to be a little devious. Maybe an anonymous letter would help.

Just after six, Denise washed and dressed and as she brushed her hair with her mother's hairbrush, she noticed how frizzy and dry her hair had become. She did have an appointment at the salon today. She'd have her beauty treatments, then the hairdo but just lately she'd thought Marcus had lost his touch with her hair and she'd have to tell him. His lifestyle wasn't something she approved of, but she did like listening to the gossip and her hearing was perfect. If she concentrated hard, she could hear interesting snippets of people's lives and somehow it compensated for her own rather quiet life.

She smiled, congratulating herself on her powers of observation and her understanding of human nature. Mandy Willens, the beautician, was a case in point. She was hiding something. When Denise had been in the salon last month, Mandy had been positively surly, and she'd been obliged to report her.

She checked her diary for the exact time. Marcus was booked for between one-thirty and two. He could never be that precise, but usually Denise didn't mind. Andrew the junior would bring her coffee and she could sit and relax, watch and listen, feeling wonderful after her manicure, pedicure, steam bath, followed by a shower and a massage. Really, the hairdo afterwards was the icing on the cake. Those two to three hours she spent in Le Salon once a month were a treat she looked forward to for the whole week before. It was only rarely that anyone ever touched her, and she so enjoyed being pampered.

Janine walked into the kitchen at seven-thirty. "You look tired," said Denise. "I've cooked you some kippers."

"I'm not hungry. And you know I hate kippers. I'll just have tea."

"I'll make a fresh pot," said Denise, anxious to please, wanting to be on better terms.

Janine shrugged and began pouring herself a cup from the teapot. It was half cold but she didn't care. She had to be at work by eight-thirty and she wanted to be out of Denise's presence as soon as possible.

"I've got an appointment at the salon for twelve," said Denise. "I should be out by two to half-past. What about us having a late lunch in town?"

"I'm having lunch with Mike. I'm meeting him after I finish work."

"Well of course, he has to come first."

Sarcastic bitch, thought Jan, but she didn't reply.

"I suppose you're seeing him tonight," said Denise, as she stared at the uneaten kippers, wondering why she'd forgotten Janine didn't like them.

"I always see him on Saturday night."

Denise's mouth tightened. "I'll see you later, then. I'm cooking steak and kidney pie tonight. I don't suppose you'll be going out to eat."

Of course, the inference there was that Mike couldn't afford to take her out to eat and the truth hurt. Jan glared at her sister. "Why don't you . . . get a life instead of interfering in mine?"

As she walked out of the kitchen, she heard her sister say in a whiny voice, "I don't mean you any harm."

Jan was still furious as she scraped the frost from her car windscreen, but when her old Mini started first time, it cheered her a little. Mike was good to her and for her in so many ways, she knew they could work things out. If only they could afford to move in together. Jan earned very little as a dentist's receptionist and Denise took quite a large part of that, although Jan was convinced she didn't really need the money. The house was in Denise's name and Jan was convinced there was money, too. Maggie had distrusted banks and took to hiding money around the house in her latter years. Although Jan had searched, she'd never found any.

Parking the car in the staff car park, Jan noticed she was the first to arrive – as usual. Not that she minded. Without distraction, she could make herself tea and then, at her leisure, take messages from the answering machine and open the post. By nine, she had easily done that and from then she manned the phone.

The dentist, Henri De Souza, arrived at nine-fifteen every Saturday to see emergency patients only. They closed at one, and usually it wasn't too busy, but the other two dentists in Fowchester had decided to 'go private', so more patients were joining the practice and soon the list would have to be closed. Although Henri was an excellent dentist, he was rather dour, and his appearance seemed to make nervous patients rather more so. He was well over six feet tall and incredibly thin, with a gaunt face, chiselled features and rather sad brown eyes. His closely cropped black hair gave him a convict-like appearance and it was only after several visits that patients warmed to him.

By nine-fifteen he still hadn't arrived. Angie the dental nurse arrived, and busied herself in the surgery as Jan checked in three very unhappy dental emergencies who sat flicking through magazines with nervous, unseeing eyes.

Henri, when he finally arrived at nine-thirty-five, looked slightly flustered, nodded at Jan, frowned at the waiting patients and walked briskly into his surgery. A few moments later, Angie called in the first patient. The morning had begun.

For Mike, the morning had begun more memorably. He'd sold a car. His first sale in over a week and so hassle-free. The customer had viewed the upholstery, looked under the bonnet, kicked the tyres, offered a price which Mike easily refused and had then abruptly, and rather oddly, given in and agreed the asking price.

Mike had finished the paperwork, the customer had paid cash and it seemed they both felt more than satisfied. With the commission, he could afford to take Jan out tonight and buy something for the kids. He felt today was going to be a good day.

Denise had bleached the kitchen tiles, done some ironing, vacuumed the lounge carpet and prepared the pie, all before eleven. She'd have a talk with Janine tonight, she decided. After all, she was her only relative, and all the more precious since Mother had died. She didn't want Janine to leave Fowchester again, so she would have to plan a campaign to encourage Mike to leave instead. Something dramatic that would cause Janine to really turn against him. After all, it was for her own good.

At eleven-fifteen precisely, Denise left the cottage. No one saw her, for they had no close neighbours. The town was a good five miles distant and, although Denise had a car, she preferred not to drive to town on a Saturday when parking was a nightmare. Anyway, she knew the bus times so it wasn't a problem.

Today it was bright and crisp and she was used to the cold. En route she would decide her plan of action. It had worked before, with unworthy people, and it could work again.

Four

O n Saturday afternoon at Fowchester Police Station, Chief Inspector Connor O'Neill and Detective Sergeant Fran Wilson sat drinking coffee. They were both refugees from other forces. O'Neill had been in the Met, was Irish by parentage and inclination, and occasionally returned to his birthplace, West Kilburn. There he met a variety of relatives, drank draught Guinness until the early hours, enjoyed the 'crack', and came home again with his spirit and his accent revitalised. He was proud of being Irish and always would be.

Fran had been transferred, having 'grassed up' a violent boyfriend. O'Neill was proud of her spirit and her honesty. He wasn't so proud of working in Fowchester, sometimes he despaired of the old-fashioned set-up and the general failures. Today the computers had gone down yet again, the uniformed staff had, in large numbers, also gone down with a serious flu virus, and O'Neill and Fran had been expected to deal with matters normally dealt with by the uniformed section.

That morning, they had already dealt with two drunks kept overnight in the cells, plus two cases of domestic violence. O'Neill's sympathy appeared to be with the two men and Fran was hotly defending the women. "How can you say it was provocation, just because she complained when she got home that he hadn't done anything all day? The man was a complete waste of space. She was the breadwinner. I expect she was very stressed but that was no justification for him to pour lumpy gravy all over her head . . ."

"Or for her to retaliate by punching him on the nose," interrupted O'Neill, smiling. "And as for the other woman, she was a total harridan. I'm not surprised they chose saucepans at dawn."

"Domestic violence isn't funny . . . sir."

"I didn't say it was, Fran. And don't call me sir. Somehow, you always make it sound like an insult. Most domestic violence isn't funny but women these days aren't always hapless victims. Sometimes it's the men, though of course they can't be admitting it until they really are at the end of their tether. They're ashamed, I suppose . . ."

"And women aren't?"

O'Neill stared at his DS. Her dark eyes were bright with irritation and he knew she felt right was on her side. She was a young woman with courage and integrity, but sometimes he felt she was . . . naïve. For her there were no shades of grey. He occasionally wondered whether she refused to see him socially simply because she considered such a relationship improper. Or was it because she worried that if it became known they were an item, it might interfere with her chances of promotion? Either way, O'Neill knew he would continue not only to hanker after her, but also to keep trying.

"Boss?" queried Fran.

O'Neill vaguely remembered the question and was just about to answer when a police sergeant, Frank Miller, appeared suddenly at their table. "Just heard, sir, there's a suspicious death at the hairdressers in Lime Avenue."

"How suspicious?" asked O'Neill.

"Murder or as near as damn it, sir. Ninety-nine point nine nine recurring."

"We're on our way, sergeant. Wilson – grab the bag."

As Fran left the canteen to collect the murder bag, O'Neill turned to the sergeant. "Does Superintendent Ringstead know?"

Miller nodded. "Just said to get it sorted and quickly, sir. He also mentioned that money was tight and because of the flu epidemic, don't expect any help from other divisions."

O'Neill nodded. "To be sure, sergeant, the man is consistent."

Ten minutes later O'Neill and Fran were in Lime Avenue and so, it seemed, were half the population of Fowchester. Small groups of people stood outside the salon and the mood, although sombre, was permeated by a general air of muted excitement. Fran could hear the whispers going round, "What's happened?", "Who is it?", "What's going on?", as they watched the police cordon off the frontage of *Le Salon*. A chilly wind blew the ribbons of yellow and black, and a child's piercing scream seemed strangely appropriate.

"Move them on constable, move them out," said O'Neill briskly to a young PC whose nose was red with cold and who seemed mesmerised by the situation. O'Neill rushed ahead of her, but Fran needed a little time to prepare herself. She'd found, in the past, the feeling of going to a murder scene was entirely different to going on a raid or into a disturbance – then you could afford to be a little excited, a little hyped up. A murder inquiry in contrast needed less adrenalin and more detached coolness. Fran tried to cultivate that by taking in the surroundings, slowly.

She watched for a few minutes as the bystanders moved reluctantly to the further end of Lime Avenue. The afternoon sky was already darkening with bulky grey clouds forming, and their ominous appearance seemed just as appropriate as the scream of the child, who still screamed but now from the inside of one of the houses. The sound reverberated eerily in the otherwise strangely quiet street.

Le Salon was a double bay-windowed establishment with dark pink frilly curtains swathed in the corners of the windows, pink blinds half-way down, and an assortment of fronds and potted plants occluding a view of the inside. As the door opened to a short burst of tinkling from a gold bell above, Fran was taken aback by the scene. A PC stood to the side to allow her to enter. He looked a little pale and shell-shocked, and he nodded somewhat wearily at her warrant card. To his left and not far from the door, the receptionist sat at a pine curved unit, sobbing quietly beside a potted gardenia. In the main part of the salon, four women sat in various stages of hairdressing, and their bewildered expressions were matched by that of the four members of staff who stood in a huddle, still and quiet as if in a tableau.

At that moment, it was a relief when O'Neill appeared. "Don't just stand there, DS Wilson. Come on through."

'Coming through' meant parting the beaded curtain of red and gold that hung from a white archway, with the words *'Le Beauty'* embossed in gold paint on the arch itself, and entering the inner sanctum of the salon via an open door to the right.

At first, Fran couldn't see the corpse. A drawn pink curtain shielded one corner of the room. The rest of the room was taken up with a toning table and a massage couch. O'Neill took her by the arm and pulled back the curtain. There, in a box contraption, was the corpse or at least the head of the corpse, because only the head was visible. A woman's head with dark brown eyes, bulging and wide open. Her mouth wide open too, but she couldn't have screamed because her mouth overflowed with thick white foam. Even her nostrils seeped foam as though the alien fluid came from within her. The foam, the head, the white towel encasing the neck within the coffin of the hot box bought images of decapitation, of heads on stakes. Fran couldn't take her eyes from the head but it wasn't the mouth or the nose that horrified her, it was the sheer terror in those eyes. Terror that even death couldn't obliterate.

"Fran! Stop your staring, for God's sake, or it'll send you mad." Only the sound of O'Neill's urgent voice and the feel of his arm holding hers brought Fran back to reality.

"I'm okay now," she lied. She felt slightly sick and light-headed. No other corpse she'd seen could compare with the awfulness of this one. She'd seen blood and gore, shootings and stabbings, but in their dead faces she had seen only blankness and the end of suffering. In this woman's eyes the fear seemed tangible, as though it lingered in the atmosphere, as real and as nauseating as the smell of the hair mousse. Fran just succeeded in forcing down the bile that rose in her throat.

"I've not seen anything like this," muttered O'Neill, shaking his head as though he too couldn't quite believe a murder as gruesome as this could have happened on Saturday lunchtime in Fowchester. "The poor woman," he said, glancing at her once more, murmuring a prayer and crossing himself.

He turned from the body, pulled the curtain, and stared around the beauty salon for a moment. Then, in his usual quiet calm voice, he said, "Forensic have been notified and the Scene of Crime boys are on their way with, so they promise me, the best video man around. No one, of course, can leave the premises until we've taken everyone's statement."

Somehow, the routine words had a calming effect

that made Fran respond normally. "What about the customers?" she asked. "They can't be left with their hair half cut or half permed."

"Jasus! They'll have to put up with the inconvenience."

"Boss, it's not just a question of that. Some of the substances could be harmful if left on for too long."

"Not as harmful as a lung full of mousse, but I'm taking your point. Tell the staff to be carrying on as best they can, but no one leaves until I say."

In the hairdressing section, the staff, obvious by their white trouser suits with red rose emblems on the breast pockets, still stood together either for comfort or as a show of solidarity.

"Who's the boss?" asked Fran. "I'm Detective Sergeant Fran Wilson."

A man in his early to middle forties, with neat greying hair and blue eyes, leant forward and nodded at Fran. "I'm Dale – the owner."

Fran smiled, took him by the arm, and moved him away from his staff to the reception area. It wasn't exactly private, but at least the staff couldn't hear their conversation. With notebook and pen poised she said, "Dale . . .?"

"Dale Dunbar. I can't tell you how shocked we all are. My poor staff. We've got later appointments . . . I mean, what are we going to do? I tell you, I feel like crying."

"Please don't do that, Mr Dunbar. I know this is very traumatic but you have to be in control of your staff. No one is to leave here without permission, but we want you to finish the customers you've already started."

"Well, of course we will. The show must go on, but I feel like a wet rag at the moment."

Fran listened to his voice and observed his carefully

manicured nails and hand movements, which could only be described as . . . exaggerated. She couldn't decide if he was camping it up or if this was his normal behaviour pattern. He was, she decided, very attractive in a fey sort of way, but not to women.

Fran gave him an old-fashioned look. "You can be wrung out later, Mr Dunbar, but for now please organise your staff and tell them we will want to speak to everyone in the building. That includes the customers."

"No one liked her," he muttered. "A terrible death, but no one liked her."

"We'll be asking you about that later, Mr Dunbar."

"Do call me Dale. I'm Dale to everyone."

"Fair enough . . . Dale. Just carry on please, and reassure the customers."

"Okey-dokey," replied Dale as he walked back to his row of expectant-looking staff.

Fran was about to return to the beauty salon when the door opened and the SOC team burst in, quickly followed by the police surgeon Graham Gretton, whose head was down and whose body language said, 'What the hell am I doing in this place on a Saturday afternoon?' Fran merely pointed them *en masse* to the beaded curtain under the arch and they clattered through.

It was at this moment, with blush-inducing embarrassment, she realised she didn't know the victim's name. Trying to appear casual, she approached the young constable guarding the door. "Do you know the victim's name, Officer?" she asked, as though testing him.

"I was first on the scene. I'm the beat officer in this section of town," he told her, sounding like a robot. "Her name's Denise Parks; she's a regular customer. It shook me when I saw the body . . ." He paused thoughtfully. "I've never seen a murder victim before. I suppose I'll get used to it."

Fran smiled sympathetically. "You never get used to it, and by the way, she *was* a regular customer."

In the beauty section, O'Neill looked vaguely uncomfortable surrounded by various people in white boilersuits looking frantically busy, collecting various samples. Suddenly he, O'Neill, was in the way and he felt a strong urge to tell them to hurry up and get out, but of course their job was vital and he just had to be patient.

Fran stood for a moment watching the video technician filming and noticed the doctor's vague shadow behind the pink curtain that shielded the victim.

"Be drawing a plan of the premises, will you?" said O'Neill.

"Do we need one if we have a good video?" she asked.

O'Neill sighed irritably, "Don't be arguing. I can carry a piece of paper in my pocket. I can't be doing that with a video."

Fran's drawing ability hadn't progressed much beyond junior school level and she had about as much artistic flair as her erstwhile mouse, but on a previous murder enquiry she had drawn a plan that had proved fairly useful, so she began drawing.

She'd nearly completed the main working areas and was about to investigate the rest of the building when Graham Gretton reappeared from behind the curtain. Even *he* had paled slightly. "It seems self-evident," he said, "that death was caused by suffocation. Time of death can only be related to the moment she went into the hot box. Body temperature is unreliable due to the heat of the steam."

"Nothing else?"

Shaking his head, the doctor's right eye gave its usual wink-like tic. "No, nothing, unless the slight bruising on her chin is indicative of anything other than being held there while she was suffocated. The post-mortem might show something, but I doubt if forensic will be able to glean anything from the body. She was killed in a totally helpless condition, she couldn't have kicked her assailant or scratched or fought back in anyway. She was the perfect victim. Death would have taken two minutes or so . . . at the least."

"God rest her soul," murmured O'Neill, thinking just how long two minutes could seem.

As Dr Gretton left, the video man moved into the hair-dressing area and continued filming with Fran following close behind him so that she could announce, "Please ignore the camera everyone. These shots are for police eyes only."

"Well thank goodness for that," said Dale loudly with hands on his hips. "We wouldn't want to be in the *News of the World*, would we?" An elderly customer in the middle of a perm gave a brief laugh, and for a moment there seemed to be a lifting of tension. Then she added anxiously, "We won't be kept here long, will we? My husband's ever so poorly and he'll be worried sick if I'm not home soon."

Fran walked over and knelt down next to the chair so that she didn't tower over the tiny bird-like lady with hair in small tight rollers, deep worry lines in her forehead, and a thin lower lip that had begun to tremble. "Please don't worry, Mrs . . .?"

"Mrs Hankins. Who are you, dear?"

"I'm Detective Sergeant Fran Wilson."

"Are you really, dear? You look so young . . . or perhaps it's me just getting older. All this is so upsetting, I feel all wobbly."

Fran couldn't think of a suitable response except the usual remedy – tea. "Would you like some tea, Mrs Hankins? Then I'll get someone to ask you a few questions and you'll be able to leave."

Mrs Hankins smiled gratefully. "That would be lovely dear. I don't usually come on a Saturday but I've got my daughter and son-in-law coming tomorrow, and you like to look your best, don't you?"

As Fran looked up to find a member of staff to make tea, she could hear the general rumble of discontent, "I've got to be home soon", "How long will it be?", "I'd like a cup of tea".

One of the staff, a young man of about eighteen, stepped forward. "I'll make tea," he said. Fran couldn't help noticing that he was tall, rather gangly, but good-looking with a big friendly smile, perfect teeth and disarmingly large brown eyes. "I'm Andrew – the junior."

Fran smiled. "Well, Andrew the junior, I'd be very grateful if you could supply all the customers with tea."

"Yeah," he said in a whisper, "I think they need it, otherwise they'll get 'hairsterical'."

Fran found herself smiling at him again, and felt a little guilty for having recovered her cheerfulness so quickly, but she realised that any spark of humour that lifted the mood of everyone involved at this moment was welcome.

She went to find O'Neill to relate the little joke but she could see by his face he wasn't in the mood, and anyway he was ahead of her. "Don't tell me," he said grimly. "They're getting 'hairsterical'."

"Things not going well?"

"Well – no, they are not going well. Forensic doubts if we'll get much at all. Bloody mousse canisters are all over the place."

Fran was unsure about what either to say or do next, so she stood there waiting for instruction.

"Have you got the names and addresses of all the staff?" asked O'Neill.

"Not yet boss, it's all a bit chaotic at the moment."

"Chaotic? It's a bloody nightmare. I'm telling you Fran, this case is going to be an absolute bitch."

"Or the male equivalent."

"What's that?" he asked.

"An absolute bastard."

Five

It was dark by the time they reached the Parks' cottage, and frost had begun to settle on the surrounding fields. It had taken O'Neill some time to find. He'd found the nearby hamlet easily enough but this cottage seemed an afterthought, being set back from a narrow lane of bushes and stark, moribund-looking trees.

Although the cottage was thatched and some ivy clung to the walls, it had a joyless aura, although O'Neill guessed that his mission might have prejudiced his appreciation. In some ways he was glad to have left the virtual chaos of *Le Salon*. The uniformed branch had completed the Personal Descriptive Forms – known as PDFs – as quickly and efficiently as possible, relatives had been informed of their loved ones' delay, and forensic had completed their examination of the minutiae of murder. It seemed ironic that the last person to know of the murder was the dead woman's only next of kin – her sister.

Fran shivered as they stood under the porch and she took a deep breath to steady herself. Only the hall light was on, giving the cottage an empty feel. The leaded windows downstairs reminded Fran of thick, old-fashioned bifocals and dead, unseeing eyes.

A young woman with neat features and shoulder length, biscuit-coloured hair eventually answered the knocking. She had only a slight resemblance to the dead woman, or at least in death there was little likeness.

27

"Janine Parks?" queried O'Neill.

"Yes." A puzzled frown wrinkled her forehead.

"Detective Chief Inspector O'Neill and DS Wilson – may we come in?"

"Yes, what's happened? It's not Mike, is it? He hasn't had an accident, has he? Is he all right?" Her questions merged in a nervous rush.

"It's not about Mike," said O'Neill, quietly. "Let's be going in and sitting down."

A coal fire in the first throes of life burned in the grate of the front room. It was, thought Fran, giving out as much heat as a candle. The room felt icy cold. A bulky, floral three-piece suite took up most of the floor space. Janine switched on a standard lamp with a maroon shade that cast less light than the flickering, but silent, black and white television in the corner of the room.

"We don't normally sit in here until the evening," said Janine apologetically as she switched off the TV, and then turning, stood expectantly watching O'Neill, her eyes anxious and bright.

"Sit down, Miss Parks," he said. Janine perched herself on the edge of the sofa as though far too nervous to sit back.

"I'm bringing you bad news, I'm sorry to say," said O'Neill. "This afternoon, your sister Denise . . ." he paused momentarily, struggling to find words that wouldn't sound so stark, so cruel. None came, so he continued, ". . .was found dead at the hairdressers."

Janine stared at him blankly for several seconds. Then she laughed, high-pitched and jarring. "Don't be silly. There's been a mistake. Denise is very healthy – she is . . ." She broke off as though wanting to confirm that it had all been a ghastly error.

"There *is* no mistake," said O'Neill.

Janine stared wildly, her eyes flickering from O'Neill

to Fran and back again. "I haven't seen your ID cards . . . you could be bogus . . ." O'Neill took his warrant card from his pocket.

"Oh God . . . no . . . please," Janine's eyes began to fill with tears. "Was it a heart attack?"

O'Neill shook his head. "I'm afraid it was murder."

She began to tremble, her shoulders and hands shook. "No . . . No, I can't believe it. She couldn't have . . . Not on a Saturday afternoon . . . not at the hairdressers."

O'Neill sighed inwardly. This part of the job often made him feel physically ill. Murder, like suicide, was the most incomprehensible of deaths. An obscenity when life was so fragile anyway. He knew the pain, the fear, and the guilt from his own experience, and at times like these he could barely distinguish his own remembered suffering from those to whom he imparted tragic news. Janine cried openly now and Fran sat beside her, holding her hand and providing tissues. At times like these, Fran knew there were no words of comfort, except perhaps to reassure relatives that the end came unexpectedly or painlessly, but she couldn't say that about Denise's death, so she stayed silent. Eventually, Janine's sobs subsided and were reduced to sighs and gulps. "How did it . . . happen?" she asked brokenly.

O'Neill paused. She would find out, of course, so he would have to tell her now, this minute. "She was . . . suffocated – murdered."

Janine's head shot up. "How? What happened? How could anyone be killed in the hairdressers? Who did it?"

"Try to be calm," urged O'Neill. "I'm sorry to be telling you this, but she was . . . killed . . . whilst she was having a Turkish bath."

"How?" Janine demanded.

"You'll be finding out, so I'll tell you now," he said

quietly. "Someone . . ." he swallowed hard, "suffocated her with hair mousse."

Her head slumped abruptly, and she began silently rocking backwards and forwards.

O'Neill once more felt that sickening feeling of being totally powerless, the same feeling he'd had when he'd found his wife dead in their garage.

"Is there someone we can contact for you?" asked Fran.

Janine continued rocking but she murmured, "Mike – he'll come. I want him."

"Would you like the doctor?" asked O'Neill.

She stopped rocking. "I don't want to be drugged. I'll be better when Mike's here."

"I'll ring him. What's the number?" asked Fran.

"I can't remember," she said, as she stared anxiously ahead. "My mind's blank."

"It's the shock, Janine. Where will he be?"

"At work till six. Best Motors. It's in the phone book."

In the dim hall, Fran rang Best Motors saying that Janine had asked her to ring him.

"Is it that urgent?" he asked, sounding slightly irritated. "I'm supposed to be here until six."

"Janine would like you to come to the cottage now."

"What's up? Is she ill? Who the hell are you, anyway?"

Fran told him.

"Police. Oh my God. What's happened? I'll be there as soon as I can."

"Drive carefully, sir. We'll stay with her until you get here."

While they waited for Mike, Fran made tea. By now Janine had started to shiver and O'Neill slipped a coat around her shoulders. Janine held her cup in her hands for the warmth and after a while said, "I prefer mugs, but

30

Denise likes cups. She wants everything to be the same as it was when Mother was alive."

Fran, ignoring Janine's use of the present tense, asked, "How long ago did your mother die?"

Janine thought for a moment, her head on one side, "Five months, I think, or perhaps six. July last year. She'd been ill for years."

"Did she die in hospital?"

Shaking her head, Janine said sharply, "No, of course not. At the end we both looked after her, but most of the nursing was done by Denise."

"What about her job?"

"She took unpaid leave for the last month or so. She works in a solicitor's office – a secretary."

"What about her friends?"

Janine looked thoughtful and puzzled, as though trying to hang on to the idea that there was no longer 'is' or 'does', but only 'was' and 'had' and 'once'. Eventually she said, "Well, no one ever came here. She went to church sometimes and occasionally she saw a friend, Monica, who lives just outside Fowchester."

"We'd like her address," said O'Neill, looking up from his cup. Then he added, as though talking to himself, "I haven't seen real tea leaves in years."

"Denise likes real tea, real coffee," said Janine, then realising her mistake again, added brokenly. "I shall miss her funny ways."

A sudden banging at the door caused her to jump up. "It's Mike," she announced as she ran to meet him. O'Neill, right behind her, was conscious of the fact that he needed to be there, and although an intruder on a private moment, he wanted to see and hear Mike's reaction at the time of impact. O'Neill also knew the suddenly bereaved who waited for a trusted loved one, nursed a subconscious belief that somehow their arrival meant events could be changed, that they would say 'Everything will be all right,' as their mothers had done. But they couldn't, and it wasn't.

Mike was, O'Neill guessed, about five feet ten, 180 pounds and in his late thirties. He wore a smart grey suit, white shirt, and a yellow and blue shiny tie. His dark hair was slicked back, giving it a wet look, and O'Neill noticed his rather full lips also had a somewhat wet look.

Janine had already begun sobbing into Mike's chest and Mike's expression was of total bewilderment. "What's happened? What's going on?"

"Oh Mike," she sobbed. "She's dead. She's dead."

"Who's dead? What are you talking about?"

"Denise is dead . . . she's . . ." Janine broke off with a choked gasp, as if trying to control herself.

Mike's mouth opened in surprise, and then he glanced swiftly at O'Neill, as if for confirmation. O'Neill nodded.

Mike eased himself into the cottage and closed the front door, still keeping an arm round Janine and murmuring, "There, there, calm down." He stroked the back of her neck, and gradually she began to quieten.

"Bring her through into the front room," said O'Neill. "And I'll be explaining."

O'Neill's explanation was blunt. "I'm sorry, but Denise was murdered this afternoon at the hairdressers."

Mike's lower lip trembled slightly. "Christ Almighty," he muttered. "She was a bitch . . . but murder?"

Janine, sitting beside Mike on the sofa, pulled away from him as if scalded. "Don't say that, Mike. She was my sister and she loved me."

"I know, sweetheart," he said, as he brushed the tears from her face with his hand. "Tell me all about it."

O'Neill noticed the tone of voice and noted that the 'Tell me all about it' seemed more appropriate for a girlfriend relating a row with her boss. O'Neill used the same expression to hardened criminals and was well aware it worked – occasionally.

Fran meanwhile watched Mike with interest. When he'd first walked into the room she had thought that she might have met him in the line of duty; then she remembered she'd seen him on one or two occasions on the forecourt of Best Motors. He was obviously fond of loud ties and hair gel and Fran wasn't sure if she'd trust a car from Best Motors, or the salesman.

"I'll be telling you about events," O'Neill said, adding, "perhaps Janine would like to make us another wonderful cup of tea." She stared at him suspiciously through red swollen eyes, obviously thinking he was either being cruel, or was trying to get her out of the room. As she hesitated he said, "Fran will help you."

"So what happened, Inspector?" asked Mike, when both women had left the room.

"Chief Inspector," corrected O'Neill, then he paused and chose his words carefully. "Denise was killed whilst she was having a Turkish bath."

"Have you got him?" demanded Mike. "Surely he hasn't got away."

"What makes you be thinking it was a man?"

Mike shrugged. "Aren't most murders committed by men?"

O'Neill didn't answer. He was beginning to dislike Mike.

"Have you got any suspects . . . Chief Inspector?"

"Not at the moment, sir, but the wheels, as they no doubt say in the motor trade, are in motion." O'Neill, enjoying the flicker of irritation that crossed Mike's face, added, "Before I forget, sir, where were you this afternoon at about one?"

Indignation replaced irritation. "Me?" Mike blustered.

"You don't think I'd murder my girlfriend's sister, do you?"

"I'd not be knowing yet, sir, but please answer the question. Where were you?"

Mike paled slightly but answered in a firm voice. "I was in my flat. I live on the premises."

"Can anyone vouch for you?"

He shook his head. "The Saturday salesman David saw me go upstairs."

"So how long were you in your flat?"

"Till about two."

O'Neill stared at him, trying to decide if he was lying. "Of course, we'll be checking your alibi, sir."

"Do what you like," said Mike, shrugging. "I may not have liked Denise but I didn't kill her. Anyway, someone would have noticed me in a women's hairdressers."

"Did I say it was women only?"

Confusion showed on Mike's broad face. "No, I just assumed."

O'Neill smiled, "In my job, I try not to assume anything. I don't even assume I'll see the sun rise in the morning. No doubt Denise thought she'd see the sun rise."

Mike's stony face relaxed slightly at that moment, as Janine and Fran came back into the room.

"DS Wilson, do you have any questions you wish to ask Mr Sanderson?"

Fran nodded. "Just one or two," she answered, giving Mike a deliberately cold stare. "How long have you two known each other?"

"Two years. Janine bought a car from me and then lived in London for a while. We've been together now for six months."

"Are you engaged?"

Mike smiled at Janine. "We're getting engaged soon."

"And marriage?"

"That's our business," he snapped. "The nature of our relationship has nothing to do with Denise being murdered."

Fran wasn't deterred. "I'd have thought you two would have been living together by now."

"We can't afford it," interrupted Janine. "It's not easy when a man has to support children from a previous marriage."

"I can appreciate that," said Fran. "But of course, circumstances have changed. I presume the cottage will be solely yours, now."

Fran watched their reactions carefully. Janine seemed genuinely surprised, as if the thought had only just occurred to her. Mike though, seemed totally unsurprised but managed to bluster, "We don't know anything yet, do we? For all we know, she could have left everything to a cats' home."

"Is that likely, sir?" asked Fran. Mike's lips tightened in anger and Fran, looking directly at Janine asked, "Are you Denise's only relative?"

"Yes," she murmured miserably. "I'm her only relative."

Fran paused for a moment before asking, "Is there any money involved?"

"Can't you leave her alone?" interrupted Mike. "You can see she hasn't thought about anything like that."

"But you had, sir?"

Fran noticed how Mike's hands clenched and unclenched before he answered. "Do you mind leaving us alone now," he said. "Aren't you meant to be investigating the crime, not harassing bereaved relatives?"

"Fair enough, sir," said Fran calmly. "Thank you for your help. Tomorrow there will have to be a formal identification of the body. Perhaps you'd like to accompany Janine."

Janine shuddered visibly, but Fran noticed that Mike's eyes reflected both hope and a degree of satisfaction.

"There is just one more thing," said O'Neill. "We'll be needing to see Denise's room now. We'll also need to take away her birth certificate for the coroner, and anything else that may be pertinent to this enquiry."

"Yes . . . yes, I suppose so. She wouldn't like it. She's a very private person . . ." she faltered. "She *was* a very private person."

"You can be accompanying us, Janine," said O'Neill, with an encouraging smile. "If you want to."

Shaking her head slowly she said, "No thank you, Chief Inspector. I didn't go into her room when she was alive, and I don't want to now that she's dead."

"Sure," said O'Neill, grateful that he and Fran would be alone whilst searching the room. A grieving relative in the background always felt inhibiting and seemed to add a voyeuristic edge to the proceedings.

"It's the third room on the right upstairs," said Janine dully.

Upstairs, O'Neill opened the door of the room on the right. "Are you thinking," he said, "what sort of person slept in a room like this?"

Fran scanned the room as though searching for the essence of Denise Parks. The room had both an odd look and an odd feel and yet Fran couldn't at first pinpoint exactly why. The bed was neatly made and covered with a candlewick bedspread. On the bedside table, three paperbacks, all historical romances, were neatly piled, next to them a pink shaded lamp and a single red artificial rose. O'Neill had begun to open the drawers, bottom drawer first, as burglars do.

"Boss . . ."

"We're on our own, Fran. Don't call me boss. What have you found?"

"That's just it. It's what I haven't found."

O'Neill raised an eyebrow and waited for an explanation.

"There's no alarm clock and look . . ." she opened the wardrobe door and moved the coat hangers along noisily. There were no clothes apart from two items, both coats. "It's as if she's been away or perhaps was planning to go away. The dressing table is virtually empty as well."

"I was thinking the same thing myself. There isn't much in her chest of drawers, but what there is . . . is unusual."

Fran agreed when she saw the few contents – three sets of lingerie in black and red, all size twelve and very tarty-looking. The underwear was still in its cellophane wrapping and next to that were several home-made cards, presumably birthday cards. Each one was made of a small sheet of white card, the inside was blank but on the outside was a pressed flower – a forget-me-not.

"Any private papers, any correspondence?" queried Fran.

O'Neill shook his head. "Nothing."

They stood in puzzled silence for a moment. "Of course," said O'Neill thoughtfully, "those two downstairs could be responsible."

"What for? Clearing the room or murder?"

"Both, probably," said O'Neill. "Let's go downstairs and find out."

Six

Dale Dunbar turned in bed and snuggled into the warm curve of Marcus's naked body. It was six a.m. and the room was dark, except for the tiny flashing light on the clock radio. He enjoyed this time of the morning, before Marcus woke up properly, when he was *there*, safe beside him.

Occasionally Marcus didn't come home at night, and Dale would wake and feel the cold empty space beside him, and that coldness seemed to penetrate his heart and his day was ruined. Today though, they were staying in, and that was how he liked it. Sometimes, he fantasised that he kept Marcus as a prisoner in the flat, locked in but happy, and then Dale could feel secure that Marcus would never be tempted, but tempted he often was, and it was a jealous cross Dale had to bear.

He resisted the urge to stroke Marcus's strong young arms that lay, pale and visible, even in the dark. If he woke him now, Marcus would be angry and Dale didn't want that. He wanted Sunday to be a special, lazy sort of day – breakfast together, listen to some music, make love, then some food shopping, or maybe a pub lunch. He just wanted the hours to while away until the evening when they might fall asleep together on the sofa, wake up, have a few drinks, perhaps watch a video, then fall into bed in the early hours, make love again and then drowsily fall asleep once more. That was Dale's dream day . . . then he remembered. The police were still on the premises. How could he have forgotten? He listened, alert now, no longer in a dreamy state, but he couldn't hear any noise from downstairs. Maybe they'd gone.

He continued to listen to Marcus's slow, regular breathing until seven, then, realising his lover wasn't going to wake, he carefully slid out from under the duvet, left the bedroom, closing the door silently behind him, and went into the bathroom to shower.

After his shower, he stared at his face in the mirror. That he was getting older was self-evident but now he realised it was really beginning to show. His chin sagged a little now, and his hair being silvery made him look older than . . . he refused to think about all those years. Marcus was only thirty, still beautiful, still attractive to a wide range of men. In his darkest moments, he wished Marcus could be maimed or disfigured in some way, so that he'd never want to leave, never attract the attentions of predatory bastards who could never love him in the same way. He'd always been ashamed of some of his fantasies and thoughts regarding Marcus, but they were there in his subconscious, and however hard he tried, they resurfaced time and time again.

He sat at the breakfast bar in the kitchen with the local radio station on low, drank coffee, and wished Marcus would move his butt and join him. By nine, his patience was exhausted. He walked noisily into the bedroom, pulled back the curtains, and placed a mug of coffee on the bedside table. Marcus grunted, pulled the duvet over his face and muttered, "Fuck off. I'm tired."

Dale felt acutely disappointed. He knew Marcus well enough to know the day wasn't going to be his dream day after all.

Marcus eventually ambled naked into the kitchen at ten.

"And about time too," said Dale, aware he was sounding peevish but unable to stop himself.

"Don't start, DD. I've got a headache." Marcus sat down, leant across to switch off the radio, then swung his long shapely legs round on the stool so that he was facing Dale. "It's your turn to make breakfast," he said. "I made it yesterday."

"It's nearly time for lunch." Dale paused; he wanted Marcus in a good mood. "What do you want?" he asked, smiling.

"Scrambled eggs would be nice. You make the best scrambled eggs in the world."

Dale smiled again, and this time he actually felt like smiling. "Flatterer. Do you want garlic?"

Marcus liked garlic puree added to his eggs, unless of course he was planning to meet someone. As Dale waited for his answer, he noticed how Marcus's long blond hair, freed from its usual ponytail, hung shining and magnificent like a golden mane.

"No garlic today, DD. I'm seeing someone."

Those three words – 'I'm seeing someone' – struck Dale like a blow to the face. His day was in ruins. "I expect you'll be doing more than seeing."

"Calm down, sweetness. I'm seeing a woman."

"What woman?"

"Just an old friend. No one you'd know."

Then, seeing Dale's pained expression, Marcus smiled. "DD, stop being such a jealous old queen. You know it's you I love."

This time, one more word caused him pain – 'old'. Dale stomped to the fridge, took out three eggs, broke all three harshly into a glass bowl, then began to whisk furiously. He added the garlic puree in abundance. The tart shouldn't get that close to him, anyway.

Neither spoke until the eggs were on the plate. "No

toast?" said Marcus, as the plate of overcooked scrambled eggs was thrust in front of him. "And do I smell garlic, contrary to my wishes?"

"Call me an old queen and think you're going to get toast as well? Get stuffed."

"Tut tut. We are crabby today. I'm only seeing this woman for a quick drink. We'll have the rest of the day together."

That thought cheered Dale a little and, although he was longing to find out who the mystery woman was, he knew better than to ask. Marcus liked to keep little secrets and Dale had enough pride to bide his time. Marcus would tell him one day, when he was ready.

Dale waited for the verdict on the eggs.

"Scrambled eggs were okay, DD. Not to your usual standard, but okay," said Marcus, giving his hair a grand theatrical flick with his right hand. "Are the police still downstairs?"

"I haven't heard them. The big chief says they'll be here for at least a week, but we'll get compensation at some point."

"We'll need it," said Marcus. "But it's a break for us, I suppose. It could be fun."

Dale shrugged. "It could be hell. After all, everyone's a suspect."

Marcus stood up and put an arm round Dale. "What do think of that Irish Chiefie?"

"What do you mean by that?" demanded Dale.

"Nothing at all, DD," said Marcus with a sly smile. "I just know you're a sucker for an Irish accent, and mixed with a bit of authority . . . well!"

"You . . . trollop . . . you tart!"

Marcus laughed, "I love you, DD. You're such a joy to wind up."

Later, as Dale dusted and polished, Marcus lounged

on the sofa, flicking the remote from one channel to another. Since they'd bought cable TV, channel hopping seemed to be his main hobby. It caused Dale intense irritation. "Are you going to do that all morning?" he asked.

"Might. Might not. I thought maybe I'd pop downstairs and have a chat with the coppers."

"What for? They'll summon us soon enough. Anyway, you haven't got any information to give them, have you? You should be careful. You hated that woman – that's a motive according to the police."

"DD, come off it. *No one* liked her. The whole population of Fowchester and surrounding parts is probably suspect."

"I expect her sister liked her," muttered Dale, as he passed a duster lovingly over a china figurine of a border collie his mother had once given him.

Marcus propped himself up on one elbow. "Every cloud has a sliver lining."

"What's that supposed to mean?"

"It means," said Marcus, "someone is going to benefit from her death – the murderer and the sister."

Dale glanced sharply at his lover. "If I'd murdered someone, I wouldn't think I'd benefited – I'd be sick to my stomach. I'd think everyone could see the guilt on my face."

"You are a sweet old-fashioned boy, but I'd say anyone can get used to anything, in time."

Dale paused with the duster in his hand and thought about that comment. Would he ever get used to Marcus cheating on him? And was Marcus trying to tell him something? As he caught Marcus's eye, the younger man looked away and continued channel hopping. A little niggle of doubt crept into Dale's mind. Surely not, not Marcus. Dale knew his own potential for violence, but he'd never seen Marcus react violently – except the once. Just that one time.

O'Neill spent Saturday night at Fowchester Police Station. Reluctantly, he'd sent Fran home at one a.m. and then he'd started co-opting any able-bodied, seemingly wide awake police officers to collate and examine the Personal Descriptive Forms.

The computers were still inactive and as much use as Morse code to the blind and deaf, but there was a rumour that Superintendent Ringstead had promised they would be fixed on Monday. This caused laughter because Ringstead embraced all forms of information technology with an evangelical fervour usually reserved for cult followers or Born Again Christians. The irony was that he rarely used a computer for anything, other than writing letters to the Police Federation or playing Patience. He'd been caught once or twice and the joke was that Ringstead wasn't paying 'hush' money, he was paying 'patience' money. A feeble joke, O'Neill thought, but a siege mentality developed strongly in a murder enquiry and any humour, however feeble, lifted everyone's spirits.

Working with Fran also lifted O'Neill's spirits, not just because he was attracted to her but because he found it generally easier to work with women. Women could be efficient, intuitive and often ambitious, but there wasn't the competitive edge that male officers seemed to generate. Being a good detective, being organised and meticulous often wasn't good enough. They had to be the better *man*. O'Neill found the macho attitudes hard to take. He liked a drink, more than one, although he was trying to be less dependent on using alcohol to help him sleep – but he didn't want to compete with men on any level other than a purely professional one.

Since his wife's suicide he had to admit he felt far more vulnerable, which was strange, because he had always been the strong one. Now, without her, he seemed to drift through life without any real aims. He didn't want promotion, he didn't want a better car, and he'd recently sold his house and bought a small flat so he had money in the bank. What he really wanted was a relationship, preferably with Fran, but that seemed more and more unlikely. Now, especially, it was time to put all his effort and concentration into finding Denise's killer.

So although he felt utterly weary, he sat through the SOC video three times with a total lack of concentration, and on the third showing he fell asleep.

At three-thirty he decided to bed down for the night on the sofa in the rape crisis room. It was against Superintendent Ringstead's rules, but those were made to be broken and hopefully he'd never find out. The room did have a soothing effect with its soft pastel colours, table lamps, potted plants and draped curtains and O'Neill slept until eight-thirty when Fran walked in carrying a huge mug of coffee. He opened one eye to view her and felt dishevelled and unkempt in contrast to her fresh face and perky smile.

"How dare you look so bright this time of the morning, Fran. I bet you've even had your breakfast."

Fran laughed. "Of course. I feel raring to go this morning."

O'Neill groaned and sat upright on the sofa. "I like enthusiasm," he said, "but not when I feel as creased up as a tramp's brolly."

"What's the plan for today then, boss?"

"Plan? DS Wilson, the way I feel I feel at the moment, I'm waiting for divine guidance."

"Shall I go away and come back when you feel better?"

O'Neill nodded. "Give me ten minutes or so and I'll meet you in the canteen. And you can arrange a briefing for ten a.m. I'll make it short because we need to see Janine again, and Dale and partner."

"Wouldn't it be better to do the briefing tomorrow after the post-mortem?" suggested Fran.

O'Neill shook his head. "Don't be arguing Fran. I can't see the PM will tell us much we don't know already. And I want the whole team to see the video."

"Anything significant?"

O'Neill smiled. "There might be. But I want to see if anyone else notices."

In the incident room just before ten, as many of the CID who could be mustered had arrived, and stood around chatting and bemoaning their lost Sunday. Fran guessed that most were grateful to have escaped household chores and demanding children, but felt they had to seem to resent being called in on a Sunday.

O'Neill walked in at ten past ten. He didn't bother with a preamble, simply drew a circle on the white board in red felt tip pen, wrote 'Denise Parks' in the centre, then turned to the group.

"Right . . . what do we know so far about the victim?"

There was a short silence, then from somewhere in the room a male voice muttered, "Sod all."

"Quite right," said O'Neill. "We know sod all really, *but* we do know certain things." From the circle, he drew a line and wrote 'Next of Kin – Janine, younger sister'. Aloud he said, "They lived together." Then in brackets he wrote 'boyfriend – Mike Sanderson'.

"Anything else?"

No one else spoke, so Fran said, "We know she worked as a secretary for a firm of solicitors, Longman and Bateson."

O'Neill nodded. "Friends? Interests? Hobbies?"

There was no immediate response. "We do know, "O'Neill continued, "that she was not a popular woman. In fact, she seems your average, middle-aged, unmarried woman who is rather crabby and prone to gossip."

O'Neill paused and waited for some sort of response and when there was none, became irritated. "When I make a sweeping generalisation, I would expect some reaction. Your average middle-aged woman doesn't get murdered in the local hairdressers. So we look at ways in which Denise Parks is different. One, she has drawers full of sexy underwear. Two, she owns a thatched cottage worth a small fortune, even though it's somewhat in need of attention. And three, I suspect she may have money in the bank or life insurance. Any questions at this point?"

"DC Tony Jarvis, sir," said a tall young man with a thin face, wistful expression and a receding hairline. "Was she a regular at the hairdressers?"

There was a ripple of laughter. "It's all right Jarvis, you're on the right case," said someone to his left. "Hair today and gone tomorrow."

Jarvis blushed but he did manage a nervous laugh. It was known throughout the station that he was fixated with his increasing hair loss. He was often to be found gazing in windows and mirrors and wearing a wistful expression. He was, of course, the butt of teasing and jokes at his expense.

O'Neill cast a quelling eye over the room. "Good question, Jarvis. Does another question immediately spring to your mind?"

"Yes, sir. Whoever did it must have known she had an appointment."

"And who would have been likely to know that?"

"The staff and her sister, sir."

O'Neill nodded. "Denise Parks was a creature of habit. Customers too could have known that she had a hair appointment every fortnight. *Not* that she had a Turkish bath every fortnight. That was once a month. Does that pose another question?"

Once more silence fell. "Was it planned?" asked O'Neill. "Or was it opportunistic? That, ladies and gentleman, is the question."

Seven

*L*e *Salon* always closed on Monday and usually Mandy
Willens slept until late, but today she was awake
at five following another night of bad dreams. It was
only two nights since the murder but it felt longer. She
couldn't eat and for two nights she hadn't slept, except
in brief snatches, seeing in her nightmares Denise Parks'
eyes following her every move.

Mandy wandered down to the kitchen. She stared
thoughtfully out into the small back garden at the frost
glistening on the patch of lawn, seemingly lit up by the
light cast from a full moon. Could things have been
different? she wondered. After all, she hadn't felt well
on Saturday morning. Perhaps if she hadn't gone in to
work . . .

"Good morning, early bird." Josh, her boyfriend, stood
behind her, slipping his hands round her waist and gathering her trim body to him. "You kept me awake," he said.
"I feel like death this morning."

Her body tensed at the mere mention of death. "Whoops,
sorry," said Josh, feeling the jolt and realising he'd
momentarily forgotten. Turning her round to face him,
he said, "I know it's been a shock but let's face it, she
wasn't much of a loss, was she? You told me what a
miserable old bag she could be."

Mandy stared at Josh's handsome face. Tall, with dark
hair, deep brown eyes and a well-chiselled chin – she

knew she was the envy of many of her friends. And yet
. . . he could be so insensitive, so selfish.

"Cheer up, Mandy," he said, hugging her. "I'll make
breakfast and when I get home tonight, we'll go out – it
will take your mind off things."

She smiled and kissed his lips lightly, thinking that
sometimes he could surprise her. "Thanks, Josh. But I
don't feel like going out at the moment." Then she added,
simply to please him, "Perhaps tomorrow."

He nibbled her ear and then nuzzled into her neck,
finally surfacing to say, "It'll be a good night at the pub
tonight and I want to be there with the most sexy, gorgeous
girl in the world, so you won't let me down, will you?"

Mandy sighed inwardly. He never seemed to *listen* to
her.

Later, after he'd gone to work, she slumped on the sofa,
switched on the TV, and let the bland programmes take
over her thoughts. Except that occasionally, thoughts of
Denise sneaked into her mind, triggered by the tiniest
detail of someone on the screen – a certain expression,
someone with brown eyes, a tilt of the head – all caused
her anxiety. She could feel her heart pounding, her palms
growing clammy, the nausea in her stomach rising up and
worse of all, a feeling of mounting panic.

It was eleven-thirty when she remembered she'd promised to meet a friend for lunch. In her hurry to get ready,
she almost felt normal again. Until, that is, a rush of cold
air assailed her lungs at the front door and she remembered
her nightmare – the treatment table covered with a large
white fluffy towel which she'd pulled back to reveal only
the head of Denise Parks; the eyes as steady and blind as
black marbles, but with a mouth that moved. And the
worst horror of all – she couldn't hear the whispered
sounds, although she'd strained and put her ear near
to the moving mouth. Denise Parks had spoken to her

even in death and, illogical as it was, Mandy feared that someone one day would actually interpret those sounds.

She took a few deep breaths before getting into her car, told herself firmly that she was being silly and hysterical about Denise talking to anyone from the grave, and gradually she began to feel calmer. Until, that was, she realised that Denise wasn't yet in her grave, but in a hospital mortuary, and the police would soon want to question her properly because, after all, she was the last person to see Denise alive. And her mouth *had* moved.

O'Neill had attended a few post-mortems in his police career, and the visual horrors were as nothing compared to the sheer repulsiveness of the smell. He sometimes wondered if it was a prerequisite of being a pathologist that they were nasally challenged, or was it simply that familiarity dulled the nose?

It was much to O'Neill's relief that, by the time they arrived at the mortuary, the PM was over and the body lay rearranged and recognisable. The pathologist, Charles Barratt, was a man of dour temperament, well over six feet six and seriously underweight. In the station he was known as 'Spindly' or 'Spindly Spider', because even a spider could look chubby in comparison. They stood over the body and O'Neill felt grateful that those eyes were firmly shut. Fran too felt relief that at last Denise seemed at peace.

"She was a fit, menopausal woman," said Charles Barratt. "Good country lungs. Excellent teeth. Died from suffocation. Some bruising on the neck from the wooden collar of the hot box and some on the chin, probably from being held."

O'Neill nodded sagely because all that registered with him at that moment was the smell of death. Barratt stared at the corpse's face with some intensity for so long that O'Neill began to imagine that he could actually communicate with the dead.

"Strange," said Barratt thoughtfully. "I would have thought, even in bare feet, that someone would have heard her banging. Her toes were bruised."

O'Neill glanced sidelong at Fran; neither showed any surprise, keeping a united front, as though the forces of law and order somehow had to keep a dignified silence against either the power of the doleful objectivity of 'Spindly', or his seeming ability actually to listen to the dead. Someone had once told O'Neill that 'Spindly' had special powers, that corpses 'spoke' to him. He hadn't believed it then, but now he wasn't so sure.

"Oh . . . and one other thing Chief Inspector, it may or may not be important, but she has had a child."

This time O'Neill *was* surprised. "When?"

Barratt raised an eyebrow. "I'm clever and meticulous and occasionally a corpse does talk to me, but all I can say for certain is that it wasn't recently. I'm sure you'll find out exactly when Miss Parks gave birth."

Just as O'Neill and Fran were leaving, Barratt said, "By the way, have you got her birth certificate?"

"We're still searching for it," said O'Neill

Barratt nodded. "My guess is she's around fifty – according to her teeth."

Again O'Neill was surprised. Hadn't Janine said there was ten years between them, so that would have made her forty-two? Murder was murder, whatever the age, but was a discrepancy in the age significant, and if so in what way?

Outside in the fresh air, O'Neill decided they needed a cup of coffee at the very least, so he drove into the centre of Fowchester and soon they sat in the warmth of Jennifer's Coffee Shop, drinking coffee and eating hot buttered crumpets.

"I should have insisted we searched the mother's room," said O'Neill, thinking back to Saturday night. "Do you think Janine deliberately misled us?"

Fran frowned. "I think, being in shock, she may simply have forgotten that Denise had moved into her mother's old room. If she was telling the truth about not invading Denise's privacy, then she didn't know the underwear existed." She paused. "I wonder if those cards have any significance?"

O'Neill shook his head, "Only time will tell, I suppose. But I'm thinking they were a very odd couple."

"Maybe Denise was still grieving for her mother and in some way wanted to keep everything the same."

That, O'Neill could understand. For a whole year, his dead wife's clothes hung in the wardrobe as though one day she'd return, and by keeping them in place he'd somehow remained loyal. Grief, he knew, contained only raw emotion. Logic and common sense returned only when the emotional turmoil quietened. Once that happened, the fragile, inexplicable expectation of seeing a loved one again ended with the loss of hope. That had been the worst of times for him, but slowly the hopelessness had been replaced with a quiet acceptance and a sort of peace.

"So what do you think, boss?" asked Fran, aware that Connor's eyes had a faraway look and that he was on a different wavelength altogether.

"About what, Fran?"

"The change of room."

He smiled. "I'm thinking, Fran, we're wasting time here. Lets get back to Janine's place and give the mother's room a good going over."

*   *   *

Janine was alone when they arrived, her hair was loose and untidy and dark rings had formed beneath her eyes. "I didn't expect you back again so soon," she said, as she directed them to the kitchen. "There's no fire lit in the front room," she explained. "I've been sitting in the kitchen."

"I'll be asking you a few more questions," said O'Neill, in his most soothing voice. "And then we'd like to look round your mother's room." It didn't work; Janine stared at him coldly. "Do you realise I feel as if you've raped my sister by going into her room and trying to tarnish her reputation."

"I think that's a slight exaggeration," said O'Neill, "and I trust you want us to catch your sister's killer."

"Of course, but do you need to be so . . . intrusive?"

"I'm afraid we do. We do have to find out everything we can about your sister. After all, this was a well-planned, or so it seems, murder. So far I do get the impression that your sister was not popular."

Janine shrugged defensively, "She told the truth, she was a bit blunt . . . she wasn't looking for popularity."

As gently as possible, O'Neill said, "For someone, perhaps the truth was too much."

Janine paused for a moment before giving O'Neill an almost pitying look, "Only family really matter, that's what Denise always said. Other people aren't important."

"And what do you believe?"

Janine paused momentarily, "I share my sister's belief."

"Does that include Mike?"

"Mike is almost family."

"Especially now?"

"What does that mean?" asked Janine sharply.

"You own this house now, I presume, and any money Denise may have had, so marriage to Mike is surely on the cards."

"I expect so," said Janine dully. "But quite honestly, I'm still in shock and I can't think about the future at the moment."

"I understand," said O'Neill, and of course he did.

Janine suddenly looked tearful. "There is a Will, I think," she murmured. "Denise mentioned it once."

"In what connection?"

"It was just after Mother died. I suppose it was on her mind then, she said if anything ever happened to her, I'd be well looked after."

"Did Mike know this?"

"No. Why should he?"

"What did you think she expected to happen to her? Was she scared of anyone?"

Janine frowned, "You've asked me before if Denise had any enemies and my answer is still the same. *No*. She went to work, she came home. She was a very private person. She may not have been popular, but that was because she kept herself to herself. She didn't need many friends."

O'Neill nodded, realising this line of questioning wasn't making any headway. "We'll leave it there, Janine. I would like to take a look at your mother's old room, and I'm afraid I'll be taking any documents that I deem necessary to the inquiry."

Janine shrugged. "Go ahead. I've got nothing to hide. I haven't been in that room since Mother died. And not since Denise took it over. Our family don't pry."

Fran stood up to accompany O'Neill but he said, "You stay with Janine. I won't be long."

They listened to his footsteps ascending the stairs, and then Janine managed to smile briefly at Fran. "What does he hope to find up there?" she asked.

"There might be a Will or a diary," suggested Fran.

Janine stared down at her own hands thoughtfully, "Denise was a very organised sort of person. Meticulous with paperwork but I'm not sure if she kept a diary, as such. She did have a pocket diary but she didn't seem to use it, other than for appointments."

"What sort of appointments?"

"Just ordinary things. The dentist, doctor . . ." she paused, "and of course, the hairdressers."

"Church meetings?"

Janine nodded. "She went to church some Sundays and to seasonal events. The Harvest supper, the Christmas pensioners' party, the Easter social . . . she enjoyed those."

"And her friend, Monica?"

"What about her?"

"Did they go to the church events together?"

Janine looked puzzled. "It's strange, isn't it? The more questions I'm asked about Denise, the more I think about her, the less I seem to know her. I took her for granted, I suppose." She gave a hollow little laugh. "So in answer to your question, I don't know."

Fran noticed Janine's eyes filling with tears and she thought it best to change the subject, or at least skirt round it. "Will Mike be round later?"

Janine nodded and then held her head back, trying to contain her tears. "Yes, he'll be around later. But . . ."

"But what?" asked Fran, after several seconds of silence.

"It's not the same now. Something has changed, and I don't know why."

"You're still in shock Janine, your emotions are all in turmoil."

"Do you think so?" she said, staring at Fran. "I don't think I'll ever quite feel the same about him again."

"Why do you think that?"

Janine was about to answer when they heard O'Neill on the stairs, and Fran knew the answer would have to wait.

O'Neill stood at the door with a bundle of items in polythene bags. "We'll be leaving you in peace now Janine, but we'll be calling on you again tomorrow."

Janine sighed resignedly and was opening the front door when O'Neill said, "How old did you say your sister was?"

"Forty-two. There's ten years between us."

"Fine. Thank you."

As they walked down the garden path Fran said, "What was that about?"

"There's no birth certificate that I can find, and no documentation of either Denise or her mother. All Denise's clothes are in her mother's old room, but as far as anything legal or relevant, it's as if the two of them never existed."

"It must be deliberate."

"Sure," said O'Neill thoughtfully. "I'm wondering what they were trying to hide. Why, and who from?"

Eight

That afternoon, Fran followed O'Neill round *Le Salon*.
She'd already seen the video twice at the briefing, and
O'Neill was convinced there was something he'd missed,
something vital. After the chaos of Saturday, the empty
hairdressers now had the atmosphere of a museum just
before opening time, with a bored-looking uniformed
police constable acting as both curator and security guard.
O'Neill told him to come back in an hour, and then their
tour began.

Using the key above the door mantle to unlock the side
door into the alleyway, they walked the length of the alley
to a high latched gate, which led to a long garden with
several bare trees, a patch of lawn and a stone wall, easily
scalable. The only other entrances to *Le Salon* were the
front door, a low side gate leading into the alleyway, and
from there the side door to the staff room. Outside of the
side door stood two black wheelie bins, side by side.

After their tour of the garden, Fran locked the side
door, put the key back in place, and then glanced round the
staff room that doubled as a stock room and was cluttered
with unwashed mugs, half-eaten sandwiches, and various
boxes of hairdressing equipment. O'Neill viewed the staff
room, but with a puzzled expression. "There's something
different between the real thing and the video, and I can't
work it out."

"Just this room?" queried Fran.

O'Neill nodded.

"Okay," said Fran. "Let's start with the side door. It's locked now. The key's in place. The sink's in a mess and there are boxes all over the floor. The coat hooks are empty, bar one." As she spoke she lifted the faded-looking anorak that hung there.

"Take it down, take it down," urged O'Neill, standing back as though to view a work of art from sufficient distance.

Once the anorak was removed, it was obvious this was no plain wall or panel, but a door with no handle or knob, just a keyhole. "That's it," said O'Neill. "In the video there was a shot of a row of coats, and I could see a ridge down one side, and it must have registered because its been bugging me ever since. Right . . . let's get the owner down and get him to unlock it."

"Why do you think it's important?" asked Fran.

"Because," said O'Neill. "I think it's possible that the murderer may have been on the premises for some time and where better to hide?"

"I can see that's possible," agreed Fran. "But, if the murderer was someone on the outside, how did they leave the building without being seen? Using the side door they would have had to unlock the door, and the key would have been found in the lock."

O'Neill smiled. "No one can say we're not open-minded, Fran. We've either got a murderer on the inside working alone or we've got an accomplice on the outside." He paused, as if realising the implication of that view. "Or in any other combination known only to the Great Detective in the sky."

Fran noticed O'Neill's eyes were bright with growing enthusiasm, and suddenly he seemed more like his old self, the person he had been before Fran made it clear there was no future for them together. Their only possible relationship was boss and minion, and minion was just how she felt at the moment. Consciously or unconsciously, O'Neill, it seemed, had relegated her to a sounding board for his ideas, and even in interview situations he rarely encouraged her to ask questions. Perhaps it was time for some sort of showdown, but the timing had to be appropriate; she didn't want to alienate him in case she was being unduly sensitive.

Dale Dunbar responded promptly to their knock on his door and although his 'front' door was inside in the hallway, he seemed to arrive soundlessly.

"Hello there, police persons," he said, sounding cheerful. Fran noticed he was wearing expensive trainers and that the stairs leading up to his flat were plushly carpeted in pale green, the walls on either side adorned with framed black and white photographs of male and female movie stars of the forties and fifties. Dale himself wore tight blue jeans and a cream polo neck sweater, and Fran wondered if he wore polo necks for the reason she wore them as a young teenager – to hide love bites.

"Do you want to come up," he said, "or do you require my presence in the salon?"

"I'll be wanting you down here, Mr Dunbar."

"Do call me Dale, Chief Inspector." As he spoke, Dale winked at Fran and whispered in her ear. "He wants me." Fran tried to keep a straight face and O'Neill cast them both a sharp look that made Fran want to giggle like a schoolgirl.

In the staff room, O'Neill pointed to the door. "What's behind there?"

Dale shrugged. "It's a cupboard. There's an old sunbed in there we don't use any more."

"Where's the key?" asked O'Neill.

"There isn't one, dear heart. It's been painted in – probably need a crow bar."

"Don't 'dear heart' me," said O'Neill, irritably. "I need to get this door open."

"I'll just go and see if I can find a handy crow bar," said Dale, wiggling his hips and winking at Fran again.

"You do that," replied O'Neill.

Dale returned swiftly with a long slim metal planer. "Couldn't find a crow bar but maybe this will do it."

O'Neill slipped the planer in between the edges and yanked hard. The old wood and paint split and cracked noisily, but it worked – he managed to open the door, although by now it was blindingly obvious that the door hadn't been opened for a very long time. Inside, the sunbed, covered with a cobwebbed blanket, took up all the space in the long narrow cupboard.

"We used to use the cupboard for stock," said Dale, "but then the sunbed wasn't used any more so we closed it up."

"Why did you stop using it?" asked Fran.

Dale's expression changed from confident to diffident in seconds. "To be honest, we had a terrible cock-up. A customer fell asleep, forgotten by the beautician, and she got burnt – not that seriously, but we settled out of court and it was very expensive. I sacked the girl responsible, of course."

O'Neill felt his irritation levels rising. He'd been wrong about the cupboard hiding a waiting murderer and he seriously disliked Dale Dunbar partly, he suspected, because Fran and Dale seemed to have a certain rapport going. "Right, Dale, I suspected this cupboard could have provided a hiding place but I was obviously wrong so I'd like you now to tell me all you know about the staff and customers present on Saturday – especially the staff."

"You can't be serious," said Dale, placing his hands on

his hips. "My staff are the best there is and, I assure you, *not* capable of anything so gruesome."

O'Neill folded his arms and, for a second, Fran was reminded of two rutting stags.

"Denise Parks, I believe," said O'Neill firmly, "*was* killed by someone on the premises. Unless of course you, or a member of your staff, failed to notice a person, neither customer nor staff, acting suspiciously."

"Of course not," blustered Dale. "He would have been noticed."

"Or she," said O'Neill calmly.

Dale shrugged his shoulders in defeat. "Oh, very well. You'd better come up to the flat. I've got the staff details there."

Upstairs in the flat, they sat round the kitchen table and Dale produced a meticulously kept ledger of staff names and addresses and began reeling them off. O'Neill interrupted him. "I've got the names and addresses of everyone except the girl you sacked over the sunbed incident, of the others I shall want you to give me more personal details."

"It sounds like telling tales to me."

O'Neill glared at him. "Don't be petulant, Dale. Tell me first about the beautician, Mandy Willens."

Dale crossed his legs, gave an exaggerated sigh and said, "Lovely girl. She's been with me about three years, lives with her boyfriend Josh . . . very handsome boy. Mandy is very well liked by the customers; she—"

"What about Denise? Did she like Mandy?"

"Denise didn't like anyone, Chief. She complained once or twice about Mandy, but then Denise complained about everyone."

"What sort of complaints?"

"Being kept waiting, her hair or nails never being quite right – that sort of thing."

"And did Mandy get annoyed by this?"

"Well of course she did. But if you're suggesting she lost her temper, then you're wrong. She can get a bit tearful and nervous at times, especially of late, but then we all get like that sometimes, don't we?"

"Why 'especially of late' has she been more tearful and nervous?" O'Neill asked.

"That's something you'll have to ask her, isn't it?" said Dale, sounding resolute. "All I can say is she's worked here for three years, she's never caused any trouble, and Denise was the only person who complained about her."

"Okay. What about Tara?"

Dale thought for a moment, "Different kettle of fish, that one, and along with the fish she does have a small chip on her shoulder."

Fran smiled at his little play on words, but O'Neill stayed stony faced. "Tell me about it," he said.

"I feel awful telling tales—"

"Just get on with it, Dale," interrupted O'Neill, "unless you want to be plagued by us from now until Easter."

"Give me a chance," said Dale, folding his arms. "You policemen are so macho. As I was about to say, Tara has worked here for about a year. Before that she worked as a stylist, quite a good one too, by all accounts. But she developed an allergy and her hands become all red raw, poor lamb. It could happen to any one of us. Anyway, the doctor said it was a severe reaction, and that her dermatitis would only improve if she stopped working as a stylist. Hence I employed her as a receptionist."

"At less money?" queried O'Neill.

Dale raised an eyebrow. "Of course. A stylist is creative, an artist; a receptionist just has to be polite and have neat handwriting."

"Did she get on with Denise?"

"Well they weren't exactly lovers," said Dale with

forced sarcasm. "Denise could wind Tara up with just a look, but then Tara can be wound up fairly easily. But I make allowances."

"Why would you make allowances?"

Dale shrugged. "You should see what she's married to. When anthropologists talk about the missing link, I think they had her husband in mind. Even she calls him the Thing. He's a drunken scumbag, to be honest, and he can be violent."

"Why does she stay with him?"

Dale gave O'Neill a pitying glance. "She doesn't earn enough to rent a place of her own, and when she does threaten to leave, he says he'll change, he loves her, all that crap. And I suppose she wants to believe it." .

O'Neill nodded. He knew some abused women who suffered not so much from stoic resignation as from misplaced optimism, always thinking life would get better – when for most of them life merely got worse.

"Tell me now about Andrew," said O'Neill. "I suppose Denise complained about him, too."

Dale frowned slightly and then said thoughtfully, "I think he was her favourite. She made it clear she didn't like men, although she could tolerate me and Marcus because in her eyes we weren't real men."

"Did she think Andrew was gay?"

Dale shrugged, "I really don't know. The sexuality of my staff is their business. Believe me, I hear enough tales of sexual adventuring every day to make a *Sun* reporter blush, but it goes in one ear and stays there."

O'Neill nodded briefly and then turned to Fran. "DS Wilson, take over for a while. I just want to wander round."

Once O'Neill had gone, Dale smiled and stroked Fran's hand. "He's getting uptight, isn't he?"

She nodded. "He doesn't like you much."

"Because I'm gay?"

"No. I think it's more that he thinks you're a barrier to finding the truth, and you take a light-hearted approach that he resents." Fran wasn't sure if this *was* the reason, but from her knowledge of O'Neill, it seemed the most likely explanation.

Dale frowned. "He doesn't actually suspect *me*, does he?"

"He suspects everyone. But then, so do I."

"Well, delicious DS Wilson, I'll have to watch my step, won't I?"

Fran smiled, "Dale, you just be as helpful as you can, and we'll be out of your hair pretty soon."

"Or out of my salon."

Fran nodded. "Now then Dale, tell me what happened from the moment Denise came into the salon. Where did she go first of all?"

Looking thoughtful, Dale said, "To be honest, I didn't see her arrive. Saturday is so busy, but first of all she would have seen the receptionist, Tara Watts. I expect Tara had to tell her that Mandy was running a bit late. That wouldn't have gone down well, and Denise would have been irritable."

"How long had Denise been coming here?"

"Since I've been open, nearly ten years now."

"And has Denise changed in that time?"

"She got more crabby, and I sometimes wondered why she bothered."

"I don't understand. Why should she not bother?"

Dale placed a hand under his chin and paused. "To be quite honest, she didn't seem interested in men or women – one of life's neutrals, I suppose – but I'd swear she came for reasons other than vanity or wanting to be pampered. I think she came to hear the gossip."

"Did she gossip herself?"

Dale shook his head. "No, strangely. I think the staff were unnerved by her, they rabbited to her, she made them so nervous."

"So, just because she was crabby, they told her bits of gossip?"

"You're putting words in my mouth, dear heart. They talked to her because she made them nervous. I didn't say they told her any gossip. I said I thought she came for the gossip. There's a lot of difference."

Fran stared into Dale's blue eyes for several seconds and suddenly she knew.

"*You* were terrified of her, too. Perhaps you were more unnerved by her than the rest of the staff."

"I wouldn't go as far as that."

"How far would you go, Dale? Fear can trigger murderous rage. Did you go that far?"

Dale's eyes flashed as brightly as any angry lover described in a romantic novel and his voice, when he found it, sounded tremulous. "Okay . . . I *was* a bit scared of her, but not for any real reason. I certainly didn't kill her. I haven't got any nasty little secrets, everyone knows I'm gay, so why would I get into a rage?"

"Don't get so upset, Dale. The sooner we catch the killer, the sooner you will get back to your normal routine. Now, tell me about your partner – Marcus."

"He had nothing to do with Denise's death, he's a gentle type. We had mice in the flat once, he wouldn't even put down a mousetrap down."

"That's a spurious argument, Dale. The odd fly or mouse doesn't produce the necessary incentive to murder – there's no emotion involved, maybe mild irritation, but not murderous rage."

"Stop trying to confuse me. Talk to Marcus yourself. He's got a sweet nature, he can be . . . "

He broke off, realising he'd said too much.

"He can be what?"

Dale sighed, "If you must know, he's not entirely faithful to me. I'm not saying he sleeps around, but he likes his freedom."

"We'll be talking to Marcus of course, but I want you to tell me what you remember about Saturday from the moment Denise arrived."

Dale looked puzzled.

"For instance, did you see her go into the beauty salon?"

He shook his head.

"Did you go through to the staff room while she was in the beauty salon?"

He frowned. "On a Saturday, I don't stop. I'll drink coffee on the job, I don't eat and sometimes I don't even go for a pee. And to be honest, I don't actually remember seeing her at *all*. Except when she was dead."

Fran watched him intently. Some people could lie so convincingly but somehow she didn't think he fell into that category. Strange though, the only thing that interested her was the reference to the 'nasty little secrets,' implying that they were rampant.

Nine

Tara Watts stared despairingly at the overweight body of her sleeping husband. He'd fallen asleep straight after his evening meal and now stretched out on the sofa, his mouth wide open and, with his bare stomach exposed above his jeans, he had the look of a man settled for the evening. And yet tonight was his night out with the boys, it was eight o'clock and he usually left the house at eight-thirty. So far, he hadn't showered or changed his clothes and although she'd tried to stir him, she'd only received grunts in reply. She watched the clock anxiously until eight-twenty. "Please Jimmy, wake up or you'll never get to the pub."

"Leave me alone, woman. I'm shattered," he muttered, before turning his bulk over like a pig on a spit.

"I'm popping next door," said Tara, as she slipped a coat on.

"Don't be too bloody long then."

Next door, her friend Yvonne seemed pleased to see her, but noticed Tara's anxious expression. "What's up? Has *he* upset you again?"

"He's not going out," she said, by way of explanation.

"What time are you meant to be meeting him?" asked Yvonne, putting an arm round Tara.

"Nine. His parents are away for a few days and I was looking forward to the evening."

Yvonne laughed. "Well, it makes a change from saying

67

you're baby-sitting for me. I'll make some tea – you ring him."

"Thanks. You're a pal."

"Well, I'm an alibi," she answered cheerfully.

Tara picked up the phone and dialled the number.

"Hi," came his cheerful reply.

"It's me," she said. "I can't make it tonight. He's not going out. I'm really sorry, darling."

There was a long pause before he said, "Not as sorry as I am. I'm gutted. You've got to leave the old bastard. I just want us to be together. We could find somewhere . . ."

"We don't earn enough."

"You mean *I* don't."

"Please don't start a row. I get enough of that at home."

There was a long silence before he spoke again. "I'll ring you tomorrow, about ten."

"Okay, darling. Bye."

"Bye," came the swift response.

Tara's eyes filled with tears, but she struggled not to cry. She didn't want Yvonne to think she was a complete wimp. Yvonne had problems of her own; her husband was in prison and she had two children under five, whose only good points were that they slept well and were reasonably bright. Tara found them ugly, with their round faces, squashed noses and small beady eyes that were inherited from their father. Whereas Yvonne, although a little round faced, had a neat straight nose, big blue eyes, long blond hair, wonderful big breasts and clear skin.

Tara often compared herself unfavourably with her friend, envying her big breasts, good skin and her ability to cope cheerfully with life's problems. Yvonne, in Tara's eyes, was all woman. Sometimes when she looked at herself naked in a mirror, Tara felt unfinished, like a child. Her body was all angles and bones, she had no definable waist and she always had dry skin and hair. Yvonne always told her she had wonderful cheek bones and lovely grey eyes but that didn't compensate her for not feeling womanly. She was only twenty-six, but sometimes she felt old. Perhaps it was being married to 'the Thing' next door.

When Yvonne occasionally provided some cheap wine or cider, they would sit all evening, never getting drunk, just more giggly and honest. Tara had told Yvonne about 'the Thing', who was twenty years older than she and whose idea of a good time was an Indian takeaway on a Saturday night, watching *Match of the Day*, followed by a war video or an old Clint Eastwood movie. The 'dessert' was a quick flick of the nightie in an upwards direction, some heavy breathing – usually hers, because of the weight of him on her chest – then came the pulling down of the nightie, followed by him rolling over in bed and promptly snoring happily and loudly. Their acts of copulation were always in the dark, not so much because she was ashamed of her body, but so that she couldn't see his expression, or let him see hers.

Yvonne returned, not with a tray of tea but with a bottle of sherry. "Sorry I took so long, but I knew I'd stashed away a bottle somewhere, I just couldn't remember where."

Tara smiled although she felt like crying. "What am I going to do, Yvonne? I can't stay with the Thing for much longer. I hate him. He's so . . . lifeless. I wouldn't mind if he let me have some freedom but here's just about the only place he lets me come to, and that's only because you're next door."

"You could leave him," suggested Yvonne.

"I'm scared, I suppose," said Tara. "I couldn't live on my own and I don't earn much at the salon."

"I heard about the murder. What exactly happened?"

"A silly old bitch got murdered in the hot box."

"Not a friend of yours, then?"

Tara sipped her sherry. "I couldn't stand her. She was creepy."

"Was she married?"

Tara shook her head. "No, she lived with her sister, their mother died about six months ago."

"Have the police got any suspects?

"I don't think so. They're going to interview everyone. I'm not looking forward to that. Once you say you didn't like someone, you're bound to be a suspect."

Yvonne laughed. "Come off it, Tara. If the Thing had been found murdered you'd be a definite suspect, but not some old biddy."

"Don't put ideas in my head. Believe me I could be tempted."

Yvonne stared at her friend. "You're joking. At least I hope you are."

Tara shrugged. "We discussed divorce once. He turned very nasty. Sometimes there seems no way out."

Yvonne moved along the sofa to reach the sherry bottle so that she could refill their glasses. "I'm surprised the Thing has got enough life in him to turn nasty."

"I don't tell you everything, it's too depressing."

Tara often glossed over the awfulness of her life because she wanted Yvonne to think well of her, and lately she had come to realise that her friendship verged on hero worship. She admired Yvonne not only because of her looks, but because she managed without a man. No, that wasn't quite true, she didn't just manage – she thrived. Tara had always hoped that one day, Yvonne's brand of courage and independence would rub off on her, but at the moment all she felt was a sense of desolation.

She had a lover but he had nothing to offer her, other than his love, and was that enough? Once they were living in a tiny flat, worried about the bills, would their love last? And if her husband found out, she wasn't sure which one he'd kill. Maybe both of them. Calling him 'the Thing' was making light of her husband's laziness, but if that had been his only fault she could have coped. Basically, the man was a thug, jealous and possessive and prone to violent rages. If she was entirely honest, she knew her only way of escape was to be under the protection of another man, because the Thing would come after her. If only, she thought, he'd been the one to die on Saturday, she'd have been free.

Mike finished work at six, and by seven he had showered and changed into jeans and a sweatshirt. He was hungry, but he had only tins of beans and rice pudding and he didn't fancy either. The 'flat' seemed smaller and grimmer than ever. He'd just enough room for his sofa bed, a small table and a bookcase; the kitchen – an extended cupboard – contained a sink, draining board, Belling cooker and one cupboard for everything. He had no fridge, but with little or no cooking and not much eating, it didn't matter too much.

Tonight he felt restless. Switching on the black and white TV, he stretched himself out on his sofa bed but still he couldn't settle. His thoughts centred on his children. Probably they would be having their baths now, then it would be story time and their mother would spend half an hour reading to them. Where had it all gone so wrong? Janine had been his replacement 'wife' and yet they wanted such different things. No, that wasn't true, he wasn't sure what he *did* want and he wasn't sure now, since Denise's murder, what Janine wanted. She had become so distant with him, as if she didn't need him anymore, and yet he would have imagined that losing her sister would have brought them closer.

He kept looking at his watch. He had to make a decision, knowing that he was far too restless to stay in. He could go to Janine's but she seemed to want to be alone, although if he was on her front doorstep she wouldn't turn him away. Or he could go home . . . old home, he corrected himself. If he left now, he'd still be in time to see the kids. He didn't like to admit to himself that he wanted to see his ex-wife just as much. After all, he was still in love with Janine, wasn't he?

Later, as he stood on the front doorstep of the house that he was still paying for, he could hear his two children laughing and then his ex-wife joining in. He wanted to clutch those happy sounds, feel their closeness; instead he felt choked, as though a dagger had pierced his heart and now he was for ever the outsider. And all the 'if only's in the world wouldn't make any difference.

Ten

Fran couldn't believe how tired she felt one week into the investigation. It was Sunday morning, snowing and cold, even on the inside. Fran wandered around in a blue tracksuit, giving her home a renewed acquaintance with its owner. This was the first time she'd seen the house in daylight for a week and she wasn't impressed. The rag-rolled walls looked even less arty and more plebeian, now that their colours had faded into a vague sludge. She no longer noticed the smell of damp or missed the mouse, but what she did experience was a sense of not belonging. Not belonging to the house, or the job, or anyone.

She had no friends in Fowchester and although more people spoke to her now in the course of a day, she was never invited anywhere. She'd heard the saying 'once a grass, always a grass' and used to think it was only used by the criminal classes. Now even her view of criminality had changed. There were, of course, professional criminals, those who made their living by theft and fraud and drug dealing. The more middle class the criminal, the greater likelihood of them carrying on undetected. Prison, for the lower rank professional criminals, was seen by them as inevitable and acceptable. It was part of the life of a criminal.

It was the others who worried her, the amateurs. Those who committed violent crimes and were either never caught, or were caught when the damage had been done.

Someone like her ex-boyfriend. Outwardly a good police-man, but inwardly as vicious as any so-called criminal. When she'd seen him beating up a prisoner in the cells, it was his expression she'd noticed – he was enjoying himself, he felt vindicated and, she knew instinctively, he'd done it before.

Had Denise Parks been like that? Fran wondered, honest and respectable on the outside, not popular but certainly not a 'criminal', and on the inside, nasty and vicious, so much so that the only way to deal with her was to kill her.

The whole team had worked solidly for a week and achieved little. The customers present when Denise's body had been found had all been interviewed and cleared of suspicion. The staff were still being interviewed, Marcus King being rather elusive at times, but O'Neill planned to talk to him again this afternoon.

Just before one o'clock, Fran toasted two slices of bread, made a cup-a-soup and sat at the kitchen table, slipping a Tina Turner tape into her radio cassette player to cheer herself up. She was about to start eating when there was a knock at the door. She ignored the knocking, undoubtedly it was either the Pentecostal Church or the Salvation Army or a duo of Jehovah's Witnesses. Whoever it was, she felt divorced from any form of organised religion and she was hungry. The knocking continued and eventually a familiar voice shouted through the letter box. "I know you're in there, Fran. Open the door, it's the police."

O'Neill seemed cheerful and was casually dressed in a brown leather jacket that Fran had never seen before, a chunky cream sweater and brown trousers. In comparison, she felt incredibly scruffy and he seemed to agree. "Get yourself dressed, Fran," he said. "We're on a mission."

She dressed hastily in black skirt, black boots and a

red sweater. Quickly brushing her hair, she then flicked mascara on her eyelashes to give her a more wide awake look. Finally, she applied what she hoped was a lipstick that complemented the red of her sweater then, grabbing a warm jacket from her wardrobe, she went downstairs.

O'Neill stood in the kitchen staring at her lunch. "It's no wonder you're losing weight, Fran. And I have to say, I'm worried about you."

"Why? I'm fine. I just haven't done much shopping."

"I think I'm working you too hard," he said.

"No harder than you. You're working all hours."

"I work long hours because I've nothing else. What's your excuse?"

Fran shrugged. "The same. It's crossed my mind just recently that there must be more to life than work."

O'Neill smiled. "And what happened to my ambitious DS? I thought you wanted to make inspector, at the very least."

Fran thought for a moment. Did she still want that? "To be honest, I don't know any more," she said. "I feel totally isolated, I have no friends here, my house needs attention but since no one ever comes here, there doesn't seem much point in making any changes."

"Well, be Jasus," said O'Neill, in his corniest Irish accent. "I think you need cheering up. I know a place that does a wonderful mushroom risotto and an apple pie to die for."

"With custard?"

O'Neill laughed. "Would I offer you any less? Come on, let's go."

O'Neill drove out into the country. It was still snowing, more half-heartedly now but driving conditions were poor.

"Couldn't we have gone to somewhere more local?" asked Fran.

"I have my reasons," said O'Neill. Then he added, "Talking of reasons, what about Denise's stock of underwear? What have you found out?"

Fran sighed, "Nothing, really. It wasn't bought via a catalogue, but an older sales lady in a lingerie shop thought it was years old . . . which is strange."

"The buying of it?

"Yes, the whole thing."

"So we're looking at a lover that she buys the underwear for," murmured O'Neill, thoughtfully.

"Or used to, if it's that old?"

O'Neill thought for a moment. "The question remains, was it bought for a male or female partner?" Before Fran had time to respond he said, "Female, I should imagine, perhaps her one and only friend. And we'll be paying her a visit very soon."

The pub – The Firs and Thicket – when they eventually arrived, was on the outskirts of a small village. The sprinkling of snow over the rooftop added to its rather twee, country pub appearance. Inside, a log fire and lamplight added to the cosy feel, although there were no old men playing dominoes, or burly young men playing bar billiards. This pub seemed definitely up-market to Fran and the sound of one or two 'Hooray Henrys' talking in loud voices confirmed her impression. It wasn't until she looked up from her menu that she realised she was the only woman in the pub. Not that that in itself was unusual; what was unusual was the fact that so many of the men in the pub were either holding hands or staring passionately at each other.

"This is a gay pub," she said.

"Correct," said O'Neill. "Take a Brownie point."

"And I thought," said Fran, "that you'd trekked out here just for the apple pie."

"An ulterior motive. I want to talk to Marcus."

"Couldn't it have waited until he was in the salon?"

O'Neill looked round the pub. From the window seat he could see the bar directly and a few of the tables. Marcus either hadn't arrived yet or he wasn't going to show at all. Dale had given him the impression during the week that this was his favourite Sunday lunchtime haunt, so a visit was definitely called for. Finally, he answered Fran: "I've spoken to him briefly, but like all the other staff members, he was blind, deaf and dumb at the time Denise was murdered."

"Is it possible they were *all* involved?"

"Sure, I'm beginning to think even the milkman might have had a hand in it."

"I'm not being funny Connor, but did they have milk delivered?"

He shook his head, "I've no idea. What's the significance?"

"I must be hungry because I keep thinking about food and I remembered there were half-eaten sandwiches in the staff room."

"So?"

"They were pre-packed, shop-bought sandwiches. The same-day sandwiches. Someone had to have bought them on the Saturday."

O'Neill nodded. "What you mean is, a member of staff left the salon . . ."

"Via the side door."

"Brilliant, Fran. You'll make inspector yet."

"If I survive the hunger pangs."

O'Neill grinned as he stood up. "I'll chase it up."

It was minutes later their meals arrived and at the same time, Marcus walked in with a young man, snake-hipped in black leather trousers, the closest fit Fran had ever seen.

"Don't stare at them, Fran, let's eat first. I don't want them to spot us just yet."

"I think he's seen us anyway. I do stand out like a sore thumb."

For a moment, O'Neill looked puzzled, then he realised Fran meant her gender.

They were waiting for dessert when Marcus walked over to them, leaving Snake Hips with only a glass of lager to stare into.

"Am I being harassed, Chief Inspector?"

"Sit down, Marcus," said O'Neill. "I'll only take a minute."

"As the bishop said to the actress," he said, smirking as he sat down.

"Quite," said O'Neill coldly. "I'll ask you the same questions I asked you before. Did you leave the salon at any time on Saturday morning?"

"And I'll give you the same answer. No."

"Who did, then? Who opened the side door?"

"Dale told you no one opened the side door in case of thieving, except for Tuesday when the rubbish was collected."

"What about the sandwiches?"

"I don't know what you're talking about."

"Didn't someone always buy the sandwiches on a Saturday?"

"Yes, but . . ."

"Who bought them?"

Marcus looked over towards Snake Hips, managing to give his ponytail a toss as he did so. "I suppose it was Andrew, he does run all the errands. But he was always supposed to use the front door."

"Why didn't you tell me this before?"

Marcus shrugged. "You didn't ask me about the sandwiches and anyway, I didn't know he'd used the side door. Is it such a big deal?"

"If someone knew Andrew had left the side door

unlocked, they could have been waiting for the opportunity."

Marcus frowned in an exaggerated way. "I'm sorry, Chiefie, but don't you think we would have noticed a stray murderer in our midst?"

"Quite honestly Marcus, I don't think the staff of *Le Salon* would have noticed if Attila the Hun had walked in, in hobnail boots. And I get the feeling that, even if they had noticed, they would have ignored him."

"That's your opinion, Chief Inspector. We were very busy that morning. Hairdressing takes concentration and care. We didn't happen to be on the alert for the odd homicidal maniac, but I'm sure we would have noticed someone behaving suspiciously."

"Yes," murmured O'Neill. "And, in a way, that is my point."

"Have you finished with me?"

"For the time being."

Marcus, looking relieved, stood up. "By the way," said O'Neill, "who shall I tell Dale you were drinking with?"

There was a long pause during which Marcus's face and body grew rigid with anger, but eventually he managed to say between clenched teeth. "Don't worry about that. I'll tell him." Then he strode back to Snake Hips, his ponytail bouncing in what seemed to Fran like an angry postscript. They talked for a few minutes, then they left together.

"That got him rattled, didn't it?" said O'Neill thoughtfully.

"He didn't thump you."

"No. But given the right needling, I think he'd be more than capable of shoving mousse down Denise Parks' throat."

Fran thought about that. "Given the 'right needling' as you put it, I think many people would fall into that category."

O'Neill stared into space for a while. "I think, after our apple pie," he said thoughtfully, "we'll pay young Andrew a visit, and this time, Fran, you do the talking."

Andrew's parents opened the door. They were, supposed Fran, both in their late forties. Mrs Baines looked vaguely anxious and ushered them in quickly, as if the fact they were CID was signalled to the neighbours by supernatural means. The detached house, situated in a tree-lined avenue, was neat on the outside and pristine on the inside. Fran noticed a strong smell of bleach and the sitting room gleamed with polished surfaces. Mrs Baines had short red hair and matching hands and looked anxiously at their shoes, as though willing them to take them off. Fran ignored the unspoken request and noticed Mr Baines had a clipped moustache and an equally clipped style of speech.

"Andrew?" he queried.

"Yes," said Fran. "We won't keep him long."

"Do sit down," said Mrs Baines.

Fran and O'Neill sat gingerly on one of the two black leather sofas, low backed and adding to the general impression of shine and polish. Mr Baines left the room and shouted, "Andrew!" loudly from the bottom of the stairs.

Moments later the boy appeared, tall and gangly and trying to appear unconcerned; although his hands gave him away, he couldn't find a place for them. He sat down on the other sofa, stretched out his long legs, and sat on his hands. "Is it about the murder?" he asked.

"Is there anything else it could be about, Andrew?" asked Fran.

"No, of course not."

Fran stared at him deliberately for a few seconds then said, "Tell us about buying the sandwiches."

He stared back, looking slightly relieved. "What about the sandwiches?"

"Do you always go out for sandwiches on Saturdays?"

He nodded. "I'm the junior. I have to."

"What time did you go out for them?"

"Early, about nine."

"Were there customers in the salon then?"

"Yes, two."

"Did you use the side door?"

He paused. "Yes."

Fran smiled and waited a moment before asking bluntly, "Why?"

Hesitatingly, as if trying to think of a reason, he said, "I'm just bone idle, I suppose. It saves going through the salon."

"So you left the side door unlocked?"

"No."

"Who locked it then?"

"Tara, the receptionist."

"So you were together in the staff room?"

"What do you mean?"

"I mean, Andrew, you must have been together in the staff room, or else you would have had to go to the reception desk to ask her to lock up after you. Rather defeats the object of using the side door, doesn't it?"

"She was late that morning. We open at eight-thirty on Saturday and she didn't arrive until nine."

"Why was she late, Andrew?

"How would I know?"

"Who would know?"

"The boss, I suppose."

"Back to the sandwich run. How did you get back into the salon?"

"Through the front door."

"I see," murmured Fran. "And at no other time did you open the side door?"

"No."

Fran gazed steadily at him. "Do you see what this means?"

He shook his head.

"You are assuring us that no one could come in via the side door. So therefore, only someone on the premises could have killed Denise Parks. Would you like a list of our suspects?"

"No."

"Well, I think you should know and maybe you'll think of something. There's Dale, Marcus, Mandy, you of course, and Tara."

"Hang on a minute," interrupted Mr Baines. "I've had enough of this. My son is a good lad, he couldn't possibly have had anything to do with this woman's murder."

"Your son has just confirmed it must have been someone on the premises that committed murder. I was just pointing out our suspects."

"It could have been a customer," said Andrew, beginning now to sound a little nervous.

"What makes you say that?" asked Fran.

"Well . . . they go to the loo. They have to walk through the beauty salon. One of them could have done it."

"Old Mrs Hankins perhaps?

"No . . . not her."

"Who, then?"

"I don't know."

"Well, maybe you could think about that, Andrew. After all, you must know the customers pretty well. You wash their hair, don't you?"

He nodded miserably. "I do all the odd jobs."

"Including making coffee or tea for the customers?"

Again he nodded.

"So you're backwards and forwards between the salon and the staff room more than most."

"Yes. What does that prove?"

"Not a thing," said Fran. "But it's rather surprising you didn't actually see or hear anything."

"Well, I didn't."

"Fair enough. I'll leave it there, but obviously we'll have to talk to you again. Next time the Chief Inspector will want to interview you, so if there's anything you do remember you can save it for him."

Andrew's eyes caught O'Neill's grimmest expression and he could no longer sit still. "Is it okay if I go now?"

Fran nodded. "*Au revoir*, Andrew."

He swiftly left the room, leaving his father looking red faced with anger and his mother near to tears. "He's a good, honest boy," she said. "He's never been violent. He doesn't have girlfriends. What possible reason could he have for killing a middle-aged woman?"

"Someone had a reason, Mrs Baines," said Fran. "And we'll find the reason and then the person."

Outside in the car, O'Neill said, "Well done, Fran. I felt quite the ogre. Silent but omniscient."

"What do you think of him?" asked Fran.

"I think," said O'Neill, "he's a lying little git."

Eleven

Janine heard the knocking but ignored it – she'd seen Mike approaching the front door. She'd spoken to him on the phone briefly the previous day and said she didn't want to see him yet. The knocking continued and he kept calling her name. For a while she blocked her ears but then he became threatening, shouting that he'd call the police if she didn't answer the door.

Finally, unable to stand any more she opened the front door. Mike wore a pair of old jeans and a scruffy black anorak, he'd got caught in the rain coming from the car and a damp smell seemed to emanate from him. Rain or beads of sweat clung to his forehead and she feared his shoes would be wet too. She didn't want him to come into the house.

"Please leave me alone, Mike," she said calmly.

"I've been worried about you. Aren't you going to ask me in?"

"Why?"

"Why? Because I want to talk to you."

She paused. "You'd better take your shoes off. I've just cleaned everywhere."

As Mike took off his shoes in the hall he looked more closely at Jan and couldn't believe the change in her. Now she appeared pale, a pallor intensified by the dark rings under her eyes. She wore no make-up and she'd scraped her hair back from her face. Somehow she seemed thinner, smaller, older, as if she were fading. Perhaps it's the dress she's wearing, he thought, pale blue, well below the knee with a little white Peter Pan collar. It took him a moment to register the fact he'd seen the dress before. On her sister! He wasn't sure now what to say to her, especially as she was staring at him . . . blankly.

"You don't seem well, Janine. Would you like me to call the doctor?"

"I'm fine, thank you. What did you want to talk about, Mike?"

"I wanted to talk about . . . us."

"Us?" echoed Janine.

"For Christ's sake, Janine. I think you owe me that."

"What for?"

Mike's hands clenched and unclenched. This woman seemed like a complete stranger. Confusion caused him to stutter, "We . . . were talking about getting married."

"Would you like a cup of tea?" she asked.

"Forget the frigging tea," he snapped, then added in a softer tone: "You make one, then perhaps we can sit down and talk."

She didn't answer but walked slowly towards the kitchen. He followed her, feeling a growing sense of unease.

In the kitchen, she put the whistling kettle on the gas cooker and he noticed she'd watched the running tap as intently as a snake charmer eyeballing the poised snake. With the kettle filled to capacity she sat down at the opposite side of the kitchen table, folded her arms in front of her chest and stared at him. He tried to keep his voice calm and even.

"I know you're still in shock about your sister, but you don't have to shut me out."

There was no response so he tried again. "I know I didn't like your sister but I didn't wish her any harm."

"You were jealous of her."

"I wouldn't put it that strongly. I did resent her, I suppose. I know she didn't approve of me and she thought I wasn't good enough for you."

Janine stared at him coldly, her eyes dull, her mouth set in a thin line, almost defiant. She said nothing and when Mike spoke again, he was aware he sounded needy and slightly whiny.

"Jan, darling. I'm the same person I was before. I haven't changed. You loved me then."

"Did I?" she said, looking puzzled.

"You said you did. Were you lying?"

"I don't lie."

"So you did love me?"

"I suppose so," she said grudgingly. It was that grudging quality in her voice he resented.

"Why are you being such a bitch? I really care about you and it's like talking to a brick wall."

"I've changed."

"I'll say you've bloody changed. You're like a different person."

"I am different."

Mike stood up, he couldn't stay seated any longer, he felt so angry. Janine hadn't been responsible for his divorce but . . . but what? He couldn't think straight any more. "For God's sake Jan, what did I do wrong?"

"You know," she said pointedly.

"Don't talk in bloody riddles. Say it! What did I *do*?"

Janine's expression remained impassive. "You killed her, didn't you?"

"Don't talk such crap. Why would I kill your sister?"

"You thought she got in the way. I think you wanted this house and her money."

"Do you think I'd risk everything by committing murder? I do have children to consider."

"And an ex-wife."

"What's that supposed to mean?"

"You still see her."

"Of course I do. She's the mother of my two kids."

Janine turned her head away. "Did you have to see her into the early hours? Denise told me you were always being seen leaving the house in the early morning."

"Once. Bloody once. My son was ill. I had to stay. Your sister was the jealous one. No man would ever want that stony-faced old cow."

Janine uncrossed her arms and stared him full in the face. "You're the only person in the world who could have wanted my sister dead. I think that once we were married you would have wanted me out of the way so that you could go back to your ex-wife."

Mike's mouth dropped open in surprise. She was totally mad . . . paranoid.

"So it's true," she said calmly, as if he had made some sort of admission of guilt.

"You're a sick bitch," said Mike, struggling to keep his temper. God . . . he wanted to hit her. Wipe that smug expression from her face. Instead, he took a deep breath. "I don't think you know what you're saying. You think I had a motive for killing your sister, but I reckon everyone who ever met her would like to have choked her. She was a smug, self-satisfied, sanctimonious, evil old bitch who loved other people's misfortunes. You need to open your eyes and grow up."

Janine's eyes flashed and her body tensed, her mouth opened but the only sound was the harsh sudden noise of the kettle whistling. It sounded to Mike as loud as a siren. "Turn the sodding thing off," he shouted. She got up slowly, turned off the gas and then removed the whistle. The sudden silence calmed Mike a little. There was nothing more to be said. She still stood with her back to him and a sudden feeling of pity came over him. She was sick, deranged. Talking to her was as pointless as arguing with a drunk.

"I think it's better if I go," he said.

She still stood with her back towards him. "Just promise me you'll see the doctor or a counsellor. You're not yourself, Janine. You really need help. If you were your normal self, you'd know I could never kill anyone. I'm not the violent type, you know that. I'm an old softie really."

"She wasn't anyone," said Janine. "She wasn't just anyone . . ."

Mike could hear the rising tambour of her voice. "No, of course not. Of course you loved her, she was your—"

Janine swung round, her eyes wide and bright. "You stupid bastard . . ."

Mike started to get to his feet as he noticed she held the kettle in her right hand. "You stupid bastard," she repeated, "Denise wasn't just anyone . . . she was my *mother*."

He saw the raised arm as if in slow motion, saw the boiling water in mid-air, realised she was aiming for his groin. The pain didn't register immediately and when he opened his mouth he couldn't hear himself screaming, yet he knew he was. He fell to his knees, knocking over the chair, the table, crawling on all fours, the pain so intense he felt he would explode. She was kicking him now, shouting obscenities, screaming. He hardly felt the kicks, he had to keep crawling away, had to escape. One kick sent him sprawling. He was still crawling as he got into the hall. She was still behind him, kicking and screaming. He saw the front door and knew he had to get to his feet. The initial shock and pain gave way to the fight for life and there was no doubt he was fighting for his life. He *had* to get to the front door.

Her ranting stopped for a second as she paused for

breath, and he raised himself on his knees and dragged himself upright. He felt a kick in the back of his leg and he turned and lashed out with all his strength. He heard, rather than saw, her fall. In moments, he had the front door opened and then closed. He propped himself against the door feeling the pain in his groin throbbing and burning, then he vomited and as the vomit hit the front porch steam rose. He wiped his mouth with the back of his hand, lifted his sodden jeans from his crotch and began to run.

As he started the car, he was aware his face was wet. It was no longer raining and he realised his face was wet with tears. He drove on, his eyes misty, trying to ignore the pain, trying to be thankful he had survived.

The doctor in casualty rang the police, but Mike didn't mind seeing them. He'd been given an injection for the pain, the blisters had been dressed and he'd been reassured that his manhood would recover. He felt euphoric now, his ex-wife was on her way to see him and he was going to make sure that Janine was either charged or the mad bitch was locked up. He lay between white cool sheets and watched the nurses, especially their legs, then he drifted off into a hazy, drug-induced sleep.

When he woke, Chief Inspector O'Neill sat by his bed. Mike was a bit disappointed the sergeant wasn't with him, she might be a bit sharp in manner but she was very attractive.

"Well, Mike," said O'Neill, "I've spoken to the Doc and he says you'll only have to abstain for a few weeks and then you'll be as good as you ever were."

Mike managed a wry smile.

"You'll be wanting to tell me all about it," said O'Neill.

Mike nodded. "She's gone mad. Really flipped her lid. She thinks I murdered Denise for the house and the money. The fact that I was working that morning and I saw her at lunchtime seems to have escaped her logic."

"You could have hired someone," suggested O'Neill.

Mike stared at him stonily. "I couldn't afford to do that, even if I was the type."

"Fair enough. Tell me what happened."

Mike related the row and the assault in vivid detail, so vivid O'Neill had a desire to place his hand protectively between his own legs.

"She was screaming something about Denise being her mother. I think her mind has gone completely."

"Did you hit her?

Mike shook his head. "I swiped at her, I wanted to get out alive. She's okay, isn't she? I mean physically."

O'Neill nodded and murmured, "She's fine, Detective Sergeant Wilson is with her at the moment."

"Jan should be committed. She was even wearing one of her sister's dresses. Can you believe it?"

O'Neill didn't answer. Instead he said, "Tell me what you know about the family."

Mike's eyes strayed to a passing nurse, then he said thoughtfully, "Not much really. Mother Maggie had been ill for some time and she died about six months ago. I do know Denise did most of the nursing and towards the last few months of the old girl's life she worked part-time. In the past, Janine worked in London but when things got tough I think Denise sent for her."

"Did Janine talk about Maggie?"

"A bit," said Mike thoughtfully. "She bought Jan and Denise up alone and I don't think there ever was a man about. I think the cottage was where Maggie herself was born."

"Did she work?"

Mike paused, "I think so. Jan did say once that she did some housekeeping and when she retired she took in mending."

"If you had to sum up the three of them, Mike, what would you say?"

Mike looked puzzled. "That's a funny question." He paused. "I knew Denise was odd, a real old crow and I guessed Maggie had been the same, but I thought Jan was different. Now I can see they were all man-hating . . . nutters."

"Why do you think Denise was murdered?"

Mike smiled. "Do you want me to do your job for you?"

"Do you think you're up to it?"

"I won't be up to anything much for some time, will I? But I'm not surprised someone bumped Denise off."

"Why is that?"

He shrugged. "It was something about the way she looked at you. Like she was a mind reader. As if she knew your secrets."

"And that made you uneasy?"

"Not particularly, but then I haven't got any guilty secrets."

"What surprises me," muttered O'Neill as if talking to himself, "is that she didn't have that many contacts and yet so many people disliked her. She wasn't in the conventional sense a gossip but she seemed—"

"To know things," interrupted Mike. "Perhaps she really was a witch."

"Or she was a very good listener," said O'Neill.

As he left Mike's bedside the question remained. Who exactly did she listen to and how did she respond?

Fran had found Janine tearful and bruised on one side of her forehead. She was also very talkative.

"I should have listened to Denise. She was always right, you know. She could see through people. She said Mike was no good, that he was still sleeping with his wife – his ex-wife. That makes it worse somehow, doesn't it? Her being his ex."

Fran nodded. They were sitting in the kitchen and Fran had made a pot of tea, and now Janine had started talking there was no stopping her.

"Denise was my mother, you know. I'm not stupid. Once I found out she'd been lying about her age, it didn't take much for me to work out why. The trouble is, I don't know the full story and I suppose I never will." She paused, "I'll never know who my father is or why she didn't tell me. Really, Denise was an angel. No one knew her the way I did. She sacrificed her life for the both of us . . ." she broke off tearfully. "Why would anyone, other than Mike, want to kill her?"

"Mike couldn't have done it, Janine," said Fran gently. "His alibi is good – cast iron."

Janine stared at her blankly for a few seconds, sipping her tea. Then she said, "Aren't most people murdered by someone they know?"

Fran nodded.

"Well then. Denise was well thought of at work. Have you been to her office? She almost ran that place. She often said the place would fall apart if she wasn't there to keep them on their toes."

"What did she mean by that?"

Janine shrugged. "They needed organising, I suppose. She was good at organising people."

"Did she ever talk about her colleagues?"

Jan nodded. "Yes. I think she took an interest."

"In what?"

"Their problems."

"Was she an expert?"

"What's that supposed to mean?"

Fran smiled. "I only meant some people can solve other people's problems and perhaps not their own."

"She didn't have any problems to solve."

"You're sure?"

Janine scowled, "I don't know what you're trying to get me to say."

"Nothing at all. We just want Denise's killer found. Now, I'll ask you again, did Denise have any problems that you knew of?"

"No. She didn't. She said other people had the problems."

"What did she mean by that?"

Janine sighed in irritation. "Denise was quite uncomplicated. Ordinary, old fashioned. There wasn't anything darker about her, anything secretive."

"What about all those new, unworn undies?"

A slight flush showed on Janine's cheeks. "She was buying them for me, it's obvious."

"Why is it obvious?"

"Who else could they be for?" snapped Janine.

"As it happens," Fran paused, "almost anyone. You're a size twelve, I should imagine." Seeing Janine's angry expression, Fran chose her words carefully. "They seem a little tarty for you."

Janine slammed her cup onto her saucer. "It's not illegal to buy stuff like that."

"Of course it isn't," agreed Fran, "but it is out of character and it might be important."

"I don't see how my sister buying a few undies could possibly be important."

Fran smiled. "It might just be a quirk, like collecting . . . beer mats. But only time will tell."

Janine stared into her cup for a moment. "Can you read tea-leaves?" she asked.

The unexpected question surprised Fran. "No. Can you?"

"No, but my sister could."

"Really? Whose leaves did she read?"

"People at work. One or two pensioners in the village. Not many, but she enjoyed it."

"I thought reading tea-leaves was a dying art, with the advent of tea bags."

"Denise never used tea bags," said Janine proudly, as if tea bags were hell's own creation and conversely loose tea would therefore be a passport to heaven.

As she left the house, Fran wondered if tea-leaves did have some influence in projecting Denise prematurely into the afterlife. The only thing she had to work out was *how*?

Twelve

Mandy Willens ate a dry biscuit standing up in her kitchen. She took a few sips of bottled water followed by a several deep breaths. Then she threw up.

She arrived late at the salon and Dale, paranoid about getting back to normal, gave her a filthy look and told her she had a customer already waiting. Since the murder they had been far busier, several customers coming from outside the town, hoping to hear the gruesome details. They hoped in vain, because the police and Dale had warned the staff not to talk to anyone about the murder.

Thankfully, the customer waited in the reception area drinking coffee, so it gave Mandy a chance to compose herself and make sure she checked her diary for customer details. She had hoped that Mrs Favell, a new customer, wouldn't want either a pedicure or a manicure but she wanted both. Mandy dreaded sitting on the low stool for any length of time. She felt less sick now but she felt safer on her feet. She took a last look around before going out to call Mrs Favell. There was much more space now that the hot box was gone and although she'd rearranged a few items, the horror of finding Denise Parks with those wild staring eyes still haunted her at times. If only she hadn't left her. Sometimes Mandy felt responsible. If she'd been more organised that day, had the towels been ready, she wouldn't have walked away. She also felt guilty because she was glad, so glad, that the know-all old biddy was dead.

Mrs Favell was about forty, wearing riding boots, cream jodhpurs and a black polo-neck sweater. Her complexion showed the ravages of wind, sun and rain and Mandy felt her heart sink. The horsey set usually had fingernails that looked as if they'd scraped out hooves with them, and they never tipped.

Mrs Favell ('call me Fliss') obviously wanted to talk.

"I usually go to a little place in London," she said, "but I'd heard you were good, via a friend of mine – Anna De Souza – so I thought I'd give you a try."

Mandy wasn't sure if she was supposed to be suitably grateful, so she merely smiled and began cleansing the worn hands and raggedy nails of Fliss Favell.

"I'll have to file your nails right down. They have been rather neglected, you know."

Fliss didn't answer for a while. She lay back in the comfort of the Parker Knoll with both hands stretched out and eventually said, "This is such luxury. I do neglect my hands, I know, but the horses do have to come first." She smiled. "Even before men."

Mandy, sitting on the low stool at Fliss's feet, began gently filing the nails. Her stomach was in knots and she knew these nails would take forever to look even half-way decent.

"I heard all about the murder, of course," Fliss was saying. "It must have been dreadful for everyone."

Mandy nodded and began buffing the nails of her right hand.

"Anna was here that morning," Fliss said. "She left before it happened, thankfully. She and I ride together sometimes. Do you ride?"

Only Mandy's stomach rode at that moment and the idea of a horse jumping over fences made the bile rise in her throat. She took hold of Fliss's left hand and began buffing the nails briskly.

"Are you all right, my dear? You're looking a little green around the gills."

Mandy remembered nothing more until she saw a blank rose-coloured space above her head. It took her several seconds to realise she was looking at the ceiling. And a few more seconds to realise she was lying on her own massage table.

"Mandy, dear heart, thank goodness. Are you okay?" Dale asked her, his face so close to hers she could smell his sweet cloying aftershave. She felt her stomach heave. "Mrs Favell," she murmured.

"Don't worry your pretty head about her. She's quite happy to come back tomorrow for a freebie."

Mandy struggled to sit up. "Now just stay there," said Dale, pushing her shoulders back onto the leather headrest. "There's no point in getting up, anyway. The fuzz are on their merry way here. They want to see us *en masse*. But if you're not up to it dear, you just get yourself home. I'll call a taxi, you're in no fit state to drive."

"No thanks, Dale. I'd rather stay here. Just give me a few minutes."

Dale laid a cool hand on her forehead. "You could have a virus," he said thoughtfully. "Meningitis, even. Have you got a headache, stiff neck, purple rash, dislike bright lights?" He didn't wait for her reply. "I think I'd better call the doctor."

Mandy sat up swiftly. "No, Dale. Please, I'm not ill. I feel fine now."

He stared at her quizzically, then he said, "Sometimes I'm slow to catch on."

"What do you mean?"

"I may be an old queen, but that doesn't make me stupid."

Mandy lay back, she felt defeated. "It was an accident," she said by way of explanation.

"It often is," said Dale, patting her hand. "Aren't you pleased?"

He was being kind and this made Mandy feel much worse, and she had to make a real effort to hold back the tears. "Josh won't be pleased."

"Are you sure? He's not a complete pillock, is he?"

"That's why we're not married. He's always said he doesn't want kids. He'll blame me."

"It takes two to tango, dear. How far are you gone?"

"Two months, at least."

"He or she is pretty well settled in, then. I shall have to get my knitting needles out."

Mandy managed to smile.

"Don't laugh hysterically, Mandy. I'm a great knitter. I love it. But Marcus refuses to wear my wonderful creations. For you, I'll knit like an angel."

"You won't sack me, then?"

Dale threw up his hands dramatically. "Sack you? Why should I do that?"

"Because I'll grow as fat as an elephant and no one wants a pregnant beautician lumbering about."

"You, my dear, will look like a peach, glowing with health, fecund and ripe. And anyway – I shall boast it's mine. That'll get the tongues wagging."

"Thanks, Dale."

"No need to thank me, Mandy. Get your bot off there and go and sit in the staff room, make yourself a cup of tea and compose yourself for the police persons."

It was about half an hour later that they arrived and by then, Mandy felt much more composed. She heard Dale telling them she was indisposed, that she should be interviewed upstairs in the flat, and she felt relieved and grateful to Dale that so far, no other members of staff seemed to have suspected the real cause of her fainting fit.

DS Wilson followed her up the stairs to the flat and they had only just sat down in the lounge when Mandy found herself blurting out, "I'm pregnant."

Thankfully, the policewoman didn't congratulate her, she just said, "How do you feel about it?"

Mandy shook her head in bewilderment. "I don't know. I've known for ages but I didn't want to believe it. My boyfriend doesn't want children. He says he'll never change his mind. I've been trying to tell him for weeks, I just can't seem to find the right moment."

"Don't you think he might suspect already?"

"He hasn't shown any signs."

"Are you worried that he might leave you?"

Mandy thought about that for a moment. She knew it was a possibility, but surely he loved her enough. Her thoughts were interrupted by the sergeant:

"Mandy, I'm really sorry, but I'm going to have to ask you about the day Denise died."

"I did write down everything in my statement."

"Yes, but a brief statement just throws up more questions. For instance, you left Denise alone in the salon to fetch towels. Who was responsible for the towels?"

"That was Andrew, but I had used about three. Denise kept saying she was in a hurry and she wanted to go in the hot box without the towel. But I told her it would be too uncomfortable and some of the steam escapes."

"Did she say why she was in a hurry?"

"She was always in a hurry. When her mother was alive she was even worse, although she usually managed . . ."

"Managed what?"

"A cup of tea."

"Why did you hesitate, Mandy?"

Mandy shrugged. "I don't know. She . . . well, she always had a cup of tea, now I think back. She had one of those little silver double spoons. We even kept a packet of loose tea for her."

"Did she read the leaves?"

"How did you know?" asked Mandy in surprise.

"Just a guess. Did you participate?"

Mandy nodded. "Once or twice, reluctantly. She was very bossy, she didn't like anyone to argue with her."

"What did she tell you?"

Mandy looked away, "It was about six weeks ago. She stared into my cup and said she thought I was pregnant. I wasn't sure then, but she said even if I wasn't pregnant now, I soon would be."

"Anything else?"

"She said I'd lose my job . . ."

"And?"

Mandy stared at Fran, her eyes filling with tears. "She told me the leaves were telling her that my boyfriend would leave me as soon as he found out."

"A regular doom merchant, wasn't she," said Fran. "You're sure she didn't have tea that morning?"

"I didn't give her any."

"Was there anything else unusual that morning?"

Mandy shook her head. "Nothing I can think of. Saturdays are very busy and I don't really see what's going on in the main salon."

"What about unusual sounds?"

"It always seems noisy, the dryers, Dale and Marcus laughing, sometimes singing. Nothing out of the ordinary." Mandy swallowed hard. She wanted to tell the DS what else Denise had told her, but it wouldn't make any difference now. It was best to keep quiet. No one need ever know.

"Thanks, Mandy. I'd just like to go back to the time

that morning when you went to get the towels. How long exactly were you away for?"

"A few minutes."

"Three? Four?"

"I wasn't looking at my watch."

"Where did you go for the towels?"

Mandy felt distinctly uncomfortable now. Of course they'd found out in the end, the police always did. "The towels were upstairs in the flat. I had to ask Marcus for the key."

"Why Marcus? Why not Dale?"

"I suppose I saw Marcus first."

"So you went up to the flat. Where were the towels?"

"We'd used a lot of towels that morning and normally there are extras in the linen cupboard in the flat, but that morning the only towels were still in the tumble drier."

"Were they dry?"

Mandy shook her head and tears sprang to her eyes. "No. They were running short of towels in the salon, so I had to wait until they were dry. I knew Denise would be in a paddy at being left and I didn't look forward to the confrontation. I was sure she'd have shouted for Dale and complained about me."

"Had she done that before?"

"She complained about everyone. Dale didn't take much notice but he always made us apologise to her."

"So how long were you away, Mandy?"

"More than ten minutes I suppose. I came down with the towels, gave the key back to Marcus, put a pile of towels in the salon and . . ."

Fran waited for her to continue. "And what, Mandy?"

"And nothing."

"Come on, Mandy. You were going to add something."

"No, I wasn't." Mandy gritted her teeth. She'd already admitted far too much.

"I'll leave it there, Mandy," said Fran. "For the time being. You now admit to leaving Denise for at least ten minutes on her own. Marcus must have known that Denise was on her own. Was he the only one?"

"Marcus wouldn't have done it. He wouldn't."

"Was he the only one?" repeated Fran.

Mandy shrugged. "I don't know. I suppose he could have told someone or someone could have seen me leave the salon."

The sergeant watched her for a while and Mandy became aware that she no longer felt queasy, but her left leg trembled and her hands were wet with sweat.

"Thank you, Mandy. I hope you feel better soon. I'll probably speak to you again tomorrow. Or maybe the big chief will want to speak to you."

After the DS had gone, Mandy sighed with relief, wiped her damp hands on her white uniform dress, and noticed how large her belly seemed. At two months, it already seemed much bigger. She didn't know how long she could keep it a secret from the others and it didn't seem right that her boss knew before Josh.

Then she broke down and wept.

Thirteen

O'Neill and Fran sat side by side in their office at Fowchester Police Station, drinking black coffee and watching the computer screen as if total concentration could solve any mystery. It was late, the rain poured down, they were both tired and yet neither of them wanted to go 'home'.

"I need a wife," said O'Neill suddenly.

"So do I," said Fran.

"I'm serious," said O'Neill. "I'm losing motivation."

"You're just tired. You need to sleep in your own bed instead of the rape room. If Ringstead finds out he'll . . . have a turn."

O'Neill shrugged. "I'll start sleeping in my own bed when I've got a real suspect. At the moment, I feel everyone we speak to is telling us some of the truth, but holding something back. Sometimes I think we're the only people who don't know who did it."

"Mandy is definitely holding something back. I know she's scared her boyfriend will leave her because she's pregnant, but it's more than that. Denise was on her own for ten minutes, maybe longer. I'm surprised she didn't kick up more of a fuss."

O'Neill rubbed the back of his neck thoughtfully. "Unless, of course, she wasn't alone in that time. Maybe more than one person spoke to her, or the murderer held a conversation before killing her. A chance remark may have triggered a violent reaction."

"What do you think of the staff as suspects?" Fran asked.

O'Neill shrugged. "Dale and Marcus aren't closet gays, Dale knows Marcus plays around a bit. They're both consummate actors, they appear to love each other and I don't see they could have a motive. Tara, the receptionist, seems a bit downtrodden but again, I couldn't find out anything from her. She was mostly on the reception desk, said she didn't hear or see anything. Then there's Andrew and although he doesn't seem the hot-headed sort, I think he's hiding something. And apart from pregnant Mandy, who could have been tipped over the edge by an unwanted pregnancy, that's it."

"It may not be a member of staff," suggested Fran.

O'Neill thought about that for a moment. "The other customers present at the time have all been eliminated."

"What about those who left the salon *before* she was found?"

"I'd thought about that. The team have checked on two of them and eliminated them, mostly on the basis of time. There are two who left shortly before the body was found. A Mrs De Souza and a Miss Richards. We'll see them tomorrow."

"De Souza rings a bell," said Fran. "He's the dentist Janine works for."

O'Neill sighed. "I feel as if I've interviewed everyone but the lavatory attendant so far and we're only into the second week. We'll split up tomorrow. You go to Denise's office. I sent a DC there but he couldn't smell a rat at five paces. You go and work your feminine wiles on the boss man. I'll check on Janine and Mike."

"Are you going to charge Janine?"

"I'm not sure. Mike isn't sure about pressing charges.

I think he wants to get back with his ex-wife and wants the minimum of fuss. Janine might get let off with a stiff warning, being recently bereaved, et cetera."

O'Neill turned his attention back to the computer, but all he could think about was food and drink. "Shall we go out for some fodder, Fran? I could eat a horse's bollocks between two slices of bread."

Fran laughed. "Why not? I'm not that hungry but I do have a craving for a big jacket potato and a huge pile of melting cheese."

"I'll swap that for the horse's bollocks any day," said O'Neill with a huge smile. "By the way I don't like that word, 'craving'. You're not pregnant, are you?"

"If I was, I'd be selling my miraculous story to the Sunday papers."

Tara had spent the evening cleaning. It was more interesting than watching the Thing sleep. One day, she thought, she'd forget and call him 'Thing' to his face. That would be the day she left, and maybe it wouldn't be too far away. She had to make plans, find a way of leaving, a place to go that he'd never find her. She had tried to leave before; she'd gone to a woman's refuge but it should have been called a family refuge. She was the only woman without kids and at first the other women had been sympathetic but when they found out she hadn't been hospitalised or had any broken bones, she became a 'victim' there. "Would you mind the kids, Tara, while I go to the shops?" or "Tara, you can cut hair. Do the kids, will you, love?" The sound of those children sometimes haunted Tara; some of them were poor lost souls, like zoo-bred animals reared in cages too small for them, bored and stressed.

The Thing had found her on her second trip out to the shops. She'd turned round and there he was; sheepish, apologetic and professing his love as though his very existence depended on her. He had looked ill, thinner and pale, and pity overcame common sense.

He'd improved for a while, she'd found a part-time job as a stylist, but then he started drinking again. He got legless at home at least four nights a week, ignored her all evening and then, when she refused him sex, the slapping and arm twisting would begin until she gave in and did her impression of a log. Not that it mattered to him if she enjoyed sex or not. She just had to be there and available.

At the moment, he was becoming paranoid that she was seeing someone. Strangely, she felt angry about that. How dare he suggest, without evidence, that she was having an affair? Anyway, it had only just become a proper affair. They had so few opportunities and she'd wanted it to be right; sweet and romantic. She'd realised long ago that nothing in life turned out quite as you imagined it would.

She'd just finished cleaning and had removed her rubber gloves when the Thing stirred from the sofa and lumbered up to the bathroom. She stared at her hands despairingly, even wearing gloves they had become red raw and angry looking.

"Tara!" he shouted from upstairs. "Get your arse up here."

To others that might have sounded crass, but she sensed he was actually in reasonable humour. She began walking upstairs – he stood waiting for her at the top, his trousers were undone. As she reached him he said, by way of his idea of foreplay, "Show us your tits then, girl." She could smell the alcohol on his breath, his eyes were as glazed as if they were sightless. Total revulsion swept over her. She stepped to one side and began to remove her sweater, he turned to watch her and, caught off guard, her push sent him headlong down the stairs.

"Whoops!" she muttered as he thudded to the bottom. He lay still, one leg splayed on the last step. "Oh dear," she said aloud. "Drunk again."

She came down the stairs slowly, praying silently. *Please let him be dead. Please God, let him be dead.*

For several seconds, she was elated. Then, he began to snore. She straightened his leg, went upstairs, took a blanket from the cupboard, a pillow from the bed and then covered him with the blanket. She held the pillow within an inch of his face, and in that moment she felt incredibly powerful and she knew there would be other opportunities. Then she slipped the pillow under his head and, crouching down beside him, she watched the barely human husband of hers breathe and snore.

Tara didn't know how long she crouched, only minutes perhaps, but it felt longer until he opened his eyes. "Where am I?" he asked, thick voiced. Before she could answer he said, "My bloody ankle is killing me."

"You fell down the stairs, you've been lucky. Shall I help you to bed?"

"No, leave me. I can get myself to bed."

"If you're sure, dear," she said sweetly.

As she entered the bedroom, her eyes savoured the sight of the empty bed. With any luck he wouldn't move all night, maybe he'd hobble back to the sofa. Tonight she would have the joy of sleeping alone. As she drifted off into an easy sleep, she realised this had been one of the best evenings she had ever had.

Josh was watching soccer on TV when Mandy arrived home. His long slim legs were stretched out in front of him and he'd made himself a mug of coffee. "You're late, sweetheart," he said. "What kept you?"

"We were running late all day. The police came and I didn't feel too well."

"Oh," he said. "This is a good game." His eyes didn't stray from the TV.

In the kitchen she opened the fridge and then closed it again. She had once enjoyed cooking, but since she'd been pregnant she'd become sensitive to smells. Josh hadn't seemed to notice her meals had got simpler and simpler, something in breadcrumbs usually, plus an innocuous vegetable with no smell, like broccoli or frozen peas. At the back of the freezer she found something round and flat, wrapped in breadcrumbs and then cellophane. She hadn't a clue what it was but it would have to do.

She'd just started cooking the unidentified frying objects when she felt a real craving. It wasn't a stomach craving, it was purely oral. She wanted to drink pickle vinegar. The urge became so strong she stood on one of the kitchen chairs and began searching her cupboards. She'd bought pickled onions at Christmas, that was the only time she ever ate them, so there must have been some left. In her efforts to get to the back of the cupboard, a jar smashed onto the floor. She paused, waiting for Josh to come into the kitchen. When he didn't, she carried on looking and, sure enough, right at the back was a half-full jar of pickled onions.

The lid was difficult but she was determined. She removed the lid and put the jar to her lips. It was . . . nectar, sweet and sour and bitter. In her haste, some of it dribbled down her chin, she wiped it away swiftly and carried on drinking; she wasn't sipping, she was gulping.

"What the hell is going on?"

Her eyes swivelled to see Josh at the kitchen doorway, his mouth open in surprise. Her 'thingies' in breadcrumbs were sending up smoke signals and were obviously burning.

"Have you gone mad?" he asked.

She shook her head. "Here, take this," she said handing him the pickle jar and scrambling down from the chair. He'd turned the cooker off by now and opened the kitchen window.

"Be careful," he said. "There's glass and jam all over the floor."

He cleared up the jam and glass, all the time watching her warily, as though at any moment she might start foaming at the mouth or fangs would appear. Then, taking her by the hand, he led her into the front room and sat her down on the sofa. He glanced casually at the TV as the half-time scores came on and then he switched it off via the remote control and sat beside her, taking her hand in his and saying gently, "What's the matter, darling? What is it?"

"I'm pregnant," she blurted out. "I'm pregnant."

He dropped her hand and his expression was as shocked as if she'd slapped him.

"How?" he said. "How? I've always been careful. I'll sue the bloody condom company, the bastards!" He stroked her hand for a while then he added, "Don't worry darling, we can fix it."

Mandy suddenly felt icy cold. "It's too late," she lied. "I'm over three months gone."

He dropped her hand and said coldly, "You stupid bitch. Why didn't you tell me sooner?"

"I was scared, scared you'd be like this. Please don't be angry."

"'Please don't be angry'," he mimicked. "What do you bloody well expect? I told you right from the start I didn't want children."

"It's not my fault—"

"It's your fault for not telling . . . in time."

The 'in time' sounded so ominous that Mandy burst into tears.

"Crying won't help," he said coldly. "We've got to think sensibly."

She continued to cry but he ignored her. Then, after a few minutes he sprang to his feet. "I'm going out. I can't stand any more of this."

"Where are you going?" she asked, as she struggled to stifle her tears.

He didn't answer but the front door slammed, and a thunderous sound echoed throughout the house.

She sat for a while, simply staring into space. It was done now. He knew. He'd reacted in the way she'd expected but she still felt disappointed, although it was tinged with a sense of relief. Now at least she didn't have to try to hide the way she felt. If she wanted to throw up, she could. If she wanted to come home and go straight to bed, she could. If she wanted to eat raw food, she could. There would be no more having to rush home and cook something in breadcrumbs or watch endless football matches. She was free. She patted her stomach. "We'll be free," she said aloud. The house was in her sole name. Josh could leave in the morning.

She put her feet up on the sofa and smiled to herself. The chances were the condom hadn't split. After all, she had had unprotected sex with someone else. Only once, but once was enough.

Fourteen

In the bathroom, Marcus brushed his hair and couldn't decide whether to wear it loose, or up in his usual ponytail. It was Saturday night and he hadn't yet told Dale he was planning to go out, and he knew it was going to cause a row. He was a party animal and Dale was a home bird. He loved Dale, but sometimes he found the differences between them irksome. Dale was a control freak, never happy if Marcus was out of his sight, but they both knew that love and business kept them firmly together, and that was a powerful combination. It was Dale's capital that had started the salon, Marcus had just qualified and was penniless but Dale had offered him a straight down the middle partnership; since then money had never been a source of friction between them. His friendships had, however, been a major cause of rows. Marcus never admitted sleeping with anyone else, mainly because he didn't want to cause Dale unnecessary pain but also because he felt it wasn't important. Sex was just sex and he liked variety in that, but love was love and he couldn't find that elsewhere. He also knew that if push came to shove, he'd forego sleeping around to stay with Dale.

Dale was outside the bathroom door when he came out. "Why are you lurking?" asked Marcus.

"You took long enough," said Dale. "Wearing the black leathers, I see. Hoping to pull, are we?"

"No, I'm just a vain bastard."

"You said it."

"Dale baby, you know you could come with me. I'm going to Peacocks – you'd like it there. They play all the old crap you like."

"It's well named, anyway."

"Come with me."

Dale felt tempted, at least if he went with him he could hold off the predators. He had to admit, Marcus looked fantastic; he wore tight soft black leather trousers with a black leather shirt open at the neck to reveal a gold necklace bright against his pale skin.

"Come on Dale. Don't stand there with your mouth open – make your mind up."

Dale still hesitated. If he was honest with himself, his soul wanted to go but his varicose veins didn't. They throbbed like crazy; he never complained about them and he tried as far as possible not to let them be seen by anyone, especially of course, Marcus. Young people too suffered with varicose veins, and they were common amongst hair stylists and people who stood to work, but that didn't stop Dale feeling that his varicose veins were a sign of ageing, like a receding hairline or crow's feet.

"It's not my scene, Marcus. I'd rather put my feet up."

"And rest your varicose veins, dearie."

"I haven't got varicose veins – you bitch."

"They're as big as tramlines, sweetie. I'm not blind."

Dale felt a mixture of anger and humiliation wash over him. He turned away so that Marcus couldn't see his expression. But he came up behind him and whispered in his ear.

"Come on, don't get upset. I'd still love you if they were bigger than tramlines. I'm going to call them your varicose 'vains' with an 'a' – get it?"

Marcus began to tickle the back of his neck and Dale felt his ill humour melting away.

"Will you still love me when I'm old and grey, Marcus?"

"I will and I do," he answered, laughing.

Marcus wasn't going out for a while so they sat together on the sofa, their arms around each other, listening to ballads on CD. They were silent for a long time until Dale said, "Remember the day Denise was killed?"

"How could I forget?"

"You disappeared for a few minutes – when Denise was in the hot box."

"Did you tell the police that?"

"Of course not. I wouldn't grass on you – whatever you'd done."

"I didn't do anything," said Marcus defensively.

"Where were you, then?"

"What is this?" demanded Marcus. He sat upright, glaring. "We're having a nice quiet time together and you give me the third bloody degree. Why now? You haven't asked me this before."

"It's been on my mind. After all, you talked to her more than anybody. I think she quite liked you."

"Rubbish," snapped Marcus. "She thought I was a real oddity."

"It takes one to know one."

"You can be so . . . trite."

"I want you to tell me," said Dale evenly, "where you were for those few minutes, and this time Marcus, I want a straight answer."

Marcus had heard that tone of voice before. The lower the tone, the more angry Dale was getting. And Dale, once roused, had a nasty temper. "Oh, all right, sweetness, I'll come clean. It was all quite innocent: I was going to get my customer a cup of coffee. I couldn't see Andrew anywhere so I thought I'd get it myself. I was just passing by, the curtains were pulled, of course, and she called out: 'Marcus, I know that's you. I recognise your heavy tread.' I stopped still in my tracks and then she said in that bossy tone of hers, 'Come here, Marcus. I want to talk to you.' First of all, she complained that there weren't enough towels, more or less accused Mandy of being deliberately dilatory. Can you believe it? She actually said that – 'deliberately dilatory'. I tut-tutted sympathetically and said I'd reprimand her for being dilatory – sounds better than slack – and I was about to move away when she said, 'By the way, have you noticed your hair is getting thinner? I bet you find more on your pillow now, and in the bath. You check your hairbrush. I'm always right about these things.'" Marcus broke off and his hand touched his ponytail as if to reassure him it was still there.

"The old crab. She always guessed a person's weak spot. It gave her power, I suppose."

He reached out to touch Dale. "It's not getting thinner, is it? Tell me it isn't."

Dale patted his lover's cheek. "It looks better than ever. I suppose you've been imagining normal hair loss was bucket loads."

Marcus nodded. "My father lost all his hair well before he was thirty-six."

"That's not happening to you so stop worrying."

"I can't seem to forget it. Every time I put my hair in a ponytail I wonder if it's doing it harm."

"Let it hang loose for a while, then. Come on, I'll undo it for you."

Dale released Marcus's hair and ran his fingers through it. "It's as thick and glossy as ever, sweetheart. It's glorious."

"You're biased."

"I know about hair, and don't you forget it."

They were both silent for a while, as if they simultaneously realised the condition of Marcus's hair was not the real issue.

"What did you do?" asked Dale.

"I didn't kill her."

"Look at me Marcus, and tell me the truth."

Marcus's blue eyes stared at him. "I walked away and that's the truth. I didn't touch her."

Dale smiled. "Good. I couldn't face you going to prison, surrounded by all those butch men."

"Jealous cat."

"And no coming in at five a.m. I'll be waiting up for you."

"There's no need for that."

"I'll be waiting up, so you've been warned."

"I'm trembling in my boots, dear heart."

Dale kissed him then, hoping, praying they would always be together.

Fifteen

When the phone rang at six the next morning, Fran guessed it was O'Neill because it so rarely was anyone else, especially at six a.m. Another week had passed so quickly, they had made no real headway and other cases couldn't be totally abandoned. The computer failure had added to their workload and evenings had been spent catching up on paperwork. When this investigation is over, Fran thought dejectedly, that's it. She'd ask for a transfer to London or Manchester or somewhere she could perhaps make friends, far enough away for the word 'grass' not to apply to her and far enough away from O'Neill to be able to forget him – eventually.

"It's your lucky day," he said cheerfully. "I'm taking you to church. St Mark's in an hour. I'll pick you up."

He didn't wait for her reply and she slammed the phone down in annoyance. Today was to have been her first time off since the murder and now she had to change into something respectable, instead of her oldest, most comfortable jeans and sweater. Undoubtedly, O'Neill would also find an excuse to hang on to her for the rest of the day.

Strangely, O'Neill was late picking her up, he didn't explain why and Fran didn't ask. By the time they arrived at the church, the congregation was just leaving – all four of them, all elderly, all women. O'Neill hung back, watching the four ladies surround the vicar for their

116

post-church chat. Eventually they drifted away and the vicar turned to go back into the church. The Reverend Donald Able was about fifty, with the round face of the perpetual schoolboy, his hair fading both at the temples and on top. "Do come into the vestry," he said in a low soft voice.

Fran loved churches – not participating, but simply enjoying that damp, old smell, seeing the wonderful stained glass and the way the sun danced and filtered through the colours. Inside a church, she hoped so much that God did exist and if he did, she thought, he might be present in such a wonderful place.

"I'll be with you in a minute," said the Reverend Able. "I'll just divest myself." He disappeared for a few seconds behind a door near the vestry, then returned wearing a dark suit and dog collar.

"I presume you've come about our departed sister Miss Parks."

"We have indeed, Vicar," said O'Neill. We're trying to form a picture of her. After all, someone disliked her enough to kill her, so she must have at least one enemy."

"I can't believe that," said the Reverend Able. "She was a fairly regular communicant and, I have to say, a sad loss to our numbers. As you no doubt saw, my faithful are dwindling, growing old and dying. The younger ones just don't come except, of course, for weddings and funerals and Midnight Mass. I'm too old to take up the guitar and go charismatic, so I expect we'll be moving on soon. Failure in the church is expected now, I'm afraid."

"We?" queried O'Neill.

"My wife and I."

"We'd like to meet your wife, if that's possible."

"Of course," said the Reverend Able.

"I presume your wife knew Denise Parks."

"Yes, indeed. My wife used to visit her when her mother Maggie was still alive. Follow me. My wife is sure to have some goodies for us to eat." Then he added, "We eat late in the evening, you see – sort of snack during the day."

In the vicarage kitchen, the wonderful smell of fresh baking was overwhelming. Mrs Able obviously baked and snacked rather more than she should have. Although quite short, she was wide and rather wobbly, she swayed rather than walked and yet her face, Fran thought, was so serene and lovely she wondered if food was the secret of her happiness.

"Guests. How lovely. Do sit down," she said with a huge smile. "Do excuse me while I commune with the Aga. It can take me rather by surprise."

"Like the Lord, dear."

"Don't be silly, Donald."

Donald shrugged, looking boyish, as if he'd just been caught stealing a jam tart from Nanny's plate. "These are the police, dear."

"All of them?" she asked, smiling.

"Chief Inspector O'Neill and Detective Sergeant Wilson."

"Well, I'm not going to call you that as you savour my soup, home-made bread, scones with clotted cream and home-made strawberry jam. What shall I call you?"

"Connor and Fran."

"You're Connor, I take it. Irish?"

"I was born over here, Mrs Able," he said smiling. "But I like to think I'm more Irish than the Irish."

She began ladling soup into large bowls, the steam rising and joining with the scent of the baking bread.

"For what we are about to receive," intoned the Reverend Able.

"Donald, if you don't mind, we may have atheists present."

The Reverend Able murmured, "I must apologise for my wife. She is apt to make assumptions."

"Donald, one should always be honest with the police," she said. "It's rare to find anyone religious in the police force. After all, they don't exactly see the best of people."

Donald was not to be deterred. "You shouldn't assume, dear, that you can determine a person's religious persuasion just by looking at them."

She flashed her husband a disapproving glance. "I can round here, Donald. Over seventy and bored with this life and ready for the next. We don't attract the bingo and tea-dance pensioners, do we? Of course not. They're still enjoying themselves."

Donald gazed upwards as though on a helpline to God and then began eating his soup.

Fran by now was really enjoying herself. The soup was delicious and now that Mrs Able, kaftan flowing and bits wobbling, had placed the hot bread on the table and began to hack big chunks off quite unceremoniously, it was improving all the time.

"By the way," she said. "I don't seem to have been introduced by my husband. I am merely an appendage, of course, but a large one. Please call me Cassie. I suppose you haven't actually come here to sample my culinary delights but to find out what I thought about Denise Parks." She paused, "I'd like to say she's missed, et cetera et cetera. But she was a sad, old, sex-starved biddy who was asking for it." She laughed. "I don't mean sex, I mean someone murdering her."

"Cassie," said her husband reprovingly. "You've been on the wine again. I do wish you wouldn't start without me. At least I can keep an eye on your consumption then."

Cassie merely smiled, "Be a dear, Donald, and open another bottle. We should try to be hospitable."

Donald obediently disappeared to the cellar and Cassie whispered, "He gets very depressed. Part of the job, I suppose. I'm a convert, you see. Quite religious before I got married, but marriage cured me. Now I believe in food, wine, good company and I'll take my chances with the afterlife."

"Do you mind talking about Denise?" asked O'Neill.

"Not at all. She gave me the creeps. I used to visit her and her mother because Donald thought I ought to and I don't do many churchy-type things, so I salve my conscience by visiting the sick. Smacks of the Lady of the Manor do-gooding, but when I wobble around to see the sick, it does give them something to talk about, and Denise tried her best to upset me. She succeeded, but not in the way she thought." She paused to sip from a glass of wine she'd hidden behind a pot plant on the window-sill. "I'm just finishing the last of a bottle, Donald will appear triumphant at any moment with another bottle so you can see how good it is. Anyone would think he grew the grapes himself, he expects so much praise."

She sipped at her wine again and then smiled at O'Neill. "I'm waffling again. You came here to talk about Denise. Well, I'll tell all I know – during my first visit to her, she asked if I'd like my tea-leaves read. I indulged her, of course. Why not? The first time, my reading was fairly innocuous. She said vague things, like she knew I had problems in my marriage. Who doesn't? So I took that with the proverbial pinch of salt. Then she said she could see via the leaves that I had high blood pressure. Being so fat, she didn't need to be clairvoyant to have a stab at that one. She was wrong as it happens, because my BP is normal." She paused to break off more bread just as Donald walked in with a bottle of wine. "There you are dear, clutching yet another bottle of Tesco plonk."

Donald smiled, "Cassie has this idea it's pretentious to keep Tesco wine in the cellar."

"There's nothing wrong with the wine. It's just that, at most, we have three bottles down there. Ludicrous really." Then she laughed loudly and infectiously. "Come on, Donald. Do let's sample the produce of the cellar."

Donald dutifully opened the wine and poured it into long stemmed glasses.

"Cheers everyone," said Cassie.

O'Neill would have happily stayed there all day, but at this rate, he realised progress was going to be slow. "Could we go back to our subject, Cassie?"

Cassie smiled disarmingly. "Yes, of course. The awful Denise. It was stupid of me to let her read the leaves again, but I was curious and not particularly vulnerable, or so I thought."

"Now don't get upset, Cassie," warned her husband. "You don't have to talk about it if you don't want to."

"But I do, Donald. I want the police to know that whoever killed her should be dealt with compassionately. A weak person could easily be tipped over the edge by her insinuations."

"What insinuations?" asked Fran. Cassie's eyes sought Donald's but he busied himself removing plates and her glance was lost to him. "I'm sure Donald won't mind me telling you . . . will you, Donald?"

"No dear, of course not," he said with an encouraging smile.

"It was my second visit," she began "The first reading had been so innocuous I thought, what the heck? She generalised a bit at first. She could see, she said, that our marriage had had past traumas but that, of course, could apply to any married couple. Then she said that she could see a choirboy, and my husband was kissing him. That could have been a clichéd guess. But, three years before, in another parish, a choirboy who was totally unreliable was dismissed from the choir by Donald. The boy retaliated by making accusations of sexual abuse. Luckily, before the case came to court, the boy retracted his statement and Donald was totally exonerated. But by then, Donald had been suspended from his duties and we had to endure insults and snubs from complete strangers which was, I have to say, easier to endure than those of our so-called friends."

"You coped magnificently, dearest," said Donald. "I couldn't have survived without your support."

"Well, it was easy. I knew you wouldn't touch a choirboy with a barge pole," she said with a brief laugh, which Fran sensed covered up a lot of anguish.

"Did she actually know about the case, or was she simply guessing?" asked Fran.

Cassie sighed. "I think she was just guessing, at the time. But she could see it upset me and later she did find out about it, or at least I think so. I was attending services then and she would stop me and make sly little remarks like, '*Such* a good thing you haven't got a choir now'. But what really upset me, and this gives you some idea of just how nasty she could be, was her reference to the dead baby she saw in the leaves. How could she have *known*?"

Fran could see that now Cassie's mood was changing, and she began swigging her wine as if trying to find the courage to say more. "You really don't have to talk about this if you don't want to," said Fran. "You're not a suspect and we are easily forming a picture of the victim."

Cassie smiled bleakly and wiped a strand of pure white hair from her forehead. "I do want to talk about it. I need to talk. Denise was merely fishing for an emotional response, I knew that intellectually, but emotionally she pole-axed me. It wasn't so much what she said; it was the smug, knowing expression on her face. At that moment . . . I could have killed her."

"Cassie," said her husband, "I think you've said enough."

"No, I haven't, Donald. All these years I've tried to bury the memories, but they never really go away. The guilt is always there."

"What on earth did you do?" asked Fran, unable to contain her curiosity.

Cassie stared ahead and murmured her story as though to herself. "I was eighteen when I got married. My parents were very religious and wanted to marry me off quickly, in case I became a fallen woman. My husband was ten years older and it wasn't a happy marriage but that doesn't stop one getting pregnant, does it? I was fine during the pregnancy, quite happy. I was slim them and I didn't think there would be any complications but my pelvis, on the inside at least, was small. The labour dragged on for three days, on and off. In those days, no one rushed to give you a caesarean. Anyway, he was eventually born by forceps delivery. They didn't let me see the baby at first. I was totally exhausted, but anxious about him. I slept, I had terrible dreams, and I hallucinated even when I was awake. I didn't know it at the time but I had an infection. I was in a single room and a nurse bought the baby to me. This was the day after the birth. And when I saw him, I thought . . ." She broke off, her voice husky with emotion. "I thought . . . I thought he was the Devil's own. His head was long and elongated. He had birthmarks on his forehead. In the state I was in, I thought they were horns. His eyes sprang open – they looked knowing and evil. I remember holding him at arm's length, terrified. I was terrified of my own baby. I can't believe it, even now. I moved to the window and his eyes bored into me and it was as if I was holding the Devil himself. I opened the window and held him out at arm's length. I

123

heard someone screaming *No! No!* But it was too late. I let go. In my deranged mind, I had let the evil go and I felt relieved. I was taken to a mental hospital, and a week later I was *compos mentis* enough to be told that I was suffering from puerperal psychosis, and that I had killed my son. I wasn't well enough to attend the funeral and I stayed in that hospital for twelve months . . . during which time my husband hanged himself."

Fran heard the clock ticking but no one spoke. Fran could see by O'Neill's expression that Cassie's confession had upset him. Donald stood up slowly and placed an arm round Cassie as she moaned and rocked backwards and forwards with remembered pain.

O'Neill's eyes caught Fran's and he nodded towards the door. Fran could see Donald and Cassie were both oblivious to either their presence or their absence.

They drove in silence back to Fowchester Police Station where O'Neill parked the car.

"You needn't think we're going in there," he said indicating the building that reminded Fran of a Victorian school. "We're going to the pub," said O'Neill. "There are some times in life when a pub with a roaring fire, copious amounts of draught Guinness, and an attractive woman beside you is one of life's best solaces, and solace is what is called for today."

Fran couldn't disagree with that and when she didn't demur, he smiled broadly for the first time in ages.

Sixteen

Janine faced her first day back at work after Denise's murder with a degree of calmness. She'd cleaned the house from top to bottom and moved into Denise's old room. She had thought about taking over Maggie's room as Denise had done, but she recognised that that move had been Denise's privilege.

Physically she felt exhausted, mentally she felt strangely serene and although she grieved for Denise as her sister, she grieved even more for her as the mother she'd never had a chance to recognise. Now that she slept in Denise's room she felt her presence more, even seeing her on two occasions. Of course, no one would believe she *had* seen her, but Janine knew she had glimpsed her at the top of the stairs and leaving Maggie's bedroom. Seeing her had been very comforting, and Janine was convinced her calm state of mind was due to Denise being in the cottage, not just her ghost but . . . *her*. The cottage could never be sold, of course, and Janine vowed she would never leave it, because how could she leave both her mother and her grandmother behind?

She was sitting at her desk when Mr De Souza arrived at the surgery. Tall, thin, nearly fifty, almost bald and slightly stooping, he had large sad brown eyes, a slightly hooked nose and an olive complexion. Janine had always thought him quite attractive, although reserved and rather shy. Denise had once said, 'What a pity your boss isn't single, he'd be a lot better for you than Mike – if you really need a man, of course.' Janine smiled to herself. *If* he had been single, Denise would have said he was too old for her. She realised now that she didn't need a man anyway, young or old. She had a home, a job, there would be some money and she would keep the cottage, as they would have liked. Nothing would change, except that perhaps she might take in a cat, possibly a stray.

"Are you all right, Janine?" Henri De Souza asked as he shook her by the hand. He was wearing a dark grey suit this morning and although it looked smart, she preferred him in his 'whites' and especially when she saw him in his mask. His eyes looked even larger then, his eyelashes longer. "Are you sure you're ready to start work?" he asked, giving her a puzzled look.

"I'm fine," she said.

"I was so shocked to her about your sister. I didn't know her of course, but I know you and you know my sympathies are heartfelt."

"Thank you, Mr De Souza. I'm still upset, but I think I'm over the worst of the shock now. Life must go on, as they say."

"Yes . . . indeed. I expect you'll be marrying Mike in the not too distant future."

She shook her head. "I'm not seeing Mike anymore. We had a fight. He attacked me."

"Oh . . ." he said in surprise. "I'm sorry to hear that . . ." he broke off as the dental hygienist and the dental nurse arrived. Janine smiled broadly at the two girls standing in the doorway but neither smiled back.

It was eight p.m. before Henri De Souza arrived home. His legs felt heavy and he had a slight headache; he'd missed lunch again. He parked his BMW in the garage and briskly walked the short distance to his large bungalow. The aroma of something delicious wafted into the hall from the kitchen. "Sorry I'm late, darling," he called out.

His wife appeared from the kitchen and thrust a gin and tonic into his hand. "You look bushed," she said, kissing his cheek. "Go and put your feet up, dinner will be about fifteen minutes."

He smiled, relieved he didn't have to eat the moment he got home. He always needed a while to unwind, drink his gin and tonic and then change into something casual. Tonight was no exception, although he did want to talk about the day and Janine in particular.

Dinner was beef casserole with dumplings, his favourite, whilst Anna ate a small plain omelette with salad because she cooked meat only for him, which Henri thought was a tremendously loving action. They had been married for twenty-eight years and he loved her more than the day he married her. To him, she had hardly changed. She was still slim; her hair, once black, was now speckled with silver, her skin was smooth and virtually unlined. And her teeth were flawless and for that he took full credit.

"I have a feeling you want to tell me something," said Anna as she served fresh fruit salad for dessert.

He smiled. "Janine came back to work today."

"You sound worried, couldn't she cope?"

"That's the trouble. She coped extremely well. Too well."

Anna laughed briefly. "Come on, darling – explain."

Henri sipped his red wine thoughtfully. "She looked strange and she was so . . . unconcerned."

"What do you mean 'strange'?"

"She was wearing a crimplene dress suitable for a woman in her seventies or eighties, she wore no make-up and her hair was dragged back with clips. The two girls were shocked at the sight of her. She was like an old woman."

"Did she actually look ill?"

"Not really. She was a little pale, but so composed. I found it unnerving. I'm not quite sure what to do about it."

"In what way?"

"She looks like a character from a pantomime. What do I say to her? I couldn't fault her work and that leaves me with the problem of broaching the subject of her appearance."

"Wouldn't one of the girls do it?"

"They've already refused, saying she's 'flipped her lid'."

"Her sister was odd, and her mother," murmured Anna.

"I didn't know you knew them."

"I didn't exactly *know* them, darling. I met Maggie the mother a few times when I was delivering meals on wheels. Usually the old girl was on her own, but occasionally Denise was there."

"In what way were they 'odd'?"

Anna shrugged. "Hard to describe really; old fashioned, prejudiced, nosy . . ."

"Those were just their good points I suppose," he said with a smile."

"Seriously, darling, they gave me the shivers. The cottage is set in a time warp, and there doesn't ever seem to have been a man around."

Henri poured himself another glass of wine. "Being odd is not a reason for murder . . ." He paused. "You don't think Janine killed her sister, do you? One reads that close relatives commit most murders."

Anna looked thoughtful for a few moments, then shook her head slowly. "I've met Janine a few times. I thought she seemed mousy and certainly not the volatile type."

He nodded, "I'd agree with that. I always thought she was pretty stable but she did get involved with that used-car man."

"Weren't they planning to marry?"

"Not any more. She told me today it was over, that he'd attacked her."

"Perhaps *he* did it."

"Doubtful," said Henri. "The police would have had him arrested by now."

"Unless he hired a hit man and they can't prove he was involved."

Henri stared at his wife quizzically. "What do you know about 'hit men'? Especially here in Fowchester."

"I read newspapers, listen to the news. It's pretty likely paid killers are as available here as anywhere. There's always someone ready to earn easy money."

"I think you've drunk too much wine, Anna," he said. "I can't believe you've just suggested that murder is earning 'easy money'. Would you find it easy?"

She laughed, "No, of course not. Don't take me so seriously." She began to clear the table, taking the plates out to the kitchen and then stacking the dishwasher. She'd just switched the dishwasher on when the doorbell rang. She heard Henri say, "Who the hell is that?" as she glanced at the kitchen clock – it was ten p.m.

"Chief Inspector Connor O'Neill and Detective Sergeant Fran Wilson. I'm sorry it's such a late visit sir, but we'd like to have a word with your wife."

Anna strained to hear above the whirring of the dishwasher. She did catch her husband's surprised, "My wife?"

When she emerged from the kitchen, the two police officers were already sitting at the dining room table. "Darling, this is—"

"I heard the introductions," she said quickly, "and I have already given a statement to one of the uniformed men."

"We're aware of that, Mrs De Souza," said O'Neill. "But you left the salon in a particular time zone and we're checking everyone's statement."

"Oh I see. Well, fire away, but I don't think I'll be much help. I didn't see anything."

"Let's start with the time you arrived at the salon," suggested O'Neill.

"My appointment was for ten forty-five, but as usual on a Saturday they were extremely busy and I had to wait."

"Who was booked to do your hair?"

"Marcus. He's the best."

"Did you leave the hairdressing part of the salon at any time?"

She tilted her head to one side. "I had a cut and blow dry, and prior to that I had a manicure and a facial."

"What time did you leave?"

"About quarter to one, I think."

"You think?" queried O'Neill.

"I wasn't wearing my watch so it's just a guess really, but that was approximately the time. I met my husband for lunch at about one."

"I see," nodded O'Neill. "Did you speak to anyone at the salon?"

"Only Marcus and Tara. Henri and I were going out to dinner that night which is why I booked an appointment on a Saturday. Normally I have my hair done on a Thursday."

"And you spoke to no one else?"

"No. I've already said. Why do you ask, Chief Inspector?"

"I'm asking because I'm wondering why you cancelled

your facial and I'm asking because you spoke to Mandy the beautician."

"I merely told her I'd have to cancel the facial. I wanted to be on time for my husband, he works long hours but on Saturday he finishes at one and having a facial takes about half an hour. Obviously, I didn't want to keep him waiting."

"When exactly did you tell Mandy that you were cancelling?"

Anna paused looking slightly flustered. "I'm not sure of the time. I wasn't wearing my watch and the clock is in the reception area."

"I see," murmured O'Neill. "Let's not be bothering with the exact time then. Was it prior to your hairdo, or after it?"

Again Anna seemed flustered, her face slightly pink. "What's wrong, darling?" asked her husband.

"Nothing," she snapped. "I'm fine. My memory of that Saturday is a bit poor, that's all."

"Well, perhaps it is rather late," said O'Neill. "Do you have any questions, sergeant?"

Fran fixed Anna De Souza with a deliberately icy stare. "Would you mind telling me where you were having dinner on that Saturday night?"

For some reason Anna smiled, as though relieved at the innocuous question. "Of course I wouldn't mind telling you. Our next-door neighbours were having a dinner party."

"And you turned up for it?"

"Yes, of course. Why not?"

"Some people," said Fran slowly, "might have decided not to go, simply because they were upset that someone had been murdered in such close proximity to them."

"It didn't affect me in that way."

"So you're a tough character?"

Anna cast Fran a glance that said, 'What do you think?' but it was Henri who spoke. "She can be tough but she isn't hard. The murder did upset her."

"When was that, sir? Lunch time on the day?"

Before he had time to answer Anna snapped, "Of course not. Well, not immediately. I overheard people talking about it in the restaurant. As you know, a town this size has few secrets."

"I'm beginning to realise that, Mrs De Souza," said Fran with feeling.

O'Neill glanced at Fran and nodded slightly as if indicating that the interview was over.

"We'll need to talk to you again, Mrs De Souza," he said with a smile. "I'm thinking of staging a reconstruction and I do hope you'll be willing to take part."

She swallowed before answering, "I suppose it might jog a few memories," she said.

"That's our aim," said O'Neill as he stood up to go. "Bye for now."

Both Henri and Anna stood at their front window watching O'Neill drive away. Then, without glancing at his wife, Henri said, "But I remember, you *were* wearing your wristwatch that day. Why did you say the opposite?"

Seventeen

"What did you think of them, Fran?" asked O'Neill as they drove away. "And why did you want to know about the dinner party?"

Fran smiled, "Easy. She's lying, but I don't know what about. I asked about the dinner because she chose to have her hair done on the Saturday instead of Thursday. It would still have looked good by Saturday, so that evening must have been very special. And somehow I can't believe that the next-door neighbours' dinner party would be *that* important unless . . ."

"Unless what?"

"Unless there was a man in her sights."

O'Neill laughed. "Only a woman could suss that one."

"I do have a strong feeling," said Fran, "that Anna De Souza is in the running as a suspect, don't you? Although I can't see what motive she would have."

O'Neill was silent for a moment, then he said thoughtfully, "We won't catch this one on forensic evidence, Fran. I just hope the reconstruction will come up with something."

"When did you decide on that, by the way?"

O'Neill didn't answer immediately because his headlights caught a startled rabbit at the edge of the road. The rabbit sensibly stayed still. "Let's hope *our* rabbit isn't so clever," he muttered, then added, "I've broached the subject with Superintendent Ringstead and he said as long as it's cheap and moves the case along, he doesn't mind."

"What did you do, blackmail him?"

"Not exactly, Fran. I'm sure he leads a life that is whiter than white."

"He's an exception then, in Fowchester," she said. "And by the way, how's Mike?"

O'Neill smiled grimly. "He is, as my aunt would say, blistered to buggery. But his ex-wife has taken him in and I think he's happier than he's been for a long time. So happy, he's not going to press charges."

"Not still a suspect then?"

O'Neill shook his head. "I think he needed more passion to commit murder for Janine's sake. He was a man still hankering after his wife and kids."

They drove on in silence for a couple of miles and Fran sensed Connor wanted to say something but was holding back. Eventually, he said, "Do you eat fish, Fran?"

"Sometimes. Why?"

"Do you fancy fish and chips?"

"And mushy peas?"

"A pea cluster, even."

"Yes. I'm starving."

"I'm glad to hear it, Fran. There is a problem though."

"What's that?" asked Fran.

"I'd like to eat it at your place,"

Fran shrugged, "Why not, boss? I trust you. We can talk about the case."

O'Neill's smile went unseen by Fran. Talking about the case was the last thing on his mind, the fish and chips a mere ploy. He wanted her body, her bare skin next to his. Being under her roof was, in his book, half-way to heaven and tonight, he thought, heaven could be his.

They ate the fish and chips sitting on the sofa. The portions were huge but they were both so hungry they ate till their plates were empty. In the post-chippie feeling of repletion, O'Neill thought he must be getting old, for his ardour had cooled and now he merely wanted to sleep.

He woke at one-thirty to find Fran asleep with her head on his shoulder and the debris of their meal still on the coffee table. He stared at it for a moment, allowing the memory of the first sight of the staff room in the salon to take over his thoughts. What was missing? The sight of other staff rooms came into his internal vision like a camera on overdrive; and then he knew.

"Hey, wake up, Fran," he said gently. "My arm's gone dead."

"Sorry," she muttered as she sat upright to battle against feelings of stiffness and sleepy confusion. "Where am I? What's the time?"

"Don't be worrying about that. I'll be making you a cup of tea while you get your head together."

When Connor returned with two mugs of tea, Fran felt oriented, but very tired and irritated that she wasn't in bed and fast asleep. As he handed her the mug of tea, without preamble he said, "Staff rooms."

"Staff rooms to you, boss."

"Fran, don't be getting tetchy. We missed something in the salon staff room."

"Well, I'm surprised. I thought we saw everything and we watched the video over and over."

"It was what we *didn't* see," he said, with a triumphant smile. "We didn't see any cigarette ends."

"It's a non-smoking salon. We wouldn't expect to. Dale's very anti-smoking and strict about it, absolutely no smoking on the premises."

"*On* the premises, yes, but outside in the alleyway? There's bound to be at least one smoker on the staff."

"I'm very tired, Connor, and I know I'm being slow up the uptake, but so what?"

"Sure to goodness, Fran," said O'Neill in one of his cornier versions of a broad Irish accent. "Don't be so t'ick. One member of staff at the very least would be opening the side door to go outside for a smoke. They could either stand just outside the door or they could go round to the back. And that means that someone could have crept in the open door."

Fran thought about that for a few seconds, "That's very possible, I can see that," she said, "but where does that get us? As far as I can see, it means virtually anyone could have murdered Denise."

"Not at all, Fran. It means one, or maybe more, members of staff took an illicit break and are lying about it, so we can't be sure exactly when Denise did die. The pathologist can only give us to within an hour. An hour. That's a long time. And of course, there is another possibility."

"What's that?"

"That someone found the body and didn't report it."

Frowning, Fran said, "Surely not. How could anyone ignore a dead body?"

"I've known it happen. People walk on by. They don't want to get involved, they don't want to become a suspect and they often have something to hide. Their attitude is, the dead can't be helped, but the living can be harassed."

"That's a cynical view of life."

O'Neill shook his head. "That's the reality of life today."

Fran didn't have an answer and when the phone rang, she jumped in surprise.

"We can't raise Chief Inspector O'Neill," said a voice. "It's Fowchester police."

"I know where he is," said Fran. There was a slight pause, as if the person at the other end had realised some significance in Fran's assertion. She listened to the message and then said, "We'll be there. Five minutes."

"What's going on?" asked O'Neill, barely able to contain his curiosity.

"There's an incident at *Le Salon*," said Fran. "A neighbour phoned. She said a man was yelling inside, screaming for help."

"Jasus," breathed O'Neill. "Come on then. Grab your coat, Fran. Let's go."

Le Salon was flooded with light, once again the road was cordoned off. One or two residents wearing dressing gowns stood at their front doors but most of the houses stayed dark, the inhabitants asleep and oblivious to the drama.

As Fran followed O'Neill into the salon, she had a strong feeling of *déjà vu* until she was faced with the scene. Dale was seated on the floor, his head resting against a bloodied wall near the sink. His white towelling dressing gown was spattered with blood and tears poured silently down his cheeks. In his arms he cradled the body of Marcus. Scissors, covered with blood, lay on the floor beside the body, alongside a blond ponytail. Marcus's hair had been roughly cut and was speckled red with blood.

A uniformed sergeant stood watching, grim faced. "This is how we found them, sir. We haven't tried to prise him away from the body . . . yet."

"Leave him be for the moment. Has Dale said anything?" asked O'Neill.

"He did mumble something. He said, 'It was only a joke' and 'He wasn't dead. He spoke to me'."

Dale's distress was painful to watch and he clutched Marcus to him as if his own life depended on it.

Fran could stand only a few seconds of what seemed like voyeurism. She knelt down beside Dale and said softly and slowly, "Dale, listen to me. I want you to lay

Marcus down. He wants to be at rest. I want you to hold my hand instead."

Dale didn't respond at first, then his eyes left Marcus and he stared blankly at Fran.

"Dale, you know who I am. Lay Marcus down gently. Do as I tell you."

Again, his responses were slow as if his brain was struggling to decode the words he was hearing. Eventually he muttered, "He wants to rest."

"Yes Dale," said Fran. "Lay him down gently and then stand up."

Dale's shoulders sagged in a sort of despairing resignation. His hands stroked his lover's ragged hair, he kissed him on the lips briefly and then gently laid Marcus down. He paused, wiped a bloody hand across his face as if suddenly becoming aware of the tears, then slowly and stiffly standing up, he put a hand out to Fran. Before she knew it, he was in her arms and she was cradling his head on her chest. O'Neill sighed. Forensic wouldn't be pleased that Fran had contaminated Dale's clothing, but it was too late now and forensic could be some time.

"Take him upstairs to the flat," said O'Neill. "Get him to strip off that robe and put it in a plastic bag of some description."

Dale had begun sobbing again and he clung to Fran as though she were a human crutch. Fran had the feeling that if she let him go he'd collapse in a heap on the floor.

"I'll get the police surgeon to see him when he comes, sergeant," said O'Neill as he guided them to the flat door. "Just get as much information as you can."

As Fran struggled to help Dale up the stairs, she thought ruefully how O'Neill always gave her the jobs he didn't want to do. Dale's distress was something he didn't want to cope with, perhaps couldn't.

She stood Dale in the bathroom and told him to take

off his dressing gown. At first he stared at her blankly, then after a short pause he asked, "Why?"

"Because you're a suspect. Forensic will want to examine them."

"Why?" he repeated.

"You were found with Marcus."

"Why?" he said, yet again.

"Dale, you've got to get a grip. I've told you why."

"I mean," he said, focusing his reddened eyes on her, "why would I want to harm Marcus?"

"I'm sure you didn't," said Fran, "but we'll talk about that as soon as you've taken off the dressing gown."

Dale stared down at his chest, saw the blood stark against the pure white of the towelling robe and paled so much Fran thought he was going to faint.

"Here, you can wear this," she said, taking down a blue towelling robe from the hook on the bathroom door.

"That's his," he said brokenly, as he snatched it from Fran and held it to his face.

"Come on, into the lounge," said Fran firmly. "I'll make you some hot sweet tea."

When Fran returned with the tea, Dale sat staring into space. Fran handed him the mug of tea saying, as briskly as though she was a nurse of yesteryear, "Drink this and I'll tell you exactly what I want to know."

Dale began to drink the tea obediently and Fran realised this was the right approach, the only approach, for if she showed too much sympathy he would simply break down again. She allowed him to drink most of the tea before she said, "Tell me about the evening, tell me what you did."

He shrugged, "Nothing much," he said dully. "Watched TV for a while, then about nine Marcus suddenly said he was going out."

"Did you have a row about that?"

Dale nodded. "I didn't kill him, you know," he said

brokenly. "I don't care if you arrest me. I might even confess so that you'll stop asking questions."

"Look at me, Dale." He looked at Fran resignedly. "All I want," she said, "is to catch Marcus's killer. This person has killed before and may kill again. Surely you would want to spare another person this sort of grief?"

Dale sighed. But eventually he said, "We had a shouting match. I called him a tart, a bitch, a slag. He called me a foppish old queen, who was so jealous and possessive that I was driving him into the arms of another."

"I bet that upset you," said Fran.

"Upset me? Upset me? I'll say it upset me. I was spitting feathers . . ." He broke off, as though remembering something.

"So what happened?"

There was a short pause before Dale said bleakly, "I slapped his face . . . Oh God, I'm so sorry I did that now."

"Did he retaliate?"

Dale shook his head, and the slightest of smiles crossed his face. "He went totally camp, put his hands on his hips and said, 'Well, that wasn't very nice, was it? You should learn to curb your temper, you naughty boy'. That was the last time I saw him before . . . He did call out, 'Ciao, lover'. I suppose that means he had forgiven me."

"I'm sure it does," said Fran. "What time did he leave?"

"Just before ten, I remember the News at Ten came on. I didn't watch it, I was too upset."

"Then what?"

Dale thought for a moment. "I played a few slushy CDs and then went to my lonely bed."

"What time?"

"It was after midnight. I was hoping he'd come back fairly early . . ." he broke off. "I can't believe he's dead, I just can't believe it. I keep thinking he'll just walk through that door and we'll be as we were."

"This will take a long time, Dale. You're still in shock at the moment."

He nodded miserably. Fran tried to curb the sympathy she felt for him and said crisply "Did you go to sleep?"

A frown crossed Dale's face, "I'm not sure, I think I was dozing, maybe I did drop off. I think I heard the door open, perhaps I relaxed then, thinking he was home. Then I sort of woke with a start . . . I couldn't tell you what I heard. I looked at the clock. It was two a.m. I put on my dressing gown and went downstairs to the salon . . ." he broke off. "Oh Jesus – he was crawling on the floor, there seemed to be blood everywhere. The scissors were sticking out of his neck . . . and his hair . . . his beautiful hair. He spoke to me, I held him, someone was screaming, 'Help! Help!' and then I realised it was me."

"Did you ring for an ambulance?"

Dale shook his head. "It was so quick, he was still alive. He spoke to me, he said, 'It was just a joke'. Then he was unconscious and then I realised he was dead."

"Did you call for an ambulance then?"

"It was too late. I knew he was dead."

"You said the scissors were sticking from his neck but when we came in they were on the floor."

He closed his eyes and hung his head, "I took them out" he murmured. "It didn't matter then, he'd been stabbed in the back as well. I suppose I knew there was no hope."

"You didn't try to mouth to mouth?"

He continued to hang his head dejectedly. "I don't know how to."

Fran was aware that Dale was near to tears again and she also knew she had to keep questioning him, regardless of his emotional state.

"Take a deep breath, Dale, and think back. Did you hear anyone leave – footsteps, a door closing?"

He shook his head. "I didn't hear anything."

"One more question, Dale. I still can't understand why you didn't ring for an ambulance."

This time, he looked up at her, his blue eyes glistening with tears. "I couldn't leave him, not for a second. How could I have done that? I did yell for help." He paused and looked at her pleadingly. "Would it have made a difference?"

Fran shook her head.

"I can't understand why his hair was cut off," murmured Dale. "Who would do that? Who would cut off his beautiful hair?"

"Dale, I'm going to end this interview now. It won't be the last, of course. Would you like me to contact someone for you?"

He thought for a moment. "Mandy. Ring Mandy." He added softly, "I can't live without him. I want to be with him."

Eighteen

It was early on Monday afternoon in his office that O'Neill finally received the post-mortem report, which showed several stab wounds. The first wound, to the back, punctured a lung and the wound to the neck nicked the carotid; the wound that actually killed him was a puncture wound to the heart. The pathologist couldn't tell if the hair was cut off prior to the attack, or when Marcus was in no state to object. The final line of the report interested O'Neill. The victim was intoxicated at the level of 150-250mg per 100ml of blood. This would be manifested by poor muscular co-ordination, slurred speech, impairment of memory, et cetera.

Fran sat at her desk ringing minicab firms to find the driver who had picked up Marcus on Saturday night. Dale had been questioned again, and he seemed convinced Marcus had used a minicab, but there had been no telephone call from the salon that evening and certainly no evidence so far that anyone had picked him up from the salon.

"Come and look at this, Fran," said O'Neill, waving the report at her. Hesitating for a moment, Fran put down the phone, then moved reluctantly to stand beside O'Neill. The whole morning he had interrupted her with various queries and chores that Fran found both intrusive and unnecessary. She knew O'Neill regarded her as his 'right hand' but she needed to think quietly and

work at least for a short time without his constant inter-
ruptions.

She read the report and then said thoughtfully, "Of
course, we only have Dale's word that Marcus actually
left the flat. So far no one saw him leave, we don't know
yet where he went and nobody saw him return."

"That's a fair point," conceded O'Neill. "It's also possible that Marcus walked to his destination or arranged for
a lift. I *do* think Dale is telling the truth, that Marcus did
leave the flat. He says he doesn't know where Marcus used
to go but when I pushed the issue, he said he sometimes
went to gay clubs in Birmingham."

"Do you think he met someone there and they drove
him home?

"No. I think he went with someone and came back with
him or her."

"Would he have risked Dale's reaction?"

"Not sober, maybe," said O'Neill, remembering only
too well the difference. "Now we know he was drunk and
obviously not thinking straight, he may have risked it.
Or, of course, the relationship between Dale and Marcus
wasn't as rock solid as Dale would like us to believe."

"Do you think the hair cutting was significant?" asked
Fran.

O'Neill smiled, "Sure I do Fran, but I don't know
in what way. Are you having thoughts about the haircut?"

Fran sat down at her desk, rearranged the notes and
files on her desk and said thoughtfully, "Either way
it seems symbolic, doesn't it? The loss of strength or
a sort of rite of passage, end of a relationship type
haircut."

"Is that common?" asked O'Neill.

Fran nodded, "I've heard of women who have ended
a relationship one day and had their long hair chopped

off the next day. I think the usual thing is to wait a few weeks, then when all hope is lost the 'chop' marks that recognition of the end of a phase. And that's when you're ready to move on."

O'Neill watched Fran quizzically. wondering if he should ask or just keep quiet. Curiosity, however, got the better of him. "You're speaking from experience Fran, aren't you?"

She smiled fleetingly and then looked directly at him. "I don't want to talk about it, Connor. Let's stick to the case, shall we?"

"Sure we will, Fran. We'll start by discussing the reconstruction I've arranged for tomorrow."

"Short notice, isn't it?"

He shrugged. "It's not as if we need the media. The team have arranged to have the customers there and, apart from Denise, it should be as it was that Saturday . . ."

"And no Marcus?"

"Shit . . . I've forgotten I'd need a stand-in for him. You find someone from the team, fair haired and slim."

Fran laughed briefly, "You make it sound easy—"

"You'll be finding someone," interrupted O'Neill.

Fran fell silent. She was annoyed. She hadn't been told that the reconstruction was taking place tomorrow and she didn't think it was a very good idea. Dale was still shocked and, judging by Mandy Willens' pallor, she wasn't too robust either.

"Why am I getting bad vibes, Fran. You seem very disapproving."

"I am. I think a reconstruction could backfire on us."

"Don't be arguing, Fran. So far we haven't solved one murder and we're not making much headway with the second. Jasus woman, don't give me a hard time."

Fran stood up, pushed back her chair and walked swiftly

towards the door. "I'll just be off then boss, to find a Marcus lookalike, and if you don't mind, I'd prefer it if you don't speak to me like a wife."

O'Neill smiled to himself as she slammed the door. He'd never seen her in a real paddy before and he'd enjoyed her flashing brown eyes and the toss of her shiny hair – a bit coltish, he thought. Was it a good sign he raised her ire? Was it a moment of passion or petulance? And was he really speaking to her like a husband?

Tara rang the bell of the flat above the salon. She hadn't wanted to come, but Mandy had begged her. She guessed it was because Mandy was nervous about the reconstruction, and being with Dale was getting to be a strain.

When Mandy opened the door, Tara thought she looked awful, all pale and with her face screwed up and creased as if she'd spent the night on a hard surface, just as the Thing had looked after a night sleeping on the floor.

"I'm so glad you've come, Tara," said Mandy, with a relieved smile. "I don't know what to do with Dale, he's in a terrible state."

"Has he seen the doc?"

Mandy nodded. "He just gave him some Valium and told him to make an appointment for next week."

As they were going up the stairs Mandy said, "I can't believe this has happened. Who could possibly want to kill Marcus? Denise, I could understand, but Marcus? Never. What harm did he ever do? He didn't even gossip . . ." She broke off as they got to the top of the stairs and the lounge door. Then, in a whisper she said, "If Dale wants to talk it'll only be about Marcus. The police have seen him twice but he's as much in the dark as the police seem to be."

Dale lay full length on the sofa, his arms folded across his chest, his eyes closed. He didn't move as they entered.

"Is he asleep?" whispered Tara.

Mandy shook her head in weary resignation. "No. Occasionally he just sits upright and tells you his latest suspect or memory of Marcus."

Dale stirred slightly. "I can hear what you're saying about me," he murmured.

"Good," said Mandy. "You can give me a rest now and talk to Tara. I'll pop out to the shops and stock your cupboard, then at least I'll know you won't starve."

When she heard the front door close, Tara sat down in the armchair opposite the sofa. The room was silent except for Dale's quiet breathing and Tara allowed her thoughts to drift. She couldn't help noticing that Mandy had put on weight, her jeans looked tight across the stomach, although her face looked thinner. It was no secret now that she was pregnant and Tara had to admit she was jealous. Not that she'd ever wanted the Thing to impregnate her; since meeting Andrew she had experienced longings, and Mandy being pregnant had made that worse. Worse still was the fact that Andrew had been so distant these past few days, and had begun to drop hints about not wanting to be tied down, about wanting to travel. In her darkest moments Tara had vague suspicions he was seeing someone else.

"Tara," Dale's voice broke into her thoughts. "Did Marcus ever say anything to you about . . . about anyone else?"

She thought for a moment. "Only sort of banter, nothing serious."

"What sort of banter?" asked Dale raising himself on one elbow and opening his eyes to reveal an expression of emptiness that Tara found quite chilling. Grief seemed to have taken the life from them, made them seem smaller, like the eyes of the dead.

"You know how Marcus could be, making comments about . . . people."

"What people?" demanded Dale.

Tara shrugged. "It was no secret that he teased Andrew quite a bit, saying he had the best bum in Fowchester and the longest thighs."

"I never heard that."

"He was only teasing, Dale. He knew Andrew wasn't gay."

Suddenly Dale sat upright his face contorted in anger. "How would he know that if he hadn't made a pass at him? I never heard Andrew talk about any girlfriends. Maybe they were having an affair right under my nose . . . and that little shit," he paused, realising the full implication of what he was saying, "and that little shit must have killed him . . ."

"No, it's not true," said Tara nervously. "Please Dale, calm down."

"Calm down," said Dale coldly. "That's the last thing I'm going to do. I can see it all – the two of them creeping back in the early hours. They couldn't go to Andrew's place, could they? Mummy and Daddy wouldn't like their son bringing home his gay friend . . ."

"It wasn't like that – you don't understand."

"Don't interrupt me, Tara. I need to get this sorted in my mind. The devious bastards. I suppose Marcus bought him back here because there was nowhere else to go. I suppose he thought I'd sleep through the night like some geriatric queen."

"Dale, you're wrong. Please listen to me."

Dale stared at her. "What are you doing here, anyway? Where's Mandy?"

"She's gone to the shops . . ." Tara hesitated. She knew

she had to tell him but would he believe her in the mood he was in? Even if he did, he might ask where Andrew was on Saturday night, and she didn't know. Worse, the thought that maybe her suspicions that he was with someone else were true. It had never crossed her mind until now that it could have been a man.

Nineteen

O'Neill and Fran arrived at the Peacock Club in Birmingham at ten-thirty p.m. It was raining hard and O'Neill had struggled with poor visibility, heavy traffic and fiendish one-way systems.

Eventually they found the club in a system of cavern-like structures in an old commercial part of the city. The silver shutters of the doors were closed tight and the only concession to there being a nightclub was a small sign just above the door arch.

When O'Neill pressed the bell on the right hand side of the shutter, it opened immediately, and there stood a bouncer dressed all in black with a shaven head and the largest neck either of them had ever seen. "What's your problem, man?" demanded the bouncer.

O'Neill felt slightly put out by this approach. He had wanted to enter the club without saying he was CID so that the clubbers might be more friendly. Before he had time to speak, Fran had answered for him. "We do have a problem," she said, smiling up at him sweetly. The big-necked bouncer leaned slightly towards her. "Yes, dear?"

"We want to enter the club incognito," she paused, looking into his rather small grey eyes intently. "You have a wonderful physique."

"I look after myself," he said, looking highly gratified. "Now what's all this about incognito? You famous?"

Fran shook her head. "No. We're private detectives investigating the murder of a member of this clu—"

"Why aren't the police here then?" he asked suspiciously.

"We've got more information than them. My assistant here . . ." she smiled at O'Neill, "knew of the place. You get my drift?"

"I certainly do," he said, giving O'Neill a broad, knowing wink. "Okay darlin', you can come in, but not dressed like that."

"Why not?" she asked. "I thought a little black dress went anywhere." She opened her coat to reveal her one all-purpose knee-length black dress.

"Very nice," said the doorman. "But this is a fetish club. You'll need to change into the proper gear."

Fran looked deliberately crest-fallen. "Not to worry," he said. "There's some stuff in the back room that will fit you. Cost you a tenner extra each."

O'Neill handed him the money and the bouncer winked at him again. "Follow me," he said. "And pay at the kiosk."

The back room contained a rack of assorted leather, PVC and rubber wear, one wooden chair, a cracked mirror and no privacy at all. Fran looked through the assortment of clothes. The only outfit in her size was a short rubber dress. For O'Neill, there were leather trousers and a leather jerkin. "Jasus. Is this worth it? I doubt if a soul will speak to us anyway." He undressed quickly, hardly looking at Fran.

Fran meanwhile began the process of squashing herself into the tightest, most odd-feeling material she'd ever worn. Once she was inside it she stared at herself in the mirror. She was flattened across the breasts and stomach, felt as if she were wrapped in Clingfilm and she realised that, for rubber, you could never be too thin.

151

"Wow," said O'Neill. "You look great."

"I feel like a trussed chicken."

Fran had to admit that O'Neill looked incredibly sexy in black leather, but she certainly wasn't going to tell him so.

The club's interior was dark and, as she'd expected, cavernous, dungeon-like. The clientele were mixed and the body parts on display, irrespective of age or shape, were mostly decorated in some way; piercings, tattoos, chains, whips hanging from well-buckled leather belts. It was a feast for the eyes, a pageant of black and silver, flamboyantly sexual and yet very unthreatening. The peacocks preened and exhibited themselves and the throbbing beat of the techno music added to the effect of its being a fashion extravaganza, rather than the predatory atmosphere of a more 'normal' nightclub.

O'Neill tried to stop staring, but when a young woman of very large proportions wearing nothing but a set of chains and silver nipple rings approached him, he had to make a conscious effort to keep his eyes on her face. Her long black hair was dressed in numerous thin plaits, stippled with silver ribbon. Her round face glowed white as if she'd applied talcum powder and her lips were painted black. He turned to look for Fran but she had sat down and a spindly young man in a pair of black leather shorts, wearing a dog collar and lead, was kneeling at her feet and gazing at her in rapt adoration.

"I'm Melissa," the big woman said brightly. "I've never seen you here before."

"First time. My name's Connor."

Melissa smiled shyly and held out her hand, the chains clanking noisily as she did so. "Is she your slave?" she asked nodding towards Fran.

O'Neill laughed. "She'd probably say yes, but not in the way you mean."

"So, do you have a vacancy?"

O'Neill, realising he was getting out of his depth, felt he had to explain their mission.

Melissa sighed. "Just my luck . . . but it's your lucky day. The submissive grovelling at your colleague's feet would know. He spends so long on his knees, or acting as a footstool, people forget he sees and hears everything. His name's Gerard."

As O'Neill kissed her hand, Melissa whispered huskily, "You belong here. Do come again."

Fran smiled broadly as he approached the table. "This is Gerard, he wants to be my slave."

"Don't we all," said O'Neill cheerfully. "Now then, Gerard. I'd like some questions answered."

Gerard's thin body seemed to shudder from his neck downwards but his pale, gaunt face stayed impassive. "I'm at your disposal, master," he said in a soft but husky voice that he'd obviously tried to perfect.

"You'll be wanting to tell me all about Marcus. Marcus with the fair hair, long ponytail – now dead."

Gerard, still on his knees, stared at the floor. "I heard someone called Marcus had been murdered, but I didn't know him . . . he wasn't my type."

"Gerard, I don't give a toss. I'm sure you don't want to upset the beautiful lady in rubber, so tell me who he saw here."

Gerard looked up at O'Neill, smiled at Fran and said, "Marcus with the ponytail used to come in here quite a bit, usually on his own, but the last couple of times I saw him he was with someone."

"Describe him," said O'Neill tersely.

Gerard raised himself to sit cross-legged on the floor, frowned slightly and said merely, "Tall, quite slim."

O'Neill felt irritated and looked towards Fran who immediately understood. "You are being a naughty boy,

Gerard," she said tapping his hand. "We want a full description."

"That's as full as it gets. Whoever it was wore a gas mask."

"You're joking," said O'Neill in disbelief.

Gerard shrugged. "Look over there." O'Neill followed Gerard's pointing finger to the other side of the club where in a dark alcove stood two black-rubber clad persons standing side by side, both wearing gas masks.

Fran's mouth opened in surprise. O'Neill gave a low whistle and then said, "I can't see much pleasure in that."

"Lots of people do," said Gerard. "It gives them a buzz and of course they're unrecognisable, which is a bonus."

"Well, I'm amazed," said O'Neill. "Where the hell do you buy a gas mask from, anyway?"

Gerard grinned, showing gappy teeth. "There are places in London where gas masks are piled to ceiling level."

O'Neill smiled, "So you're telling me the country will survive a gas attack?"

Gerard nodded, then smiled knowingly at Fran, as if implying that even a gas attack wouldn't affect his adoration of her.

"Well, you haven't been much help to us, have you?" said O'Neill. "I would have thought there would have been more loyalty amongst the members of the club. Helping to catch a killer of one of your number not on your list of priorities, then?"

"I would help you if I could," said Gerard, "but as I've said, I haven't got X-ray vision. I couldn't even tell you if the person Marcus was with that evening *was* a man. He was tall and slim but look around you . . ."

O'Neill looked around the dim club. A woman wearing a black basque, black stockings, suspenders and six inch black stilettos was leading, by a dog chain, a muscular man who wore only a G-string. The woman's long black hair fell in flamboyant curls, just skimming equally flamboyant breasts and her skin was milky white. O'Neill watched in awe as this exotic creature flicked a silver-handled whip at the man's bare buttocks. He experienced a momentary pang of lost erotic potential which was quickly ended when Gerard said, "She's really a man, married, two kids, runs a local business. See what I mean? It's hard to tell."

O'Neill sighed. "Such is life," he said. "Come on, Fran, time to go."

"Do we have to?" asked Fran. "I was beginning to enjoy myself."

"We are working," said O'Neill pointedly.

They were about to leave and Gerard had owned up to a full five feet six, kissed Fran's hand and whispered sweet somethings in her ear before he said casually, "By the way, I did see Marcus in here with a young man, tall, about twenty, slim. Good looking, I suppose, if you like that sort of thing."

"Hair colour?" asked Fran.

"Sort of mid brown. Neat looking style."

"Smoker?" asked O'Neill.

Gerard thought for a moment. "Yes, I saw him smoking."

"Andrew," they both said in unison.

"That's right," said Gerard. "Someone told me they worked together."

As they left the club O'Neill said, "What a prat."

"Who?" asked Fran.

"Gerard, of course."

"I quite liked him."

"You," said O'Neill with emphasis, "are getting to be a seriously sad case."

"Ditto."

They both laughed as they got into the car. O'Neill because he'd moved a step further in solving the case and Fran simply because she'd enjoyed herself.

Twenty

O'Neill stared out of his office window at a struggling dawn, thinking how muted Janine's reaction to finding out sister Denise was really her mother had been, as if deep down she'd known all along. Gradually the picture was emerging of a complicated family history that might or might not have contributed to Denise's murder. How Marcus's murder fitted in yet he didn't know but he knew that psychologically, for most detectives, the first murder was the crucial one – solve one and you solve the other. Providing they are both connected. O'Neill was convinced they were connected and the connection would find the killer. But what connection? Did Marcus and Denise have anything in common? Or anyone in common? His train of thought was interrupted by Fran who came into the office looking young, fresh and bouncy, making him instantly feel ten years older. She wore black leggings, a bright blue sweater and black boots; her dark hair looked newly washed and matched her general bounciness.

"You're looking cheerful this early in the morning," said O'Neill, leaning back in his chair. "And I don't want to change that, but I'd like you to visit Denise's friend Monica Ward. She may have been her only confidante and I think it might need the feminine touch."

Fran laughed, "Sometimes I think you're really a chauvinist masquerading as a normal person."

157

"I wouldn't be arguing with that," said O'Neill. "Now, off you go and be a detective."

Monica Ward lived in a bungalow in a cul-de-sac on the outskirts of Fowchester. Fran felt convinced that Monica and Denise were more than friends – not that she was a suspect, her alibi was as cast-iron as they get. The Saturday Denise was killed, Monica had been in hospital having an operation, which was why the interview had been delayed.

When she answered the door, Fran's first reaction was that whoever the underwear had been for, it wasn't for Monica. Monica was big, not so much fat as short and bulky, reminding Fran of a large parcel. This impression was formed partly by the tight floral dress she was wearing that was tied around her middle by a length of black cord. Fran's first impression was of a woman in her late fifties, even early sixties. Then she realised that, although her hair was thin, greying and combed flat, her face was unlined and comparatively youthful.

"Do come in," said Monica, before Fran had time to introduce herself. "I've been expecting you."

"I'm sure it was a shock to you," said Fran as she followed Monica's broad rear into the living room.

"I'd been half expecting it. I'd had my suspicions."

"You had?" queried Fran, trying to keep the surprise from her voice.

"Do sit down, but mind the cat," said Monica indicating an armchair. Fran, about to sit down on what she thought was an empty chair, was startled when a black cat emerged from under a cushion, eyed her with obvious disdain and sloped out of the room. "She's a little eccentric, like her owner," said Monica by way of explanation. Then she added, "How about a nice cup of tea before we get down to business?"

"Well, yes. Thank you."

When Monica left the room, Fran looked quickly around, noticing the general impression of conventionality in the neatness, smell of polish, thriving pot plants that lined the window sill, and in the line of photographs on a low bookcase. Mostly they were of Monica and a woman Fran presumed to be her mother. There were two photos of Monica and Denise together having a picnic and a group of women, arms around each other, against a backdrop of sea and beach.

By the time Monica returned with a tray of tea, Fran had sat down and was opening her notebook. "I see you're getting organised, dear. You'll want my measurements, of course."

Fran frowned in puzzlement, "I think we're talking at cross purposes, Miss Ward. I'm Detective Sergeant Fran Wilson. I'm here to talk to you about the murder of your friend, Denise Parks."

Monica, looking flustered, said, "Good Lord, I thought you were the breast care nurse. I'm so sorry. I just assumed."

"Please don't apologise," said Fran. "It was my fault. I assumed you knew who I was."

There was a slightly embarrassed silence broken by the pouring of tea and the chink of cups on saucers. "I'd better explain," said Monica. "I've just had a mastectomy. I'm expecting the nurse to help me with a falsie."

"I didn't notice," said Fran.

Monica smiled. "I'm gratified. But you don't want to hear about my operation, you want to hear about Denise."

Fran nodded. "How well did you know Denise?"

"Pretty well. We were at school together, although I was two years older. We lost touch for years and then . . . well, we had our sick mothers in common. My mother was here before I went into hospital, she's in a nursing home until I'm more recovered. Generally, we helped each other."

"In what way?"

"Company, mother-sitting, we even formed a small group of carers. Denise did have her good points."

Fran smiled. "That sounds as if she also had her bad points."

Monica frowned and sipped her tea. "I don't want to speak ill of her. She was a good friend."

"I'm sure she was, Miss Ward, but to someone she was an enemy and we want to find that person."

"Do call me Monica. I'll try to be honest about Denise, she did have a good heart, really . . ." She trailed off as if aware she wasn't being overly warm about her friend.

"Did you know about her pregnancy?" asked Fran bluntly.

Monica looked taken aback. "I'm surprised you know about that. The post-mortem, I suppose."

Fran nodded. "We've found out that Denise was Janine's mother."

Monica slightly raised an eyebrow and didn't answer at first, then she murmured, "I can't comment on that."

"Did you ever suggest to Denise that she explained the circumstances to Janine?"

"No. It was none of my business. What's this got to do with Denise being murdered?"

"I don't know, Monica, but I'm trying to find out, and for some reason that I'm finding perplexing, you seem to be keeping something back."

Monica shook her head vigorously. "Not at all. I just think you should keep to the point."

"Fair enough," said Fran. "Did Denise have any enemies?"

There was a short pause before Monica said, "No . . . not everyone liked her, and she didn't like men, and men didn't like her much. She didn't seem to meet people socially . . . except for me and occasional meetings of the group. She had a few boyfriends when she was young, but they didn't last long."

"Could one of them have come back into her life?"

Monica once again looked vaguely uncomfortable. "I don't know. But if you're trying to say she was involved with a man in some way then that's not true."

"How can you be so sure? After all, she did get pregnant once."

Monica's round face broke into an embarrassed smile. "I said she didn't like men. That wasn't quite true. She loathed men. To be quite honest, if you had said Mike had been found dead, I wouldn't have been surprised. She felt very strongly about him."

"Did she say why?"

"No one would have been good enough. Denise said she just wanted her and Janine to stay together . . . always."

Fran thought about that for a moment. "Do you think," she said thoughtfully, "there was someone else in Janine's life, who could have seen Denise as a real threat and decided to get rid of the opposition?"

Monica's pale blue eyes stared at Fran shrewdly. "Janine, from my knowledge of her, seems to be a one-man woman. I really can't imagine her cheating on Mike."

"What about another woman?"

Monica showed no sign of surprise at that question. "It's possible, I suppose."

Fran noticed that Monica's body language was becoming more defensive, her arms were now folded across her chest and her face a little set. The earlier friendliness had disappeared, to be replaced by a guarded reserve that troubled Fran. Was she lying, or merely hiding the truth?

"We did find something unusual in Denise's room," Fran paused. "Sexy underwear."

Monica smiled. "Is that a crime?"

"No, of course not. I just wondered if Denise ever mentioned it."

"Why would she?"

"You do seem to be her only friend."

"We didn't talk about underwear and anyway, are you sure it *was* hers? Could it have been Janine's?"

"She's denying that," said Fran. She studied Monica carefully until Monica became uneasy.

"I don't know why you're staring at me. I've told you all I know."

"I think, Monica, you've only told me what you want me to know. I think you know who Janine's father is, because I'm sure someone like Denise wouldn't just hop into bed with anyone. She must have thought she was in love."

"Huh . . . love. That's a joke. It was rape, and that's all I know. I'm just surprised Denise kept the baby."

Fran was about to question her again when someone knocked the front door. "That'll be the nurse," said Monica.

As Fran walked away, her main memory of the interview was Monica's expression of relief at the arrival of the nurse.

Back at the office, Fran tried to explain her unease to O'Neill. "It's not that I think Monica's lying; she's just evading the truth. Strangely enough, she got quite defensive about Denise being Janine's mother. And, far more importantly, she told me Janine's conception was the result of rape."

O'Neill realised he didn't feel surprised. "There'll be nothing reported because the two of them colluded in saying the baby was Maggie's. It seems Denise only ever visited a GP twice – both times for flu type symptoms." He paused. "Would it be worth our seeing Monica together?"

Fran nodded, then said thoughtfully, "It might also be worth seeing Monica's old mother."

O'Neill shook his head. "She's probably gaga and it would be a waste of time. We need to put the pressure on the salon staff. We should be delving into their backgrounds, but Criminal Records haven't come up with anything yet and neither have we."

"Who do you want to start with?" asked Fran, as she gazed ruefully at the ever-increasing pile of paperwork on her desk.

O'Neill stared ahead for a moment. "I've changed my mind. We'll go with your instinct to visit Monica's old mother and if it's a waste of time, you can do penance by doing some paperwork."

Fran raised an eyebrow. "Be fair boss, I do my share."

"Sure you do, Fran. I suppose I'm just feeling as bogged down with bloody trivia as with the paperwork. We don't seem to be getting anywhere. Forensic have been as much use as an accordion to an armless man, and in general I feel—"

"Jaded?" interrupted Fran. "Forensic will come up with something, I'm sure. You know how long it can take."

O'Neill smiled half-heartedly. "Come on then, let's find this poor old biddy and see if she even remembers Denise."

"I still think this visit is a waste of time," said O'Neill, as he parked his car outside the Larkswood Nursing Home. The building, newly built and low level, looked like a large bungalow. The tall trees on both sides gave it a dignified air, although O'Neill failed to see the dignity in decrepit old age itself. The sight of elderly people *en masse* struggling to walk on zimmer frames or dribbling pureed food left him feeling profoundly depressed.

Fran seemed convinced Mrs Adeline Perton could

supply information on the Parks' family background, but O'Neill's experience of elderly ladies led him to doubt his ability in that direction. Twice he'd been chosen as a long lost nephew, once as a son and last but not least, a long-dead husband. Maybe Fran would have more luck.

The manager, Mrs Hardiman, a tiny woman with greying hair, a soft voice and incongruously large shoulder pads in her pale blue suit, led them to a door marked Respite Room. "Wait here, please," she said. "I'll pave the way. Adeline has an excellent memory of the past, but a very poor memory for recent events. And please, don't be deceived by her frail appearance. She's very sharp so don't underestimate her."

"You do the talking," said O'Neill to Fran, once Mrs Hardiman had 'paved the way' and left them to it.

Mrs Adeline Perton sat, or rather slumped, in a high-back chair near the window. Her feet rested on a footstool, and a red and white crocheted blanket half covered her legs. A fine dusting of stray white hairs covered her skull and her face seemed shrunken and tiny. Fingers, distorted by arthritis, plucked momentarily at the blanket and near-blind eyes sought to focus on Fran who knelt down to speak to her.

"Do sit on a chair, dear," said Adeline in a thin, croaky voice. Fran moved an armchair near to Mrs Perton and O'Neill sat on the edge of the bed whilst their interviewee regarded them with dullish blue eyes that nevertheless seemed to miss nothing. "My daughter hasn't been in today," she said, peering intently at Fran.

"She's been in hospital, Mrs Perton," said Fran.

"I remember now," she said. "I keep forgetting."

"She seems to be doing very well."

"She's a strong girl. Comes from good stock." Mrs Perton's eyes rested on O'Neill. "Is he your bodyguard?"

Fran nodded and was sure that Adeline's left eye

winked at her. "I sit in the lounge sometimes," she said, then added: "This place is full of women – only the odd poor old man. Men don't stay the course."

"Did Matron tell you I wanted to talk about the Parks family?" asked Fran, trying to keep Adeline on course.

"Not that I know of dear, but I do remember . . ." she paused and closed her eyes. "I remember Maggie very well. Pretty girl, when she was young. We lived in the same village then. Her father was very strict, she didn't go out to play often and they all went to chapel three times on Sunday. She was hardly able to speak to a boy until she was eighteen. There was a whisper that she had to get married, but there was no baby and it was a few years before Denise was born. The man she married was years older than her, but he had a nice little cottage and some money put by and he didn't drink or smoke. They went to chapel every Sunday. Now . . . what was his name? Reg, that was it."

"Were they happy?"

Mrs Perton frowned and opened her eyes to give Fran a disapproving look. "In those days dear, married couples didn't expect to be happy. If you made a bad choice, it was your fault and you had to put up with it. I saw her occasionally when she came to the village and she seemed fine and dandy. But after Denise was born, I heard all sorts of rumours. Reg was seen with trollops and he started beating Maggie."

"Any reason?" asked Fran.

"You young girls have it so easy these easy these days with the Pill and everything," said Mrs Perton disapprovingly. "Of course there was a reason. Maggie was in labour for three days. They did that in those days, let you go on for as long as it took. It was wicked. She lost a lot of blood and it took months to get her health back. Denise was sickly and had colic and Maggie looked like a walking ghost for months. Reg, like all men, thought Maggie would be the same as before, but of course women never are, especially when they're frightened to death of getting pregnant again. Anyway, the years went by, Reg got pot-bellied, turned to drink and then when Denise was about thirteen, she had to take Maggie's place."

"You don't mean he started sleeping with her?"

"There's no need to sound so shocked, dear. Social workers didn't invent it. It's always been going on. If anything, it was less shocking then than it is now. Except, of course, when the girl got pregnant."

"You mean Denise got pregnant by her own father?"

Mrs Perton paused to put a wobbly hand out for a glass of water from the table beside her. "I couldn't swear to it, but Denise went to an all girls' school, no one ever saw her with a boy and she always came straight home from school."

"What on earth did Maggie think?"

Mrs Perton sighed. "Poor old Maggie. Denise managed to keep the pregnancy a secret for four months but then, of course, Maggie guessed, by which time it was too late to do anything about it."

"You mean . . . an abortion?"

"Of course dear, but not a nice little operation in a private hospital. Abortions then were in back bedrooms with lots of screaming and blood and pain. Wicked, it was, what those poor girls had to put up with."

Adeline Perton sighed again, closed her eyes, sagged a little more into her chair and seemed to fall asleep. O'Neill whispered, "You've exhausted her, Fran. We'd better be going."

"I am not exhausted young man," she said, her eyes snapping open. "I was just thinking . . . wondering about things."

"What things?" asked Fran.

"Such as what happened to Reg . . . probably dead now . . . bound to be. Maggie got rid of him the moment she found out, quite right too. She threatened him with a rolling pin and the police, according to the gossip. No one in the village ever saw him again."

"And Denise?"

"She left school in a hurry, and not long after started work. Maggie pretended the baby was hers. No one in the village would have given her away. She knew too much."

"I don't understand."

"Well you wouldn't, dear. You're the wrong generation. It's all so easy these days."

"What is, Mrs Perton?"

"Abortions, dear. Maggie was the one everyone went to. She was the local abortionist. That's why she wasn't very popular. Once someone knows . . . you steer clear of them."

"Was she paid?"

"Oh yes, sometimes quite handsomely. Even rich people preferred going to her. She had a good record, she was clean and very experienced and she was sympathetic."

"Do you think Denise ever helped her?"

Mrs Perton stared at Fran for several seconds before answering. "I would think so," she said slowly. "They were very close; they had the baby to care for. I should think they needed the money. What was the baby's name? No, don't tell me . . . I'll remember. Anyway, as Maggie became old, she would have needed help."

"You don't mean Maggie carried on doing abortions? Surely no woman would go to an abortionist these days?"

Mrs Perton smiled wryly. "You'd be surprised, dear. I can't remember when she stopped, but only old age and her health stopped her. It wasn't so long ago. You see, a trip to London or another big city would need explaining and money and maybe an overnight stay. Maggie was accommodating about money. She gave terms, you see, and if people didn't pay up she never chased them. It's not just young girls would want abortions; married women do, too. And they don't want their husbands to know. Sometimes its because they've slipped up with another man."

"Did Janine have any knowledge of this?"

"Who is Janine?" asked Mrs Perton.

"Janine's the name of the baby."

"Oh, yes," said Mrs Perton tiredly. Then her eyes closed and she fell asleep.

O'Neill murmured, "Well done, Fran. Let's go."

Fran watched Mrs Perton's slumped head and hoped she would wake up, if only to allow her to say goodbye and thank you. Outside there were sounds of footsteps and a trolley trundling along. Eventually there was a knock at the door and the trolley entered, pushed by a young care assistant in a pink dress who approached Mrs Perton, stroked her hand and said loudly, "Tea or coffee, Adeline?"

"Tea please, dear, and a biscuit," came the swift reply, although her eyes remained closed.

When she did open her eyes, Fran could tell Mrs Perton had forgotten who they were. The trolley trundled away and Mrs Perton sipped her tea eagerly. "What were we talking about, dear?" she asked.

"Maggie and abortions."

"I remember," she said dunking her biscuit in the tea.

"Remember what?" asked Fran feeling that at this moment she was going to find out something significant but a wrong word might spoil Mrs Perton's lucidity. "The tea has reminded me. Girls used to say they were going to see Maggie to have their tea-leaves read. A few hours with Maggie could be easily explained. If any of the family did suspect, they kept quiet. It was best all round. They were the words of comfort in the old days. If a handicapped baby died or someone with cancer, 'it was best all round' . . . country ways I suppose."

"Country ways," echoed Fran softly.

Mrs Perton's head dropped again. Fran stood up, patted the old lady's hand and said, "We'll be off now, thank you so much for your help."

Her head raised slightly and, without opening her eyes, she said, "Is that chap who's with you quite the ticket?"

Fran smiled. "He's of Irish descent."

Mrs Perton smiled sleepily, "I had an Irish boyfriend once. He could charm the knickers off a flagpole."

Twenty-One

Breakfast for Henri De Souza never varied – orange juice, cornflakes (no sugar, of course), boiled egg with one slice of toast, plus coffee and the *Daily Telegraph*. Today he couldn't concentrate on the foreign news because Fowchester was suddenly 'news'. The tabloids would no doubt have lurid headlines of the 'Gay hairdresser slain' type but the *Daily Telegraph* had a mere few lines on page three, muted and to the point, entitled 'Second murder in Fowchester'. No doubt, thought Henri, it would generate a few ghouls who would be avid to visit the scene of such sensational murders.

He looked across at Anna who nibbled on her usual one slice of toast. They rarely spoke much at breakfast time but Anna seemed particularly subdued this morning.

"Any ideas," he asked, "on how best to handle Janine?"

"In what way?" she asked, hardly bothering to look up from her toast.

Henri folded his newspaper neatly before answering; he was always neat and tidy because organisation, in general, he thought, was the key to a contented life. Luckily, Anna shared nearly all his beliefs, including politics, religion, and the need to maintain respectability and fairness in dealing with other people, especially staff. Which was one of the reasons he worried about Janine.

"I'm sorry, darling," she said, looking up at him with her wonderfully luminous eyes. "I was miles away."

"I was talking about Janine. She really is most peculiar. I'm not sure what to do about her."

"What are your options?"

"Should I suggest she has more time off?" he asked, as he sipped at the last of his coffee. "Or insist she sees a doctor? She really is behaving strangely."

Anna stared at him steadily and then said quietly, "Henri, where were you on Saturday night?"

He showed only a mild flicker of surprise, "What's that got to do with Janine?"

She shrugged her narrow shoulders almost imperceptibly. "Nothing at all. That was the night Marcus was killed."

"Darling, I don't know what you're talking about," he said, frowning. "You know I was here. I was here when you came in – very late, I might add."

"I told you I'd be late."

He held her gaze for a moment. He knew his wife well enough to know she was having an affair, but to acknowledge the fact would mean having to face the consequences, having to make decisions; decisions and declarations that would not only threaten the continuation of their marriage, but resulting in a scandal that might harm his career. Fowchester was a small town with small town prejudices and sometimes a level of hypocrisy Henri found hard to understand. Anna's private life had to be kept private at all costs.

He smiled. Anna, relieved, smiled back. "What's your agenda for today, darling?" he asked in his usual level tone.

"I'm in the Help the Aged shop this morning and shopping in the afternoon."

"And this evening?"

She smiled again. "Just a delicious meal for the two of us."

Henri nodded with satisfaction. "I'll look forward to that." Inwardly, he sighed with relief. The crisis was over.

Driving to the clinic, he decided that he should talk to Janine, judge her reaction and make a final decision based on her response. As he drove into Fowchester, he couldn't fail to notice increased police activity and he experienced a small tremor of anxiety on a level, he supposed, with the patients who would already be waiting for his ministrations with the needle and the drill.

Tara and Mandy met for coffee in the Baker's Oven. They sat at the back where they could be less easily seen for they both felt, but didn't admit it to each other, that they were being watched, not by the police, but by the curious residents of Fowchester.

"If he closes the salon, what are we going to do?" asked Tara, stirring her coffee absent-mindedly.

I'm on my own now, thought Mandy. How will I manage?

Tara placed her spoon noisily into the saucer, stared into her cup and then said quietly, "I was planning to leave the Thing but I suppose I'll have to stay now."

Mandy smiled wryly. "You've been planning to leave for years. What's so different now?"

Tara shrugged, "I'm involved with someone."

"You don't sound too thrilled about it," observed Mandy.

"He hasn't got any money or a place of his own, so unless I find the means, it's going to be difficult – bloody impossible in fact."

"Is it someone I know?" asked Mandy.

Tara paused. Secrecy seemed unimportant now that Marcus was dead and Dale seemed likely to sell up. In some ways, though, she was loath to give up her secret

172

– having a younger lover and meeting clandestinely had been the turn-on. If she were to tell all now, would she feel differently about him? She was far too astute to be swayed merely by his sexual prowess but he was what she needed now, he was her antidote to the Thing.

"Are you going to tell me who he is?" asked Mandy, almost beginning to wonder if Tara's lover was a figment of a married woman's frustrated imagination.

Tara smiled. "There's no point in keeping it a secret now. I don't suppose he'll keep his mouth shut, especially to the police. It's Andrew."

Mandy echoed the name 'Andrew' as though she'd never heard his name before. "Our . . . Andrew?" she asked croakily.

Tara nodded. "What's the matter? Why on earth are you so shocked? I know he's young but he's good looking and rampant. A bit inexperienced, but I've been teaching him . . ."

"So have I," blurted out Mandy, unable at that moment to work out who had betrayed whom and who exactly was to blame.

"You bitch," snapped Tara. "How could you? What about Josh?"

"What about your husband?"

"He's my excuse. What's yours?"

Mandy's eyes filled with tears. "I don't have an excuse. Andrew made a play for me, I suppose I was flattered. He said he loved me and I was the most beautiful girl in the world. I'd met him in a pub with a few friends. I was drunk anyway and ready to believe anything." She hung her head. "It was a one-off . . . in the park . . . standing up against a tree."

Tara stared coldly in response, then suddenly the corners of her mouth twitched and she began to laugh loudly and infectiously. Eventually, Mandy began to

173

laugh too. "Are we prize plonkers or what?" spluttered Tara.

"Yes," laughed Mandy. "At least we know what we are. That little shit thinks he's God's gift."

"Probably us that gave him that idea," said Tara. "How could we have been so bloody stupid?"

"It was easy in my case," said Mandy. "I think I was born that way."

They both fell silent then as if the full impact of Andrew's easy-won treachery had now become apparent. Eventually Tara said, "Oh well, that's life. Escape from the Thing looks a bit less likely now, at least for the time being. Murder is probably the only answer."

"You're joking," said Mandy, hoping that she was.

Tara half smiled. "I've been near to it, believe me. Sometimes I dream I have killed him and I don't wake up in a hot sweat feeling guilty. I feel happy and relieved and then I turn over in bed and realise it was just a dream and I feel the misery wash over me."

"I didn't realise things were so bad. You seem to make a joke of it."

"My life is a joke," said Tara bitterly. "A sick joke at my expense."

Mandy nodded thoughtfully and then murmured, "My life has definitely taken a turn for the worse."

"In what way?"

"I'm pregnant."

Tara stared at her. "Shouldn't that be cause for congratulations? Isn't Josh delighted?"

"He's gone," said Mandy bluntly. "Pissed off, done a runner, left, scarpered – anyway you want to put it. As soon as he found out, he left."

"He'll have to support the baby—"

"If it's his," interrupted Mandy.

"Oh my God. You think Andrew might be the father?"

"It's a possibility. He was a bit clumsy in his enthusiasm. And it was a bit squashed . . ."

"What was?" interrupted Tara. "Not his cock?"

Mandy began to giggle. "No, I was a bit squashed. If Andrew is the father, it was conceived with me squashed up against tree bark getting a cold bum."

"That's a bit sordid, isn't it," said Tara, trying to keep a straight face.

"It's more than a bit . . ." she paused and stared at Tara. "And may I say, you seem to be taking this very calmly. I'm sure if *you* were pregnant by Andrew I'd scratch your eyes out."

Tara smiled. "I just have a low opinion of men in general, formed by years of existing with the Thing."

"Is he really as . . ." Mandy paused, trying to summon up the right word.

Tara fixed Mandy with a steady gaze. "Yes, he's hell to live with. I hate him. I wish he were dead."

"You don't mean that."

"I'm quite serious, Mandy. Last thing at night, I lie in bed plotting my revenge. I've got a little money saved towards finding a hit man."

"I don't believe you."

"Good," said Tara with a grim smile. "We haven't had this conversation."

"Wouldn't divorce be the easier option?" suggested Mandy.

Tara smiled. "The only redeeming feature of 'the Thing' is the fact is he has life insurance. If I divorced him, half of nothing is nothing."

Mandy thought for a moment. She couldn't believe that Tara was serious but even if she was, there was still time to stop her doing anything silly. "There is another way," she said.

"And what's that?" asked Tara.

"You could live with me."

"And share the baby?"

"If you want."

"I would love to have children, but not the Thing's offspring," said Tara thoughtfully. Then she added, "Do you mean it? Is that a genuine offer about living with you and sharing the baby?"

Mandy nodded.

"It would be doing me a favour. I really don't think I could cope on my own and we could share expenses and baby-sitting."

"It could be fun," said Tara, smiling and feeling a surge of optimism she hadn't felt for a very long time. "The men in our lives could be mere sex objects."

"I'm finished with men," said Mandy. "Apart from gay men like Dale. He offered to keep me on and help with the baby, but that was before Marcus was killed."

"I don't think Dale will ever be the same again," murmured Tara.

"Will any of us?" said Mandy. "Let's face it, the police suspect us all. Have you heard that the Chief Inspector is planning a reconstruction?"

Tara nodded. "That's scary, isn't it?"

"I'm dreading it. I feel sick just thinking about it."

"Why, Mandy?"

Mandy blushed slightly and looked away. "I'm the chief suspect for killing Denise."

"Don't be daft."

"I'm not being daft. I was the last one to see her alive. I feel . . ."

"Guilty?"

"No . . . responsible. I shouldn't have left her. If I'd stayed with her, she wouldn't have been murdered."

"That's true," agreed Tara. "But only because she

wouldn't have been murdered at that moment. Her killer would have found another time or place."

Mandy watched Tara's expression carefully. She sounded so knowing, so sure. A shiver crossed the back of her neck. What did she really know about Tara? She wanted her husband dead for his insurance money. And she made Denise's murder seem inevitable, as though she too harboured thoughts in that direction. Or were they merely thoughts? Had she just invited a murderess into her home, her life and her baby's life?

"Why are you staring at me like that?" asked Tara.

"No reason. I was just thinking."

Mandy drank the last sip of her coffee and from the corner of her eye noticed that Tara had started to scratch her right hand, so hard that her nails raked the skin and a trickle of blood trailed lazily towards her little finger.

Twenty-Two

O'Neill stared at the ceiling of his bedroom. It had been the first night back in his flat, and he felt quite homesick for the rape suite, where he'd felt soothed by the placid pastels and by the fact that he knew there were others around. Here in the flat, his loneliness gripped him as acutely as acid indigestion but there were no antacids that could cure his feeling of isolation . . . or failure. He was failing now and he knew it. Ringstead had reneged on his promise of funding the reconstruction for the time being, pointing out that even to get on television's *Crimewatch*, a crime had to be well past its solve-by date and as yet, Fowchester's murders had not quite reached that stage.

O'Neill glanced at his alarm clock. It was seven a.m. and too early to ring Fran. Her plan of the salon had been useful, but Marcus's death had robbed him of a fairly sound suspect. Marcus had been cheating on Dale. Marcus knew that Denise knew and he didn't want anyone having that sort of power. Maybe she'd made a pointed remark and he'd simply lost his temper. Simple, O'Neill had thought. Some murders were that simple. Just a sudden loss of control, almost a crime of passion. But then Marcus was killed and somehow simple became complex and complex became bloody impossible. Some murders he'd investigated had a gender stamp – sometimes a question of height or strength or simply having a certain aura that eliminated one section of the population. In the past, female killers were rare but women had become more violent, and he knew that officers on the beat were far more scared of a violent, deranged woman than a violent, deranged man. A woman in full lunacy would have not only the extra strength, but a cunning and deviousness that surprised many young coppers.

Neither killing, in this case, gave him a hunch of gender or otherwise. In fact, he felt as open minded as a lobotomised gorilla. The team was working gruelling hours, interviewing everyone from shopkeepers to members of gay clubs. If a man had admitted to knowing Marcus even on a lustful-glance acquaintanceship, or come within a hair's breadth of his scissors, he'd been interviewed – and all to no avail.

Fran had suggested a severely disgruntled customer may have held a grudge and whilst this seemed a bit far-fetched to O'Neill, Fran managed to describe several hair horrors she'd gleaned from women's magazines. Women who had hair turn green, frizziness that bordered on freaky, clumps of hair falling out, and total hair loss and burnt scalps seemed to be fairly common. Not via *Le Salon*, however. The records from ten years previously showed a few complaints, mostly about style and excessive cutting but nothing, O'Neill suspected, that could lead to the culprit meriting death by scissoring.

Maybe, mused O'Neill, as he began the process of getting up, the motive was getting in the way of detective work. In the final analysis, it mattered not why, but *whom*. It was obvious that several people had the opportunity to kill Denise. The to-ing and fro-ing of staff and customers could never be that accurate. Staff and customers used the same loo, people moved continuously, unaware of the movement of others. They just didn't notice.

Marcus, in contrast, had been alone with his killer. He'd

obviously brought someone back that night or opened the salon door to someone whom, presumably, he knew well enough and trusted, even, to allow that person to cut his hair, or maybe . . . the phone ringing broke his train of thought.

"Yes," he said tersely.

"Chief Inspector?"

"Yes," he repeated.

"It's Sergeant Datton. We've just received a call from Miss Janine Parks. She wants you to visit her at home, today if possible."

"Any reason given?"

"No, sir. She just said it was important, but not urgent."

As O'Neill rang Fran, he glanced at his watch. It was eight a.m. Breakfast time.

"Fran, I'll be over in about ten minutes. We're off to see Janine, she's just rung the station."

Her answer was slightly muffled as if she'd just woken up.

"And I wouldn't mind a bit of breakfast before we go," he said.

Her answer to that was equally muffled, but he was fairly sure it wasn't that polite.

When Fran did answer the door, he could see why her voice sounded muffled. She had the flu. Her face was hot and flushed, her eyes streaming, her hair unbrushed. She wore a crumpled sweater and creased skirt. "You're looking as if you slept in that, Fran."

"I did. I felt really ill last night, but I'm a bit better this morning."

"Sure – you're a bit better than death. Get to your bed, I'll ring the doctor."

"It's only flu. He'll just tell me to take paracetamol and drink plenty."

"And to stay in bed," said O'Neill, "but I'll give

180

you a choice. Either I call the doctor or you go to bed."

"Just give me a few minutes, Connor. I'll get changed, have a cup of coffee and I'll be fine."

O'Neill stared at her for a moment, wanting to hold her close. Instead he said firmly, "Be going to bed. I'm pulling rank now. Just do as you're told."

"I'll be fine—"

"If you argue with me any more, I'll carry you up the stairs."

Fran shrugged and managed to smile. "You win, Guv."

After she'd gone upstairs, O'Neill rang Janine.

"Would you like to be telling me about it over the phone?" he asked.

"It's not urgent. I'd just like to show you something."

"Are you working today?" asked O'Neill.

"No, Chief Inspector, I'm taking a few days off sick."

"Are you ill?"

There was a long pause before she answered. "I'm not ill, exactly. There are things I have to do. In the house, sorting things."

"I see," said O'Neill. "I'll come this minute if you want me to but my DS has the flu and I'd prefer her to be with me."

Again there was a long pause. "Yes," she said eventually. "I'd prefer it if she came with you."

"I'll ring you tomorrow," said O'Neill.

"I'll be here," said Janine. "I'm not planning to go anywhere."

Strange, thought O'Neill, how a categorical statement can immediately place a doubt. Was she in fact planning to go somewhere? Could she be suicidal? She was definitely strange, but was she in any danger? He thought not, but decided he'd ring later in the day just to make sure.

In the kitchen, he put on the kettle and decided to make

Fran some breakfast. In the food cupboard he found a tin of baked beans, a tin of anchovies and a tin of black cherries. In the fridge he found a half-full bottle of white wine, an egg and a tiny portion of Stilton cheese, plus a few drops of milk in a jug. Suddenly he felt very angry with her. No wonder she was losing weight, no wonder she was ill. Weren't women supposed to know about healthy eating? Weren't vegetarians supposed to be attuned to a healthy lifestyle? His fridge might well be empty but he ate out for most meals and, after all, if he had a wife he would expect her to keep a well-stocked fridge.

O'Neill made Fran a mug of tea – she seemed to be out of coffee – and took it upstairs. She lay fast asleep, one arm on the back of her head, her hair damp on her flushed forehead and her breathing seeming faster than usual. He sat on the small armchair by the bed watching her. Occasionally she mumbled feverishly. Just before the tea become cool he drank it himself and continued to watch her for a while. He knew in a day or two she would be well but it didn't stop a flicker of anxiety deep in his soul, even though on optimistic days he sensed Fran *was* his destiny. She didn't know that, of course . . . yet. One day though, she would and, again in optimistic moments, he was convinced they would always be together.

It soon became clear Fran wasn't going to wake for a while so he wrote a note, leaving it propped up on her bedside table saying that he would be back at lunchtime and she was to stay in bed. He'd already decided to visit Dale at the salon, not least because the whispers at the station were getting louder: Dale had killed Marcus and O'Neill wasn't doing anything to prove it.

Le Salon, dark and lifeless, cast a depressing aura, the sign on the door saying 'CLOSED DUE TO BEREAVE-MENT'. O'Neill rang the doorbell of the flat several times before Dale's heavy footsteps descended the stairs. He looked pale, unkempt, his eyes still red and haunted looking.

"You're not sleeping," said O'Neill. "Have you seen the doc?"

Dale merely nodded. "You'd better come up."

It was obvious once they were in the lounge that Dale was awash with vodka. He'd made no attempt to hide the empties and, judging by his gait, he'd already drunk most of the bottle that stood on the coffee table.

"Do you want a drink?" Dale asked, as he snatched a clean tumbler from the cabinet.

"Why not?" said O'Neill. He didn't actually like vodka so it would be no problem merely to have one drink.

"You haven't come to arrest me, then?" asked Dale, as he handed him half a tumbler of neat vodka. O'Neill shook his head.

"Do you want tonic in it?" asked Dale, sounding as if Paraquat might be more appropriate. "If you do, there's some in the fridge."

When O'Neill returned from the kitchen, Dale was staring somnolently into his glass. His trance-like state continued, but O'Neill merely sat watching him, knowing that soon he'd start to talk.

Several minutes later Dale took his eyes from the vodka and said, "He was always too young for me. I always knew he'd leave one day . . . but not like this. People think I killed him. I know they do. I've been outside, I could see they way they averted their eyes when they saw me. I heard them whispering, too. 'That's the one who killed his gay lover. Hacked him to death with a pair of scissors . . . jealousy, that was the cause. The younger one was seeing other blokes . . . you know what queers are like.'" O'Neill couldn't disagree, the same things were being said at the station. Gays, it seemed, were more jealous, more unstable, more promiscuous than the rest of the population. But when O'Neill asked if they were more likely to be criminally inclined to robbing banks, mugging old ladies or getting drunk and disorderly, the same officers muttered uneasily that it wasn't that easy to judge.

"I was jealous, of course," continued Dale. "But I kept it under control. Hairdressing is a stressful job you know, always trying to please people, especially women. When did you last see an employed stylist of my age? Old barbers die with their boots on, but old hairdressers get burnt out and do other things. Marcus and I thought of other ventures, I quite fancied a smallholding but Marcus said, 'Duckie, if I wanted shit on my boots, I'd prefer to work down the sewers than be out in all weathers, getting a red face and worrying about the price of parsnips.'" Dale smiled at this memory of Marcus, then his expression changed and his eyes filled with tears. "He was a vain sod. His hair, his teeth, his skin. He maintained his bits, I'll say that for him. He wouldn't have taken as much care of a Rolls Royce as he did his own body."

"The night he died," began O'Neill tentatively.

"Go on," said Dale, sounding slightly suspicious.

"Was it usual for Marcus to bring . . . a casual acquaintance back here?"

"You mean someone he'd just picked up? He'd never done it before. I keep thinking about that, wondering if it was the end anyway."

"What do you mean?"

"I mean," said Dale, "he was bringing him back here either so that I'd catch them, or he wanted to tell me it was all over. On your bike, adios amigo, let's always be friends . . . you know the scenario."

O'Neill nodded. "Do you think the haircut was significant?"

Dale looked away. "I do wonder," he murmured, "if

having his hair chopped off was a signal to me that we were finished as an item."

"Was there any sign of that?"

Dale shrugged. "I didn't really think so at the time. He had his freedom, he seemed happy. Now, of course, I look back on . . . our situation and think I was just kidding myself."

"There's no way of knowing," said O'Neill quietly, "if the hair cut took place as something pre-planned or on the spur of the moment."

Dale took a huge swig of vodka and mumbled as if thinking aloud, "Why did the stupid tart let him use his best scissors?"

"It could have been a woman, Dale."

Dale seemed to think carefully about that before answering. "He did have women friends, but they all knew he was gay."

"No hint of bisexuality, then?" asked O'Neill casually.

"Certainly not," snapped Dale. "Marcus was purely homosexual. He liked women but he didn't fancy them."

"Sure, Dale. I'm sure you're right, but it's perfectly possible a woman killed him. A woman, perhaps, with hairdressing skills."

Dale stared into his glass again. "Hacking skills only, Chief Inspector. But if not a jealous man, why the fuck would a woman want Marcus dead?"

O'Neill smiled. "I keep asking myself the same question Dale, and if I knew that, I wouldn't be sitting here asking you these questions."

Twenty-Three

Fran remained in bed for two days, two days in which O'Neill visited her every few hours. He called out the doctor on the second day because Fran complained of a blinding headache, and when O'Neill wanted to search her body for a meningococcal rash, she sat bolt upright in bed saying, "Since when have you been a GP?"

O'Neill had answered, "To be sure, you're contrary, Fran. Here's me working my fingers to the bone for you and when I want a little diagnostic practice, you say you want the real thing." She'd managed a wry smile at that moment and the GP managed to convince O'Neill that it wasn't meningitis, but merely a headache due to having a high temperature. 'Plenty of fluids and paracetamol every four hours, and by the way, there is a lot of this around.' There always is, thought O'Neill.

Fran meanwhile had begun sneezing, snuffling and coughing, and O'Neill spent a small fortune buying every-thing at the chemist from lemon barley water to tissues. Then, having watched Fran drink a large tumbler of squash plus two paracetamols, he began talking about the case. At first she was fairly responsive, but then she dozed and muttered, politely and totally out of context. But O'Neill didn't mind, he just wanted to air his thoughts.

When night fell, he knew he couldn't leave her so he decamped to the sofa and spent a restless night thinking he could hear her sleep-walking, and even more time awake hearing her coughing. Fran being ill he found, to his surprise, very distressing. He knew it was only flu but he knew people could die of 'only flu'. Not young people though, he tried to reassure himself.

In the morning, he woke to find Fran standing over him. "I wasn't at the pearly gates Connor. You needed have stayed." He didn't answer. She seemed unaware she was only wearing a thin nightie and he rubbed his eyes as if still half asleep so that he didn't have to stare at her.

"But thanks anyway, for looking after me."

"Pleasure," he said. "You go back to bed and I'll make you some tea and toast."

"No bread."

"Have now – I've been shopping."

In the kitchen, Fran opened her fridge and cupboards to find them stuffed with food and she felt grateful and touched, but strangely depressed. Illness bought home how vulnerable the person who lived alone was. Who would have helped her if O'Neill hadn't? She vaguely remembered him talking about the case as she fell asleep, which probably explained her nightmares.

It was later when she was gratefully back in bed drinking tea that she related her nightmare of the birthday cards that opened up, each one containing an incredibly shrivelled head, reduced to the size of a fifty pence piece. She related this to O'Neill who perched on the edge of the bed listening intently.

"People like Denise Parks do perhaps buy in bulk," said O'Neill, "but who the hell was she buying all those cards for? And is it significant? What really surprises me is the fact that she didn't keep the names and addresses listed somewhere."

"Perhaps she did," said Fran. "Janine wanted to see you, maybe she's found them."

"I should see her today, but she wants you to be there."

187

"Why?"

"No idea, but you're not well enough to leave the house."

"I'm managing to talk today, Connor, and the headache's gone. I could manage one little trip."

O'Neill shook his head.

Fran meanwhile had her head on one side and was murmuring, "Go on, be a sport."

O'Neill, unwilling to give in so easily said, "I'll see how you feel this afternoon, but I'm not making any promises."

O'Neill stood by her bed, about to leave, and felt a strong urge to kiss her. Fran, seeming to guess his intentions said, "Don't get too close, Connor, you really don't want this bug."

He smiled, trying to hide his disappointment and merely said casually, "Sure. You're right. I'll see you later."

After he'd gone Fran slept uneasily. When she did get up to go to the bathroom, she felt dizzy and very weak, so that she was only too glad to return to her warm bed and even to relish the thought of dreaming her fevered dreams.

O'Neill returned to the office and began sifting through the PDFs and the reports on the backgrounds of virtually anyone connected with the case. Now that the computer system was back to normal, the Criminal Records Office had processed all the names. No one, it seemed, had a criminal record, except for Maggie Parks – not for performing abortions, but for shoplifting. She'd been caught only once, at the age of sixty, and the judge had given her a conditional discharge on the grounds that her memory seemed impaired and the article she had stolen – a red basque – was obviously a manifestation of a slight mental aberration. O'Neill smiled to himself; would the judge have said the same if Joan Collins had nicked a red basque?

That was one little mystery solved, thought O'Neill, but of course provided no clues to who might have killed Denise. The one person he did suspect of both murders was, of course, young Andrew. He at the moment was suspect *el primo*. He had been seen at Peacocks with Marcus and undoubtedly he had access to Denise that day. He had lied about leaving the salon, and he was learning the art of hairdressing. Maybe Marcus had suggested he cut his hair and a row started, and perhaps if Andrew had been as drunk as Marcus then he could easily have lost his temper. Was Andrew a young closet homosexual or unable to determine his own sexuality? Perhaps Denise had sensed his ambivalence or she'd heard gossip and confronted him and his reaction was vicious and immediate. Andrew's parents would no doubt provide him with an alibi for the night Marcus was killed, but maybe the reconstruction would prove so unnerving for him that he would succumb to more intense questioning. Suddenly O'Neill felt a quiet confidence he hadn't felt in ages and even though Superintendent Ringstead still balked at the cost, O'Neill intended to go ahead anyway.

He tidied his desk, feeling only a slight anxiety about Fran. Was she really fit enough for the visit to Janine? A visit that he couldn't put off for any longer.

By the time he arrived at Fran's place it was late afternoon and the low clouds and general air of wintry dankness and fine drizzle suggested it would rain all night. Was one visit worth Fran succumbing to pneumonia? He let himself in with the key Fran had lent him and was surprised to find her up and dressed. She looked pale and thin but her eyes seemed brighter.

"I feel so much better, Connor. I'm raring to see Janine."

O'Neill raised an eyebrow. "Are you sure you haven't overdosed on the hot lemon and honey?"

Fran laughed. "No, but perhaps later you could fix me a hot toddy!"

O'Neill merely smiled, but inwardly his optimism on their future relationship rose by fifty per cent. Was she inviting him back? Was a hot toddy more of an invitation than coffee? Either way, they hardly talked in the car and their arrival at Janine's cottage was equally muted by a protracted wait on a dark porch.

"Did you ring her?" asked Fran. "Because if you did, it looks like she changed her mind. There are no lights on."

"I didn't ring her today," said O'Neill, banging loudly on the door. "But I'm sure she's in."

Fran wasn't so sure, and her feeling of being in improved health was fast diminishing. She wanted to sit down and preferably to go back to her bed.

When the door did suddenly open they were startled, not only by the silent and swift opening, but also by the sight of Janine. She wore a long flowered and padded dressing gown and a pair of fluffy pink slippers, her hair was lank and unbrushed and her eyes seemed deep sunken and empty.

"I'm glad you've come," she said dully. "There are things I want to tell you."

The three of them sat at the kitchen table and Janine didn't seem to need prompting. "I've had some time to think and I need to get certain things cleared up." She paused. "Would you like some tea?"

O'Neill shook his head. "What was it you wanted to tell us?"

Janine looked at him stonily for a moment. "I think I know why Denise was killed. I found something in the loft that might be . . . helpful."

O'Neill nodded. "Would you be showing us?"

"It's in the loft."

190

"Could you bring it down?"

"You'll have to go up. The ladder's there. I'll wait down here." Then she added, "You'll find it in the tin box."

O'Neill signalled by a brisk head movement that he wanted Fran with him and she stood a little unsteadily and followed him from the kitchen towards the stairs.

"She's giving me the creeps," whispered O'Neill, half-way up the stairs. "She reminds me of a Lady Macbeth who's forgotten her lines."

Fran moved slowly up the ladder, she hated ladders and heights and she still felt light-headed. *Just don't look down*, she told herself, as though she were on a high ledge instead of halfway up a mere loft ladder. Once she was through into the loft, she remained looking ahead. Her eyes flicked over the suitcases and boxes, an old standard lamp with a dusty broken shade, a stack of jigsaws and dusty books. Finally she glimpsed a large tin box in the corner.

O'Neill struggled behind her through the narrow trapdoor and edged gingerly along the joists. The attic had a characteristic smell of dust and dry rot. The light bulb that hung in the middle rafter cast its light sparingly, and the outer corners of the attic remained gloomy and shadowy.

Fran knelt down by the tin box and then turned to look at O'Neill. "Go on, Fran," he said. "Open the box."

She lifted up the metal latch and swung open the box. On top lay a white cover. She lifted the corner and noticed it was lacy and very pretty. She held it in her hands and as she did so, realisation dawned. It was a christening robe. She moved the material between her hands then stared into the box.

She moved her mouth as if speaking but no words emerged. O'Neill now stood over her, also staring into the box. Fran looked up at him and saw there was sweat on his upper lip.

Twenty-Four

It took both O'Neill and Fran several seconds to compose themselves, but it was O'Neill who eventually said, "I'll deal with this Fran, you can move away from the box."

Fran stood up unsteadily as a wave of nausea flowed upwards and caught her in the throat, causing her to cough and heave at the same time. She had never seen anything quite so . . . macabre and horrifying; for the box contained three large glass jars, in each of which floated a foetus suspended for ever in a liquid grave.

Fran looked across at O'Neill and saw the colour had faded from his face, he looked ashen in the poor light and his eyes glistened brightly.

"Jesus Christ," he murmured sadly. "Sometimes, Fran, this job really gets to me. You think you've seen every horror and madness and then something like this happens and you realise that you're only a novice and that so called humanity can be such a stinking cesspit . . ." he broke off. "You'll have to deal with Janine. I can't face talking to her at the moment."

"Perhaps she didn't know," suggested Fran.

O'Neill shrugged. "You talk to her and find out. I'll ring forensic and stay out of your way for a while. I have a feeling she's more likely to be honest with you."

Janine sat where they had left her at the kitchen table. Now she stared vacantly into space but when Fran called out her name she obviously heard because her back tensed and when Fran sat in front of her Janine's eyes did meet hers.

"How long have you known about . . ." Fran raised her eyes upwards.

Janine clutched at the neck of the dressing gown she wore. Then she smiled bitterly. Fran thought she looked more than a little mad and she felt herself shiver and have to take a deep breath to steady herself.

"I always suspected something," said Janine slowly. "Denise and Mum warned me never to go into the loft. They said the joists were unsafe. But a few years ago, I did go up there and I saw that tin box. And I must admit I was suspicious . . ." she broke off and began staring ahead.

"What made you suspicious, Janine?" asked Fran.

After a short pause Janine began playing with her fingers while Fran tried to stay silent and patient.

"There was nothing wrong with the joists," murmured Janine, "and as soon as I saw the tin box, I wondered if that was what they didn't want me to find. Mother, I still think of Maggie as my mother, always said one of us should be in the house until the day we died. But I thought it was for another reason."

"What was the reason?"

Janine fixed Fran with an icy stare. "I thought my father's body was in that box."

Surprise made Fran stutter. "But . . . but . . . it's too small for a man's body."

"He wasn't large," said Janine, matter of factly. "I thought they might have chopped him up."

Fran swallowed hard but she said, calmly and evenly. "Why would your mother and sister want to kill him anyway?"

"He wasn't a very nice man."

Fran waited for her to elaborate but when she didn't she said, "Come on Janine, you'll have to do better than that."

"No, I won't. No one can force me to divulge anything. Some secrets have to stay secrets."

Fran sighed inwardly. "That's all very well Janine, but the contents of the bottles in the loft are a serious police matter."

"Are they? Why?"

"Because they're evidence of illegal abortions."

"Who are you going to prosecute? They're both dead. I didn't even know . . ." she broke off, a scared expression crossing her face. "They can't leave here, they can't. Don't you understand? They've been preserved for a reason."

"What reason?" asked Fran uneasily.

"It's their resting place. What will the police do with them? Give them a Christian burial?" She laughed harshly, the sound making Fran feel more uneasy. Where the hell was O'Neill? Why wasn't he supporting her? This woman really was giving her goose bumps.

"Come on, Detective Sergeant. Tell me what they'll they do with those dead babies who died so long ago. Throw them into the incinerator? Use them for research? Bury them in a cardboard box on a piece of hospital waste ground? Those babies float in liquid as if they never left their mother's womb. No one will ever touch them – not while I still live."

Fran watched as Janine's whole demeanour grew more manic. Her voice now had an hysterical edge and she seemed unable to keep her hands still.

"Calm down," said Fran softly. "We'll work this out together. But if you want them undisturbed you must tell me all you know. After all, you do want Denise's killer caught, don't you? The bottles upstairs might have something to do with her death."

Janine frowned, "How could anyone know?"

"Are you sure no one's been in the loft? Mike, maybe?"

"Of course not," she snapped. "Mike was never alone in the house."

There was a long pause before Fran said, "Tell me, Janine, whose babies were they?"

"How should I know?" she replied swiftly. "I didn't even know they were there."

"I think you do know, or could at least guess."

"I've no idea. I did know . . . Maggie did abortions in the sixties, but she only tried to help people."

"Why keep three of them? Don't you find it a bit strange, Janine, rather macabre?"

"Why should I? I don't know why she did it, but she had a kind heart. What was she supposed to do with them? Build a bonfire, flush them down the loo? She simply kept them safe."

At that moment the sound of knocking on the front door startled them both. A look of sheer panic crossed Janine's face. Fran put out a hand to calm her but it had the opposite effect and, brushing Fran's hand aside, she ran from the kitchen – straight into O'Neill's arms.

"There's no need to be frightened, Janine," said O'Neill as he patted her back. "Dr Harrod is here."

A tall, thin, grey haired woman, carrying a black leather case, came into view and smiled reassuringly at Janine. Janine, however, wasn't reassured, instead she looked even more frightened. "You're not taking them away. I'm telling you that now. They're safe here."

"Of course they are, Janine. I want everyone to be safe," said Dr Harrod softly as she took her arm. "Let's sit down and talk about this."

Janine looked round apprehensively for a moment then, gathering her dressing gown tight to her neck, began walking back towards the kitchen with Dr Harrod.

Fran and O'Neill both breathed a sigh of relief which had hardly expired when the front door was again knocked upon loudly. As O'Neill approached the front door, Janine walked past him saying, "I'm going to the loo." By the time he'd opened the front door to the forensic team leader and greeted him, he'd heard the loft ladder being lowered.

"Quick, Fran!" he shouted. "Get after her!"

Why me? thought Fran as she dashed up the stairs. It was too late. The loft door was just closing but she didn't hesitate and began climbing.

"Go away," Janine was screaming. "Go away! If you don't, I'll hang myself. I've got a rope. I can do it and I will. I will!"

Janine's hysterical voice came through the closed loft door, sounding disembodied and distant. Fran clambered up the ladder, this time hardly noticing she was no longer on terra firma. She tried to open the loft cover but it wouldn't budge. She guessed Janine was either holding it closed or had placed something on top.

"Janine, I'm going down now," Fran called out. "Just calm down and in a few minutes I'll come back up and we can talk."

At the bottom of the ladder stood O'Neill, Dr Harrod and the forensic man, all looking as nonplussed as a trio of garden gnomes.

"Did you hear she's threatening to hang herself?" asked Fran.

O'Neill nodded. "We heard."

There was a pause while they all looked up to the loft and listened intently, but all was silent and eventually Dr Harrod said, "If you like, I'll go up and talk to her. I've known her for quite a while. But I'll have to make promises."

"What sort of promises?" asked O'Neill.

"That she'll be allowed to keep the foetuses."

"Do you think she'll actually try to commit suicide if we do remove them?" asked O'Neill.

"Undoubtedly," said Dr Harrod firmly. "You see, I think one, maybe two, were her babies. I think the third may be either her mother's or her sister's. They've been kept in the family."

"Oh my God," muttered O'Neill.

"Shall I go up?" asked the doctor.

"Certainly. Thank you."

"It's probably best if you two go downstairs."

O'Neill nodded. "Sure. We'll do that. Be careful, just yell if you need help."

In the kitchen, Fran made tea and O'Neill pondered the legal and medical implications, whilst the forensic man silently read a newspaper he'd bought with him.

"Do you think she'll be sectioned?" asked Fran, as she placed a tray of tea on the table.

"I think it would be best if she was," he said, "but these days, there are so few beds it seems unlikely."

They drank the tea with an edgy awareness of the slightest sound. Occasionally, the sound of Dr Harrod's soothing reassurances seemed to drift downwards, but individual words couldn't be deciphered. After a while Fran said, "She seems to have been up there for ages. Should I see what's going on?"

"Just be patient, Fran. A siege situation can take days, after all."

This comment caused the forensic man to look up from his newspaper. "Sorry, chief, I can't hang around for another hour, never mind a few days. Anyway, the prosecution service is unlikely to prosecute a woman for having an abortion and keeping the foetus – balance of the mind and all that. At this stage, the interest in them will be purely academic and she's obviously a very sick woman."

O'Neill nodded. "I was thinking the same thing myself. You go now, we'll have to see if the doctor has any ideas."

The forensic man folded his newspaper carefully, stood up and said dourly, "In my opinion, she should try a stun gun. . . . but then I'm an old cynic."

O'Neill watched him go, finished his tea and said decisively. "Come on Fran, I think it's time for action."

Twenty-Five

When O'Neill checked on Dr Harrod, he found she'd obviously gained Janine's confidence and was with her in the loft. He heard no raised voices, but he didn't think it wise to make his presence known until reinforcements came. He'd sent for uniformed back-up, simply because he didn't think it wise to leave Janine alone in the house. She would, at least, be safe in a police cell until a psychiatrist could organise treatment for her.

Meanwhile, Fran felt that she personally was deteriorating fast. Whilst her adrenalin had been in overflow, she had felt strong and able to cope; now she felt she had as much strength as a soggy lettuce. She desperately wanted to lie down and close her eyes, but she knew she had to keep going, at least until the uniformed back-up resolved the situation.

When the burly uniformed duo did arrive, with night sticks and handcuffs attached to their leather belts and with necks as big as Tyson, Fran thought Janine would be forced to give in, if not gracefully, at least through trepidation and intimidation. Fran had seen both men in action before and she couldn't help wondering if O'Neill's call for back-up was really necessary. They were a tough and nasty pair, the sort anyone would need in a really violent situation. Luckily, in a perverse way, they both had a major drawback – they were not very bright. Intuition and experience in the police force had prejudiced her

199

against brain combined with brawn. There was always the possibility men like that could reach senior levels powered by testosterone and ambition, their aggressive instincts often wreaking havoc. She was trying to think of examples when O'Neill's voice broke into her reverie.

"Fran, you stay down here. You look all in. I'll take the lads upstairs."

'The lads', looking tough and grim but with bright excited eyes, nodded at her, and in Fran's fragile mental and physical state, it seemed their footsteps were more military and synchronised than was necessary for one poor demented woman.

Fran heard them go up the ladder and smash their way through into the loft. She heard Janine screaming and scuffling noises and swearing and she fought back the urge to go to Janine's aid – after all, whose side was she on anyway?

It seemed ages before she heard descending footsteps. Fran, all lethargy forgotten, rushed up the stairs. Dr Harrod, looking slightly ruffled, already stood at the bottom of the ladder, holding out a hand to O'Neill who had a bloody nose and the expression of a truly anguished man. He was quickly followed by one of the police constables, handcuffed to Janine, whose now bare feet kicked at him alarmingly. Janine continuously screamed out every swear word Fran had ever heard, and she tried to yank the other attached officer down the ladder so that he faltered and they all nearly fell. Fran noticed that the PCs were red faced and sweating. Janine was neither.

As they took Janine away, both men looked straight ahead, their initial excitement and bravado well dissipated. Janine continued to struggle vainly and scream various obscenities about their birth and the nature of their subsequent sexual limitations. Fran was surprised at

Janine's vocabulary, but also hopeful. She'd come alive, her spirit was still strong, and the fact that she could give three men a hard time showed she had the will and the stamina to fight back.

A little later, whilst O'Neill sat nursing his nose with a cold flannel, he told her what had happened. "She was quite calm, initially. Dr Harrod had convinced her she could stay in the house and that her 'babies' could stay. Then she saw me and I approached her, thinking she was calm. She just swung at me with both fists, I fended off her right but she caught me with her left. When the lads came up she was in her glory; kicking, spitting, trying to bite. Then she sort of sagged and became quiet, and as the lads tried to get the handcuffs on she went crazy again. Knees, elbows, stomach – you name it, she went for it."

"Demented people do seem to have extra strength," said Fran, trying not to smile.

"Demented women are the worst," said O'Neill, stroking his nose in recognition of the fact. "They're faster than men and they seem to have more stamina for a struggle."

Fran fell silent for a while; she had seen a side of Janine she hadn't known existed. "Is there any way Janine could have killed her sister and Marcus?" she murmured almost to herself. "We know the back door may have been open, we know the time of death is only accurate to within an hour or so and that Mandy left her longer than she said. Does her alibi stand up? And does she have any alibi at all for the night Marcus was killed?"

O'Neill frowned. "I expect she'd be saying she was at home fast asleep, but what motive could she possibly have for killing Marcus? Her sister, I can vaguely understand. An odd family . . ."

"Odd?" interrupted Fran. "They make the Munsters look normal."

O'Neill cast Fran an irritated glance, her interruption

had spoilt his train of thought. "As I was saying, Fran, the family was dysfunctional. And perhaps Janine could have sneaked out of the dentist's, rushed along to Lime Street, crept in the back door, murdered her sister and then sneaked back. However," he paused, "I'm sure the good citizens of Fowchester would have seen her, and she couldn't risk actually being seen."

"But maybe she was seen," said Fran. "We haven't asked for witnesses to come forward, have we?"

O'Neill ignored that question because she knew the answer already and was just being clever. Still irritated, he said, "You seem to have all the answers, Fran. What motive could she have for killing Marcus?"

"I can only think of one strong enough. She either knew or suspected that Marcus knew or suspected that Janine had murdered her sister."

O'Neill smiled at the convoluted explanation. "What puzzles me is the timing. How would she know for certain that he was going out, or what time he would be back? She would have had to lay in wait for him. Somehow, it all seems a little unlikely."

"She could have guessed that, being Saturday, he would go out and would be back quite late."

"It's worth following up," conceded O'Neill reluctantly. Then, looking round the kitchen, he said, "Something else is worth following up. Let's give this house a proper search while we've got the chance."

"What exactly are we looking for?" asked Fran, trying to disguise the weariness in her voice. A house search was the last thing she wanted to do. If she even saw a bed she would want to lie down.

"How would I be knowing that?" said O'Neill, his cheerfulness restored. "We'll know what it is when we see it."

They started in the loft. The tin box with its grisly

contents still sat there but the lid was closed. "We'll deal with that later," said O'Neill.

For the next fifteen minutes they searched through black plastic bags full of old clothes, boxes of dusty books and a few broken toys that seemed almost as macabre as the preserved foetuses. Eventually they realised there was nothing else of significance in the loft. "It's strange," said Fran. "Maggie and Denise didn't allow Janine in the loft, for obvious reasons, so what better place to hide things they wished to remain secret?" She paused and looked over to the tin box.

O'Neill followed her drift and muttered, "Oh, no." Slowly he moved over to the tin box. He had to bend because of the slanting roof and he very nearly asked Fran to remove the boxes, but she wasn't well and he didn't want her to faint on him.

He removed the glass bottles carefully, realising as he did so they were Kilner jars usually used for making jam. He didn't look at the contents, he couldn't, he didn't want to lose face by puking or passing out. It was a myth that all coppers had strong stomachs. It was like saying sailors never got seasick.

All he could see at first was a fine, lace crocheted square. He lifted that to find several neat piles of cards. Each one home-made, in plain white card with a pressed flower of a forget-me-not on the front. Inside the first of the pile, in black letters, it said 'R.I.P.' and below that the date: '2nd April 1962'.

Fran sat beside him now as they both gazed at the cards. In all, there were fifteen. All were dated. Underneath the cards was a notebook, also decorated with a pressed forget-me-not. Inside were names, addresses and dates. There was no need to search the rest of the house.

Outside in the cold fresh air, Fran felt light-headed. It was late, pitch black and as they drove back to Fowchester they hardly spoke. Except for O'Neill who said, "I'll stop off for an Indian takeaway."

"As long as it's vegetarian," Fran mumbled tiredly, not caring about food, merely wanting two paracetamol and a good night's sleep.

O'Neill stopped off at the Balti house in the high street and, once in Fran's flat, he said, "Now, you sit down and put your feet up, and I'll dish up."

By the time he returned from the kitchen, Fran was already asleep. "Fran," he called loudly. "Wake up. Can't you smell it? It looks delicious."

There was no response. He eased her feet slightly so that he could sit on the edge of the sofa and ate his meal to the accompanying sounds of Fran's rather snuffly breathing. He soon realised there was no hope of Fran waking up before morning, so he brought down her duvet and covered her. He stood looking down at her for a while. Then he slipped off his shoes, told himself he shouldn't be doing this, but that he was going to do it anyway, and eased himself beside her. She didn't stir at first but just before she fell asleep he heard her murmur, "Is that you, Connor?"

"Go back to sleep, Fran," he said softly, gratified that she didn't seem to object.

Strangely, although he felt squashed and uncomfortable, he had the best night's sleep he'd had in years.

Twenty-Six

D ale had seen his GP, who had suggested bereavement counselling. He'd had one session and had met a gay man whose partner had died of AIDS. It made Dale realise that suffering was all around and not his alone, and he found that vaguely comforting. He also found that he was beginning to miss the salon. At first, he could only stand in the reception area and remember the blood and the shock of seeing Marcus on the floor dying. He couldn't find the courage actually to be in the same space that Marcus met his death.

Now, two weeks on, he began to see that the salon was all he had, that he missed the staff and the customers, and he didn't want to lose the business it had taken him years to build up. He knew Chief Inspector O'Neill wanted a reconstruction to take place in the salon, the sort of event he would have wanted Marcus to share. But he would have to go it alone and he consoled himself with the thought that Marcus would have been proud of him.

Today was Monday, normal closing day, so he rang Mandy and Tara and Andrew and told them to be at the salon by eight-thirty the following morning. He then rang some of his regular customers, offering them reduced rates, and found that only one refused. The others offered their condolences and were glad he was back in business. After that, he rang Chief Inspector O'Neill.

"I'm being a brave old queen, Chief, and opening the salon."

"I'm glad to hear it, Dale. Keeping busy does help."

"You sound as if you're speaking from experience," said Dale, realising once more that there was no monopoly on grief and misery.

"Sure I am," said O'Neill. "If I get the go ahead from above, I'll be wanting to do the reconstruction on Saturday. I'll be ringing the customers who were there on the morning Denise was killed. I want everything to be as it was."

"So do I, Chiefie. So do I." Then he added, "You won't forget about Marcus in all this, will you?"

"I think whoever killed Denise also killed Marcus."

"I just want the bastard caught."

"It's as good as done, Dale."

"I'll hold you to that."

A few minutes after talking to O'Neill, Dale broke down in tears again. He wasn't sure now if he could get through the night; and if he didn't, who would be there to grieve for him?

Andrew had mixed feelings about the salon opening. He'd been looking for a new job with no success, but even if he had found another job, he knew he'd still have to take part in the reconstruction. He had thought of ringing Mandy but she'd seemed very sharp with him last time they'd spoken on the phone. Tara hadn't been too friendly either and he suspected they both knew he'd been two-timing them. He didn't feel guilty. They'd both enjoyed it, both had the hots for him and he'd given them a good time. Tara worried him more than Mandy; she seemed to want to get serious, mostly because she was married to a pig. His attitude with girls was to take what was on offer and never get fond of them. The moment they stopped being randy and got romantic instead, he dropped them. Tara was different; he had wanted to live with her, mainly to escape from his boring parents. Perhaps he was growing old, he thought, ever to have considered it was a good idea.

He'd been playing computer games in his room all morning when his mother shouted from downstairs that there was a phone call for him. He spoke briefly on the phone and arranged a meeting.

"Who was that?" asked his mother.

He ignored the question. "I'm going back to work tomorrow. If the police come round, tell them I'm out."

His mother sighed. Where had they gone wrong? she wondered.

Andrew felt unnerved by the phone call. He didn't want a meeting. In fact, he suddenly felt scared. There was, after all, a murderer in Fowchester and he could be next in line, although he wasn't sure why.

Fran had completely recovered from the physical effects of the flu, but the virus seemed to have left her depressed and weepy. Her paperwork had piled up and, in her imagination, was of mountainous proportions. O'Neill wanted her out and about all day and then in the office in the evening. He always saw her home and waited expectantly on her doorstep for an invitation for coffee. The last two evenings she had gone to bed while he remained sprawled on her sofa, as if her home was his. She could hardly call it sexual harassment, but it was privacy harassment.

Today they had followed up some of the names and addresses on the list of card recipients. It had been time consuming, because only those women who had been alone in the house had been interviewed, simply to protect their privacy.

Their first visit was to an Irene Jacobs, who lived in a suburb of Birmingham. The house was large and detached; inside, it was light and airy with fresh flowers, mock antique furniture and commemorative plates that covered one complete wall of the living room.

O'Neill's excuse for calling was to inquire about the efficiency the local neighbourhood watch scheme. Mrs Jacobs stared at him shrewdly from beneath her purple rimmed spectacles.

"You're very senior for such a mission, Chief Inspector," she said. "Would you mind if I verified this with your police station?"

O'Neill smiled. "I'm fabricating a reason to talk to you, Mrs Jacobs." An anxious flicker crossed her face. Fran guessed she was in her mid to late fifties, but she had a trim figure and unlined olive skin. She wore a white silk blouse and well-cut black trousers and had perfectly varnished nails and soft-looking hands which gave Fran the impression she didn't clean her own house. Mrs Jacobs certainly didn't seem the type to need a village abortionist, either.

"Yes?" she queried in response to O'Neill's odd admission.

"I'm here regarding a murder investigation – in Fowchester."

If the name of the town surprised Mrs Jacobs she remained composed. "How can I help?" she said.

O'Neill answered quietly and slowly, "I believe every year on the tenth of June you receive a home-made forget-me-not card."

The colour slowly drained from Irene Jacobs' face and for a moment, Fran thought she was going to faint.

"Yes," she whispered. "How did you know?"

"We found a list and the cards in the house of the dead woman – a Miss Denise Parks," said O'Neill.

"And we thought you might be able to help with our enquiries."

"Oh my God," muttered Mrs Jacobs. "It's a never-ending nightmare."

"It could be over now. Maggie Parks is also dead. So I'd be obliged, Mrs Jacobs, if you could tell us what happened to you."

For a few moments, she stared down at the rings on her finger. Then she began speaking in a low, flat monotone. "I got married at the age of eighteen. My parents disowned me; they were fairly orthodox Jews and my husband was a gentile. We were quite happy at first, but then he started seeing other women. I stayed with him but I got terribly depressed. I'd no family, even my Jewish friends deserted me – then I found I was pregnant. When I eventually told him, he suddenly announced he didn't ever want children and I was to get rid of it. He recommended Maggie Parks, she was cheap and fairly local. I was heartbroken, but I felt I didn't have much choice . . ." She paused as her eyes filled with tears.

She removed her spectacles, dabbed at her eyes with a lace hanky, then replaced her glasses and said, "I remember the day so well. The sun shone, but her cottage seemed dark and gloomy. I was so nervous. I felt sick and couldn't stop crying." She took a deep breath and then continued. "But she was efficient and kind and it was quick. I have to admit, I came away feeling relieved. I thought that was the end of it. Later, I became very depressed again and, some months later, I divorced my first husband. After that my parents, bless them, accepted me back into the fold as if nothing had happened. I still lived in the marital home when the first card came. I was on my own when it was delivered and I nearly passed out. I'd never forgotten, of course . . . how could I?" She broke off again in tears.

Fran put an arm around her and eventually Mrs Jacobs' tears became sniffles. Finally she took several deep breaths and said, "It's a relief to talk about it, really. Some years I didn't get a card, but every June I got depressed and anxious and couldn't tell anyone why. I remarried, a lovely Jewish man called Sam, but I'd never told him about the abortion. We have two children. They're grown up now – a Jewish mother's dream, my daughter is a doctor and my son a lawyer."

"And your husband?" asked Fran.

Mrs Jacobs sighed. "He died last year of a heart attack. I regret so much not telling him. He was a fine man and, now he's dead, it's too late to say I'm sorry for my unexplained moods and sadness. I just wish . . ." her voice trailed off miserably. Then she shrugged and with a big sigh said, "Is there anything else you want to know to know, Chief Inspector?"

"Thank you for telling us, Mrs Jacobs. There is a question. Throughout the years, the cards have continued?"

She nodded. "Yes. What really puzzles me, apart from why, is how she always seemed to trace me."

"There are always ways," said O'Neill. "Did you never think of warning her off?"

Mrs Jacobs gave a rueful smile. "I thought of killing her. Sometimes when I was near Fowchester I found myself driving towards her cottage, but I always turned back. I often wondered why she picked on me."

"It wasn't just you," said O'Neill.

"Why did you visit Fowchester, Mrs Jacobs?" asked Fran.

"I know one or two people in the area, so occasionally I visited them and I saw the dentist."

"Henri De Souza?" queried Fran.

She nodded. "I"ve known him since he first quali-fied."

O'Neill raised an eyebrow at Fran and then said, "There will be no more cards, Mrs Jacobs."

Relief flooded her face. "Thank God. You won't have to tell anyone about . . . all this, will you?"

O'Neill smiled. "It's over, I can assure you."

She smiled back sadly, her spectacles misted, her eyes red and watery. "It's never really over. I needed no reminders, but it's still a relief. Thank you."

Twenty-Seven

O 'Neill stared out from his office window onto a grey early-morning sky. Dark low clouds threatened rain or snow and Fowchester at seven a.m. was extremely quiet. Only the occasional car passed by, and so far he hadn't seen a single pedestrian.

After a while he made coffee and started more detailed lists for the reconstruction on Saturday. So far, he had two major problems regarding the planned reconstruction. Superintendent Ringstead had costed it carefully with the thoroughness of a keen young accountant and still wasn't convinced it merited the expense. A Marcus lookalike couldn't be found in the police force and the team was still visiting gay pubs and clubs in Birmingham, in the hope of finding a ponytailed volunteer.

Meanwhile, house to house enquiries were intensified, but as yet had yielded nothing new. O'Neill was convinced that in cold weather people walked heads down, totally concentrated on getting from A to B. In warm weather they looked around, took notice and lifted their heads. Consequently, the shopping population on the Saturday morning Denise was killed seemed as observant as suicidal gerbils and both the uniformed branch and CID failed to come up with significant sightings. The woman serving in the bakery remembered Andrew coming in but couldn't give an accurate time. "Time flashes by," she reported, "and I don't have time to stand around watching it."

O'Neill had been in touch with Dr Harrod regarding Janine. Eventually, a bed in a private mental hospital in the Midlands had been found for her. She was being treated for depression and was attending group therapy sessions. The foetuses had been removed and were in a local hospital's pathology department, where their future was uncertain. O'Neill planned to visit Janine when it was considered she was fit enough, and for him that would be the conclusion of her part in the investigation.

At nine o'clock, Superintendent Ringstead sent for him and Fran whispered, "Good luck." O'Neill gritted his teeth and told himself not to retaliate if Ringstead ran true to form. Which he did.

"Ah – O'Neill," he said, his round face looking more puffy than usual, his dark eyes seeming wedged between his ever plumper cheeks. "I know you're keen on this reconstruction idea O'Neill, but what exactly do you hope to achieve by it – some sort of dramatic confession?"

"No, sir."

"Would you care to elaborate?"

"The case is at a crucial point. A reconstruction will hasten the end."

Ringstead showed his teeth; O'Neill could not have described it as a smile. "What leads do you have, O'Neill? I've kept an eye on this case and, quite honestly, I'm not impressed. You haven't had anyone in for questioning and you seem to be generally floundering. Are you sure your relationship with DS Wilson isn't affecting your judgement?"

"What relationship . . . sir?"

Ringstead's eyes narrowed even more. "Don't play the innocent with me, O'Neill. You've been seen coming and going from her place like a homing pigeon. This is a small town, you know people are gossiping. Why do you do it?"

Before he knew it O'Neill uttered the fatal words: "I'm in love with her."

Ringstead's mouth opened silently like a fish. "Well . . . I see. Yes. Is it reciprocated?"

"No."

Ringstead now seemed at a genuine loss. "What can I say? After your . . . tragedy, we all hoped you'd find happiness, but if she doesn't feel the same . . ." He shook his head dolefully.

"There's always hope," said O'Neill.

Ringstead stared down momentarily at his blotting pad. "Be honest with me, O'Neill. Do you think this . . . relationship is affecting your judgement? I mean, are you working to full capacity?"

"Sure I am. I'm working all hours God sends. I couldn't be doing more."

Ringstead shrugged. "It's too late to take DS Wilson off the case but I'll review the situation as soon as you have a result – which I hope won't be long."

"Yes, sir."

As he opened the office door Ringstead said, "By the way, if this expensive reconstruction nonsense doesn't work, I'll have you both transferred to Toxeth or Tottenham. Their clear-up rates are worse than ours. Just get it done, O'Neill. I mean it – fail on this one and you'll be losing your girl and the job."

"Bastard," muttered O'Neill as he closed the door.

"What's wrong?" asked Fran, when O'Neill returned.

"Loose talk, Fran."

"Yours or his?"

"Mine. I think I may have landed us both in it."

"In what way, Connor?" asked Fran suspiciously.

O'Neill paused, "Just the usual gossip."

"About us?"

He nodded.

"So we'll be sent to the eastern front?" she asked, smiling.

"No. Toxeth and Tottenham were mentioned."

"Together?"

"That's what the man said."

"Could be worse, then," she said.

O'Neill noticed she sounded quite cheerful about the prospect and that made *him* cheerful. He knew that Ringstead's bluster meant little. It was merely chest-beating and, if they succeeded, Ringstead would probably take the credit. "Come on, Fran," said O'Neill abruptly. "Let's get on with the job, we need to show Ringstead that we do make a great team."

Fran smiled. "Was there ever any doubt?"

Over the next two days, doubts did arise. O'Neill felt an increasing sense of panic, feeling that he hadn't been focused enough and that maybe Ringstead did have a point.

Twenty-Eight

O n Saturday morning O'Neill woke into the darkness, saw it was only five a.m., but knew he would not be able to go back to sleep. He made himself coffee and stared round his soulless flat. When this case was over, he resolved, he was going to get his life in order, and that meant either pursuing Fran and risking ultimate rejection, or asking for a transfer. And to be sure, he told himself firmly, she wasn't the only woman in the world.

At seven-thirty he rang the video man to make sure, not only that he was up, but that he was well briefed. Shortly after that, he rang Dale and told him that they had found a young lookalike and he hoped he'd be able to cope.

Just after eight, he was in the station's briefing room talking to the team and showing them exactly, on a large plan of the salon, where he wanted them to be based.

"Try to be unobtrusive," he said.

Someone sniggered at the back, which irritated him, and he glared around the room before continuing. "The press will be hanging around, Superintendent Ringstead will be practically foaming at the mouth and I'll be cheerfully strangling anyone who cocks up." He paused. "Are there any questions?"

No one spoke and they left *en masse* quietly with a few more 'Hair today and gone tomorrow' type jokes, childish but cheering.

At the salon, O'Neill definitely needed his own morale

boosting; a complete fiasco seemed foretold from the moment one of the original customers rang to say she had the flu. Also, the Denise lookalike, looking nothing like Denise, kept smiling and being affable.

Eventually, though, by nine a.m., there was some semblance of order. The affable 'Denise' had been sat down in the staff room with a cup of coffee and now it seemed the only major drawback was the absence of the young actor who would play Marcus.

O'Neill wasn't the first to see him. Dale saw him the moment he walked through the salon door. The colour drained from Dale's face, and he began to tremble. A strained silence fell upon the salon and as tears coursed down Dale's face. Fran guided him to the staff room where she sat him down with a box of tissues on one side and 'Denise' comforting him on the other.

O'Neill followed them into the staff room and signalled to Fran to meet him outside the back door and there, with a chill wind blowing, O'Neill said, "This is a complete and utter disaster, Fran. Whose idea was it anyway?"

"It wasn't mine," said Fran. "Anyway, the day is still young."

That thought didn't comfort O'Neill and neither, a few minutes later, did the sight of the local press building up their forces outside the salon.

Gradually, as the morning wore on, order was restored. Dale, still pale and red eyed, began to hair-dress with 'Marcus' by his side, who brushed the long hair of a WPC in a parody of the real Marcus's professionalism.

At midday, the time Denise had been seen to enter the salon on the day of her murder, the stand-in walked in and waited at reception.

"Now then, Tara," said O'Neill. "Try to remember your exact words to Denise when she arrived."

Tara frowned and looked particularly thoughtful. Then she smiled, "I remember."

"Well, go on. Say it!"

Tara, looking and sounding self-conscious said, "Hello Denise. It's really cold out today, isn't it?"

"And how did she answer you?" asked O'Neill.

"She said, 'It usually is in January.' She always managed to put the damper on things."

"Then what happened?" asked O'Neill, resigned now to the whole exercise being as successful as peace talks in Northern Ireland.

Tara, however, suddenly seeming to enter into the spirit of the idea, said, "I'm really sorry, Denise, but Mandy is running late today, so you'll have a short wait." She paused. "Shall I take your coat?"

'Denise' looked perplexed and glanced at O'Neill for her 'lines'. "Don't be looking at me," said O'Neill. "Tara knows what was said."

Tara smiled. "I'd forgotten about her coat. We hang them in the staff room and give them a cape from the shelf. But that morning, she said, 'I'll take my coat.'"

"Was that usual?" asked O'Neill.

Tara shook her head, "No. I guessed she wanted to go to the loo."

O'Neill turned to 'Denise'. "Okay Denise, off you go." As he watched her go, he asked Tara if she looked anything like Denise.

"From the back view – yes," said Tara. "From the front, she's the same age, size, build and colouring, but Denise had a mouth that looked as if she'd just sucked a lemon and eyes that never smiled."

O'Neill looked round the salon. One of the original customers sat reading a magazine with her head under the dryer. Dale was chatting whilst he cut hair, 'Marcus' was both chatting and flirting with the WPC. Andrew was shampooing at the furthest sink, and Mandy was out of sight, but presumably in the beauty parlour. No one even saw 'Denise' walk towards the loo. It was as though she were invisible.

'Denise' returned from the toilet to the beauty salon where Mandy, looking pale and anxious, sat her down near to a chair where once the hot box had been.

"Don't you be worrying about this, Mandy," said O'Neill. "You're very brave and all you have to do is repeat your actions and try to remember the conversation of that day."

She nodded miserably. "I remember apologising to her. I was still in the middle of a manicure. I offered her usual tea and a magazine to read, but she refused both."

"Then what did you do?"

"I went behind the curtain and carried on with Mrs De Souza's manicure."

"Be doing that now," said O'Neill indicating the drawn curtain.

Mrs De Souza smiled an acknowledgment as the curtain was drawn back. She lay on a couch, one hand stretched out on an armrest, the nails painted a pale pink.

"Will you excuse me," said Mandy, as she turned abruptly and left the room.

O'Neill wasn't sure if she was feeling ill or simply couldn't go on. Mrs De Souza smiled at O'Neill's puzzled expression. "She's got frequency," she explained. "A symptom of early pregnancy."

"Did she do that on the day Denise was murdered?"

Mrs De Souza gazed at her outstretched hand for a moment. "Yes, I think so. She left me at least once, while my nails were drying."

"How long for?"

She looked thoughtful. "I get relaxed lying here, time

doesn't mean very much. It's rather like being hypnotised, I suppose. Five minutes maybe."

"Did she speak to Denise?"

"Not that I heard. I probably dozed off."

"Did you hear Denise speaking to anyone at all?"

"No. When Mandy came back she finished off my manicure – I'd already had my hair cut and blow dried by Marcus – then I left the salon."

"Did Mandy get your coat?"

"Yes."

"Where did you wait?"

"Here."

"Then what did you do?"

"Paid the bill, of course."

"You paid Tara in reception?"

"Yes."

"Tell me again what time you left the salon."

Anna De Souza sighed. "I'm not sure to the minute, but it was after twelve."

"Thank you, Mrs De Souza. I'd like you to repeat that scenario when Mandy comes back."

She smiled fully, showing her husband's expertise. "I'll do my best, Chief Inspector."

When Mandy came back she held Anna De Souza's coat over her arm, and then Anna followed her to the reception area.

Meanwhile, 'Denise' waited alone and seemingly ignored.

Twenty-Nine

O'Neill followed Anna De Souza's slim hips to the door then, as she turned, he said, "Would you be indulging me and return to the beauty salon and then walk from there to the front door?"

She shrugged her shoulders slightly. "No problem, Chief Inspector."

As she walked back to the beauty salon, it wasn't her he watched. He watched everyone else. Again, no one seemed to notice.

Mandy once more apologised to 'Denise' as she had done previously. The real Denise hadn't responded, just sat herself in the hot box.

"It was only then," explained Mandy, "that I realised I'd run out of towels. I offered her tea again but she still refused, she was in a really bad mood by then."

"I'd like you to do exactly as you did that day," said O'Neill. Mandy frowned and her lower lip trembled slightly. "What's wrong, Mandy?" he asked. "I know this is distressing, but if there is something you want to get off your chest, you'd better do it now."

Mandy appeared to sway just a little. Then, taking a deep breath, she said, "I don't know why I didn't tell you before. I've been wanting to, but I suppose I couldn't believe it."

"Believe what?" asked O'Neill, trying to hide his impatience.

She swallowed hard before replying. "I hadn't got a towel to put round Denise's neck so I went off to get one. When I came back – I wasn't gone for long – she had a towel round her neck. She had her eyes closed so I didn't speak to her. That was when I left her . . ." She broke off looking tearful. "I went to the staff room to the toilet. There was no one in the staff room, but when I came out Andrew was there, he'd been having a smoke outside. We had a bit of a chat . . . well, it was more than that. He starting kissing me and . . . I suppose I was there longer than I should have been. When I went back to Denise, she was dead. If I hadn't left her for so long she'd have still been alive."

O'Neill patted her on the shoulder. "The murderer would have found another opportunity, you can be sure of that. But why didn't you tell me about the towel?"

Mandy's eyes rounded in surprise. "Because one of the staff must have put it round her neck. It was white, you see. Dale uses white for hairdressing because he can bleach them. I use pink ones."

"I see," said O'Neill softly. "So, who do you suspect?"

Mandy blushed a faint pink. "I don't suspect anyone. That's why I didn't tell you. I didn't want you to suspect anyone on the staff."

"So why have you told me now?"

"Because of Marcus. He was one of the good guys, who could have wanted to kill him? There must be a madman around and none of us will be safe until he's caught."

O'Neill smiled. "Don't you worry, Mandy. I do have a suspect and, very soon, that person will be in custody."

She observed him doubtfully for a few moments. "Is there anything else you want to know, Chief Inspector?"

"Just one more thing, Mandy. When you first left Denise, I presume you pulled the curtains round her."

"I always do. Quite often I have two people at once in here, and I always curtain them off."

"Did you have the curtain pulled around Mrs De Souza?"

"Yes."

"More importantly," said O'Neill. "Did you pull back the curtain when she left?"

Frowning, Mandy said hesitantly, "I think so. I can't remember. You don't think someone was hiding behind the curtain, do you?"

"It's a possibility."

Mandy stood for a moment with her head on one side as if listening. "You're going to think I'm very stupid," she said.

"Tell me about it."

"There's a difference between now and that Saturday morning. I was in such a state, I've only just remembered. When I left Denise, the radio was on. It was Radio Two, quite low, middle of the road stuff. When I came back that first time to find the towel round her neck, I don't know for sure what programme it was, but there were voices discussing something or other. I'm sorry . . . I don't take much notice of radio, it's just a background noise."

"You've been a great help, Mandy. Thank you."

"Have I?" she said, looking surprised, but she did manage a half-smile and when O'Neill told her she was free to go, she looked positively relieved.

Fran, meanwhile, watched and listened, trying to be unobtrusive and two things struck her; the customers were self-absorbed and the staff were task-oriented.

Tara answered the phone several times and rarely looked up, unless she was actually at the till or dealing with a customer. When she was on her own in reception, she certainly didn't seem to be interested in what was going on in the salon.

Andrew washed hair and seemed to run various errands, usually making tea or coffee and occasionally picking up a dustpan and brush to sweep the hair from the floor. Andrew's presence or absence seemed the least important. He undoubtedly would have had access to Denise.

Dale, in contrast, being not only the boss but also the senior stylist, would have been missed in seconds. He was the ship's captain and Fran could see that he really was in control, now that he had overcome his shock at seeing 'Marcus'.

When Fran stood to the side of the mirrors, watching Dale at work, the customers glanced at her initially but, as with the video cameraman, they soon forgot or simply ignored their presence. She heard various snippets of conversation and, she had to admit, she was a little shocked by the intimacy. It was as though wet hair was akin to being naked and, once 'exposed', the small talk became more like bedroom talk. The more she listened, the more she realised that Dale's being gay made him a sort of neutral sounding-board. Somehow, his homosexuality made his female customers perceive him as broadminded, unshockable and the font of all knowledge on emotional and sexual matters. He had become, in their eyes, an honorary woman. And he gave advice, he didn't just listen.

Fran heard a middle-aged woman, half-rollered, say, "I've told her, she can bloody well leave home if that's her attitude. Good God, he's old enough to be her father."

Dale, mid-roller, said, "As old as me, Marie?"

She smiled, a strangely flirtatious smile, directed at him in the mirror. "Come off it, Dale. You're a mere boy."

"How old is he, then? Come on, tell Uncle Dale all about it."

And she did, at some length.

Fran realised that most of what she'd heard was inconsequential, but this was just one morning spent listening. How much had Denise heard over the years? She also noticed that Dale gave his undivided attention to the customer he was working on. His seeming oblivion to the rest of the salon's activity could have been a deliberately staged act, or could have resulted from his trusting everyone else to do their jobs without any interference from him.

Andrew, though, remained for Fran her prime suspect. He seemed nervous, and spent some time watching 'Marcus', who now was doing very little other than entertaining the customers waiting for the services of either Dale or Mandy. Towards midday, she followed him into the staff room.

"I'm starving," he said, as he picked up a packet of sandwiches from the rickety table that sat in the middle of the room. "Do you want some?"

Fran shook her head. "Do you always eat about this time?"

"Yeah, usually." He smiled as he ripped open the sandwiches. "I'm a growing boy."

"What time did you eat on the day Denise was killed?"

He shrugged. "I don't know," he said. "I haven't got a watch."

Fran looked at her wristwatch. "It's just twelve-fifteen. Which is about the time Denise was murdered."

"Nothing to do with me," he said, biting into his sandwich.

Fran coolly stared at him. He swallowed hard. "Why are you staring at me like that?"

"Why do you think? I'm just trying to decide if you killed Denise before or after you ate your sandwiches."

Thirty

O 'Neill and Fran spent the next morning watching the video of the reconstruction. It proved less helpful than O'Neill had thought it would, but it did show that people could walk back and forth with no one registering their movements. The customers' eyes seemed focused on the mirrors in front of them, and the staff focused only on the customer they were dealing with.

"I read once that middle-aged women often complained that they had become invisible," said Fran as she opened the office blinds, feeling relieved she didn't have to watch the video yet again.

"Depends what they look like," said O'Neill. "I can't imagine Sophia Loren or Joan Collins being invisible, even to female eyes."

Fran had to agree with that, but nothing altered the fact that, so far, the reconstruction hadn't revealed anything new or relevant. O'Neill had asked one of the team to find out about broadcasts on that Saturday, but as yet they hadn't reported back.

O'Neill stared down at his notes. "Fran, do you mind if I ask you a personal question?"

She smiled. "You'll ask me anyway."

"Sure I will," said O'Neill. "I do notice that women pay more visits to the loo than men but I noticed on the video that Tara only went once, in the late afternoon. Mandy went several times, Dale and our young actor friend also

226

only went once. Andrew went twice during the day. And you popped in and out of the loo about four times – why was that?"

Fran gave O'Neill an old-fashioned look. "Time of the month, that's all. And I'd drunk lots of coffee and not eaten much. On a busy Saturday, the staff wouldn't have the time to keep leaving customers for cups of coffee or the loo."

"Mandy did," said O'Neill.

"She's pregnant."

O'Neill stared out of the window for a moment. "What if Mandy has taken us in all along? Imagine Denise saying something to the effect that Mandy should have an abortion – that single mothers cost the country a fortune, or something along those lines. Wouldn't you want to at least biff her one?"

"I would, but I'd walk away. Anyway, at the time Mandy had a partner and, of course, Denise had been pregnant once herself."

O'Neill nodded, "True, but then all 'reformed' people have an added zeal. Look at ex-smokers – self-satisfied or what? Denise wouldn't, from our knowledge of her, have been able to resist a barbed comment. Perhaps to the effect that Mandy's boyfriend would never marry her, that could have touched a raw spot."

Fran fell silent for a while, then sat up abruptly. "It's so obvious! Why didn't we think of it before?"

"Enlighten me, Fran."

"All this talk of the staff going to the loo, et cetera. What about Denise? Why have we assumed she just sat there patiently waiting? Maybe she waited for a few minutes and then took herself off to the loo or to the staff room, looking for Mandy. Once there, she overheard or saw something. Maybe she worked out about the double-crossing Andrew and then used that information to put in the poison, but was 'poisoned' in return."

O'Neill frowned thoughtfully. "We haven't been aggressive enough, Fran, we need to come down heavily on them all. So far, all we have is conjecture and speculation."

"They don't necessarily know that," said Fran. "We could say forensic has come up with something."

"DS Wilson, I'm surprised at you. But you're right. I also think someone on the staff knows exactly who killed Denise, but they thought she had it coming. But if they thought the same person killed Marcus they might, with suitable 'evidence', be prepared to speak up."

"Who do we start with?"

"We'll have Tara in but we'll have a word with her friend next door first, because she seems to be her only social contact apart from those at the salon."

They were just about to leave the office when the phone rang. O'Neill answered it reluctantly but when he put the phone down, he was smiling. "That was the hospital. Janine is much improved and she wants to see us."

"Things are looking up," said Fran. "At this rate, we'll solve the case well within Ringstead's 'Six weeks, or forget it,' deadline."

"We haven't cracked it yet, Fran. Promise me that when we do, we'll go out together to eat, drink – maybe go dancing?"

"I didn't know you could dance," said Fran in surprise.

"I only have one dance in my repertoire."

"What's that?"

"The tango."

Fran laughed, "I don't believe it for a minute, but you're on for the eats and drinks."

"Sure you'll see," said O'Neill. "I do have my little secrets."

Fran remembered that phrase later when they visited Tara Watts' next-door neighbour, Yvonne Jenkins. Surprisingly, she seemed quite happy to receive a visit from the CID.

"You've come on a good day," she said cheerfully. "The kids are with a friend of mine."

Yvonne dressed in cheerful colours to match her personality. A crimson red sweater encased breasts so voluptuous and alive they looked about to escape the confines of her scooped neckline. Her black skirt barely covered her bottom, but she did have a good shape and, for a moment, Fran was jealous of her sheer nerve and verve. Dyed blond hair swung free to her shoulders and she had plenty of mascara on her eyelashes, but no other make-up. She didn't need any; she had what Fran's gran would have called 'a face like an angel'. Fran supposed that meant neat and cherubic with round, childlike eyes.

The hall carpet and the carpet in the living room were threadbare, the furniture was obviously old and looked second-hand but children's paintings had been framed and hung on the walls as if they were masterpieces and pots of flowering plants and crocuses lined the window sill. Yvonne kicked a large plastic tub overflowing with toys into a corner of the room and then said, "Sit yourselves down, I'll make you some tea."

Before they could answer, Yvonne had left the room and in a short time had returned with a tray of tea and chocolate biscuits.

"We don't usually get the red carpet treatment," said O'Neill.

"I've got a lot of time for the police," said Yvonne, as she handed them strong tea in large mugs. "My ex was a complete head-case, very violent. Drink wasn't his excuse. He was just nuts. But he could be persuasive and if the police were called – Tara called them a few times –

I always prayed they would believe me. And mostly they did. When I threatened to press charges, he always did a runner. Unfortunately, he always reappeared."

"Why did you only threaten to press charges?" asked O'Neill.

Yvonne's blue eyes widened as if in disbelief. "It seems so bloody simple to you, doesn't it? He wouldn't get a long sentence; then, when he *did* get out, he would have come after me. Even on the inside they make phone calls, send letters and send their new-found, just released 'mates' to frighten you. The last time I was definitely going to press charges I had a burglary. Everything of mine was either stolen or smashed up. I've only got furniture now because the local boys in blue helped me out."

"I see," said O'Neill. "Where's your ex now?"

"In the nick. He half killed a man in a pub brawl. He got ten years. When he's due out I'll move or go abroad. I haven't had any threats yet; perhaps he doesn't blame me – this time. Thank God I've divorced him now and that's what Tara should do. I keep telling her that."

"So she has problems with her husband?" said O'Neill.

"There's no love lost," said Yvonne, somewhat cagily.

"Is he violent?" asked Fran.

Yvonne smiled. "He's a pig and a slob but Tara doesn't admit he's violent."

"Why not? Aren't you her best friend?"

Yvonne crossed her legs and stared at Fran. "You wouldn't understand. She's ashamed of him and of herself for staying with him. If she told me he'd been violent, I'd just tell her to get out, but it's never that easy."

"Why not?"

"Because he'd come after her. Violent men are like that; they don't give up. He thinks of her as a possession and what do you do if you lose something you own? You find it."

"What about a women's refuge?" asked O'Neill.

"Have you ever been in one?"

O'Neill shook his head.

"Screaming kids, rotten smells, no privacy, camp beds, no money and a shared kitchen. Would you want that, or would you rather bide your time and think of another way?"

"Put like that," said O'Neill. "I think you've got a point. But what option does Tara have?"

Yvonne laughed. "Apart from murder, you mean?" She paused seeing O'Neill's disapproving expression. "Just a joke. But with some men like my ex and him next door, murder does cross your mind."

"So you think Tara may have thought of murder as a way out?" queried Fran.

"Be honest," said Yvonne. "Wouldn't you? But if you're suggesting Tara had anything to do with the murders at the salon, you're wrong. If her husband got his just deserts, I'd think she'd had a hand in it; but as for killing anyone else – no way."

"Do you mean she wouldn't be alone in planning it?" asked Fran, trying to make her query sound as casual as possible.

"I never said she was planning it. You're putting words in my mouth."

Fran smiled, "I know you're holding something back, Yvonne, and I'm afraid we do have some circumstantial evidence against Tara."

"I don't believe it," snapped Yvonne. "She's not violent . . . but . . ."

"But what? Come on, Yvonne, you want to help Tara, don't you? She obviously has been violent at least once, or you wouldn't have paused. What happened?"

"It's no big deal. Her husband got very drunk and turned nasty and she pushed him down the stairs. It was an accident, and she just left him at the bottom of the stairs until the morning. He was too drunk to hurt himself."

"Thanks for telling me," said Fran. "Although earlier on, you told us Tara didn't talk about him being violent."

"That was the only time. I think she felt proud of herself. She'd made an effort, you see."

Silence fell for a few moments, then O'Neill said, "Tell us about her relationships at the salon."

Yvonne thought for a moment. "Tara's a bit jealous of Mandy, I think, because Mandy is doing the practical stuff. Tara's a great stylist but her hands didn't survive the different solutions or wearing the rubber gloves."

"What about Dale and Marcus?" asked O'Neill.

"Marcus was her favourite. She was very upset when he was killed. I'd never met him but she said he was really good looking with wonderful long blond hair."

"And Andrew? Did she see him much after hours?"

Yvonne shook her head. "About once a week when the Thing went out. I think she was only in lust with Andrew. He was her way out, not murder. She said he was young, but at least he knew there was more to foreplay than her husband could manage – his idea of foreplay was putting his cold feet on her warm bum."

Fran smiled and then noticed that Yvonne looked a little pensive. "Is there something else?"

"I'm not sure. A couple of weeks after Denise was killed, Tara got a little bit secretive. She said she was having a drink with a man – it was a Sunday, I think. But she wouldn't say who it was."

"Who do you think it was?" asked Fran.

Yvonne shrugged. "I'm only guessing, but I think it was Marcus."

Thirty-One

The voice on the line sounded thin and worried, and at first O'Neill didn't recognise it.

"Mandy?" he queried.

"I don't know if it's important or not," she said hesitantly, "but I've remembered something. Tara remembers it too."

"Tell me about it," said O'Neill.

There was a slight pause before Mandy spoke again. "I'm sure it wasn't her, but it does seem strange and it was my fault really . . ."

"What was, Mandy?"

"I took Mrs De Souza's coat from the rack in the staff room . . . but she didn't have her handbag with her. I don't know why I didn't notice it before."

"Did she normally keep her handbag with her in the beauty salon?"

"Yes . . . but the reconstruction reminded me that I didn't remember seeing her handbag *at all*. It's a shoulder bag with a roped gold and black chain."

"You've been a great help Mandy, thank you."

"Have I?"

"Sure you have," said O'Neill as his eyes rested on Fran's shoulder bag strung from her office chair.

He couldn't resist it. What did a woman like Fran carry in her handbag? He knew that Denise carried keys, a purse, a neatly folded handkerchief, a powder compact and lipstick and a fountain pen and that her diary was missing, probably stolen. He opened Fran's bag and inspected the contents. There was a make-up bag, set of keys, a diary, a notebook, three ballpoint pens, a ball of screwed up paper tissues, half a packet of Polo mints, several scraps of paper plus a pair of thin rubber gloves. He was so engrossed he didn't hear her approaching footsteps.

"What the hell are you doing?" she demanded.

"Calm down, Fran. I'm only rifling through your bag in the spirit of genuine investigation."

"Really," she said, sounding totally unconvinced. "In that case, why not wait until I came back and then I could empty my bag for you?"

O'Neill smiled, ignoring her indignant expression. "Would you go to the hairdressers without your handbag?"

Slowly, she relaxed a little. "So your searching of my bag really is in the nature of work?"

He nodded. "Well, would you?"

"Very unlikely. My keys are quite bulky and I'd be lost without my diary."

"That's as I thought. And now I suppose you'd like to know what it's all about."

When he'd finished, Fran said, "Are we going to see her now?"

"I thought we'd interview her here."

Mrs De Souza arrived an hour later looked slightly flustered, which in Fran's experience was perfectly normal. Only those well used to police stations appeared nonchalant.

"Would you like some tea?" asked O'Neill, as they settled themselves in a bare interview room.

Anna De Souza shook her head. "I hope this won't take too long. I really don't know any more than I've told you before."

"It's about your handbag," said O'Neill.

Anna's hand tightened around the gold corded strap. Then she smiled. "Well it hasn't been stolen, Chief Inspector."

"I can see that," said O'Neill slowly. "Mandy Willens seems to think you didn't have your handbag with you the day Denise was murdered."

Coolly she gazed at him. "Well, how silly of her. Of course I had my handbag. She was mistaken."

"Was Tara mistaken too? She also says she didn't see your handbag on that day."

"Chief Inspector, if all the staff say I didn't have my handbag – so what? I know that I did. How could a woman go anywhere without a bag? It contains firstly my keys and secondly my cheque book and purse. I would be bereft without my handbag. Why is it so important, anyway?"

"I think you left your handbag in the salon on purpose and slipped back into the salon, unnoticed, to reclaim it. And for reasons I'm not sure of yet, you murdered Denise Parks."

Anna De Souza stared at him incredulously. Then she laughed and laughed. "Why on earth would I want to kill Denise Parks. That's ridiculous."

"Is it?" said O'Neill. "She seemed to know quite a few people who would cheerfully have killed her."

"Well I wasn't one of them. What possible reason could I have?"

O'Neill stared at her. She wasn't fazed, she seemed totally confident and his optimism began to fade.

"Perhaps you had a dark secret in your past, Mrs De Souza."

Her blue eyes gazed at him almost sorrowfully. "Chief Inspector," she said resignedly. "What do you suppose I've been up to? A secret love child of a Tory MP, maybe?

235

Be realistic. I'm a respectable married woman, there are no skeletons in my cupboard."

"And your husband's cupboard?"

"No, of course not," she blustered.

O'Neill saw the fear in her eyes, heard the slight tremor in the sharp retort, and knew he had found her Achilles' heel.

"We'll conclude the interview there, Mrs De Souza. Thank you for coming."

"But I . . ." she floundered. O'Neill knew she wanted to defend her husband and, not being given a chance, she flapped horribly like a dying fish.

"We'll be sending for your husband, Mrs De Souza."

"He has nothing to do with . . . Denise Parks," she said between her gritted, perfect teeth. "He doesn't need this . . ."

"Why is that?" asked O'Neill.

She sighed. "He's been under a lot of stress lately. Dentistry isn't an easy profession, it's hard work, physically and mentally. He couldn't possibly be of any help to you."

"He does have a connection with the Parks family. Janine works for him and Denise was a patient."

"So is half of Fowchester. That doesn't mean anything. First of all, you tell me some nonsense about me not having my handbag, then you suggest my husband needs to be interviewed. I think you're clutching at straws."

O'Neill smiled, "Thank you for coming, Mrs De Souza. Please ask your husband to ring me . . . soon . . . and I'll arrange to see him at his convenience."

Anna De Souza glared at both O'Neill and Fran, muttered, "Good day," and left, leaving in the air a faint trace of expensive perfume.

Henri De Souza rang at ten p.m. "I believe you want to speak to me, Chief Inspector?"

"Just to get a few things cleared up."

"Shall I come now?"

"There's no need for that, sir. Tomorrow will be fine."

There was a short pause and when he spoke again O'Neill could hear the change in his voice. "I really think I should come now," he said. "You see . . . I want to confess. My wife is entirely innocent. I'm the guilty one."

Thirty-Two

As O'Neill waited for Henri De Souza to arrive, he felt a strange sense of emptiness. "Jasus . . . how could we have got it so wrong?" he said to Fran. She stared at a blank computer screen and muttered, "We've had sexy underwear, tea-leaves, abortions, babies in formaldehyde, an assault with boiling water, a short siege in a loft, nasty cards, and now the local dentist wants to confess."

"Don't forget suggestions of rape, incest and insanity."

"Whose?" asked Fran.

"Janine's of course. Our insanity is still mere potential."

They sat in silence then, watching the main road for a sighting of Henri's car. The main road, however, remained desolate in the dark gloom of a wintry Fowchester night. The police station itself was quiet except for the occasional distant phone ringing or muted footsteps. Could be two a.m., thought O'Neill.

Breaking the near silence, Fran said, "What reason could Henri De Souza have for killing Denise and probably Marcus?"

O'Neill shrugged. "Protecting someone. Maybe Denise knew something about his mother or his sister or, of course, Anna. She might have had an abortion years ago. People may have been sympathetic to a single woman but if Anna was married and just didn't want children

. . . perhaps they thought an abortion would spoil their respectable image."

Fran thought for a moment. "Those preserved babies – we haven't yet found out where the formaldehyde came from. A dentist would be able to acquire it, no questions asked, wouldn't he?"

"Sure he would. That's a possibility, Fran. I won't be taking bets on it, though. As a motive for one murder, it's a bit thin; as a motive for two, it's so thin it's transparent. If he's risking everything to rid the world of Denise and Marcus, I'd expect something pretty devastating."

They fell silent again and Fran couldn't stop herself yawning with sheer tiredness. It was already ten-fifteen and there was still no sign of Henri.

"Don't let me keep you up, Fran," said O'Neill with a smile.

Fran heard the car first. "No chance of that, Connor. He's here."

They met Henri De Souza in reception. His olive skin looked sallow and his eyes were red and slightly bloodshot. In the interview room, he was offered tea but declined it. "Just take my statement," he said bleakly.

"Before I take a formal statement," said O'Neill, "I'd just like to ask you a few questions."

Henri nodded, then coughed harshly and seemed to struggle to catch his breath. He refused Fran's offer of a glass of water.

"My first question," said O'Neill, "if you're sure you feel up to it is: *why?*"

There was a short pause in which they could hear Henri's slight wheeze. "I have asthma," he explained, seeming embarrassed. "Denise Parks was blackmailing me," he began. "Marcus too. I thought I could get away with it. But you took an interest in Anna and it wasn't fair on her."

"I see," said O'Neill slowly. "Why were you being blackmailed?"

Henri's mouth tightened. "I don't have to tell you that at this stage, if ever. Suffice it to say it was enough to cause me to commit murder."

"Allow me to get this straight, Mr De Souza. You're telling me that Denise and Marcus were blackmailing you for money."

"I didn't say anything about money," said De Souza. "There was no money involved, but it *was* blackmail."

O'Neill studied Henri De Souza's face and general demeanour. He was not the type, O'Neill decided, to commit murder on the basis of one impulsive moment. He was an organised man, a planner, probably meticulous.

"Tell me," said O'Neill, "about the day you killed Denise."

Henri swallowed and gave a slight cough before answering. "I knew Denise would be at the salon that Saturday morning – her appointments nearly always coincided with those of my wife. I saw a patient and left the surgery by the side door. It took me less than ten minutes to reach the salon. I entered by the side door, obviously no one saw me. I killed Denise and left by the same door."

"It appears then, Mr De Souza," said O'Neill leaning back his chair, "that you arrived and left without a single soul seeing you. Not only that, but it seems you were not missed at your own surgery. Sure, we are putting our hearts and souls into finding the murderer but so far you're not convincing me that you're the one."

De Souza looked strangely crestfallen. "The fact that I wasn't seen is odd, I admit, but I can assure you, I'm the perpetrator of both crimes."

O'Neill caught Fran's eye and they both tried not to smile. O'Neill had heard many confessions, been saddened by some, sickened and horrified by others.

This was the first time he'd been both amused and puzzled. Henri De Souza had neither convinced them, nor did he seem convinced himself.

"It seems to me, sir," said O'Neill laconically, "that honesty might be the best policy. It's getting late, my DS and I are both tired and want to go home. I could question you further, especially with regard to the murder of Marcus . . . however, perhaps a stay in the cells overnight might make you want to retract your confession. We wouldn't want to be accused either of failing to take a confession seriously, or of letting a murderer off the hook."

Henri gave a faint smile as though relieved. "I'm sure it's for the best that I stay here for the night."

"That's one way of looking at it," said O'Neill. "We will, of course, want a formal statement in the morning and we'll want your wife to also answer a few questions."

"My wife knows nothing of this. I'm the guilty one . . . please don't involve her."

"Your wife *is* involved . . . simply because she's married to you. We have no choice."

Henri stared bleakly at O'Neill for several seconds, then silent tears began to run down his thin cheeks. His eyes closed and his shoulders slumped. He was a man totally defeated and both O'Neill and Fran watched him being led to the cells feeling vaguely guilty, as though somehow there was something else they could have done.

O'Neill gave instructions that Henri should be checked, without fail, every fifteen minutes, and that if he seemed overly distressed the doctor should be called.

O'Neill and Fran left the station just after eleven. As Fran opened the car door and got out, O'Neill, as usual, had a strong urge to follow her, but he resisted and merely waited until she'd entered the house before driving away.

He saw her lights snap on and watched as she drew the curtains.

He felt depressed as he drove back to his flat, because he knew the end of the investigation was nigh and it could well be the last case he would work on with Fran. Which is more important, he asked himself – your job or Fran? And the answer was as clear as the light of a full moon in a dark and cloudless night.

At seven-thirty the next morning, O'Neill walked into Fowchester Police Station to see Anna De Souza sitting in the reception area. She wore a large-collared camel-hair coat, her head bowed into it as if she were being sucked into the coat itself. He presumed she was asleep and he signalled to the desk sergeant not to wake her yet, so that he'd have time to drink coffee. The sergeant mouthed, "She's been here for hours – wants to see her husband."

O'Neill mouthed back, "Ring me when she wakes."

As O'Neill approached his office one of the cleaners, known only as 'Bluey' because of her blue-rinsed hair, was leaving carrying a black bag of waste paper in both hands.

"Morning, Mr O'Neill. You're early." Bluey was fat, nearly sixty and always cheerful. The station would miss Bluey when she retired because she raised spirits and was a font of good advice, usually ignored. The recipients would often say, 'Bluey was right' and anyone with a problem unsolved would be teased with 'Bluey was right' comments.

"I've no good woman to keep me at home," responded O'Neill.

"You need a bad woman," she laughed. "By the way, I found a slip of paper stuck to the bottom of your waste bin. I've put in on your desk – just in case."

"Just in case of what?"

"It could be important," said Bluey. Then she added

with a slow shake of her head, "You should get more sleep."

The note was placed in splendid isolation in the middle of his newly polished and tidied desk. Hand-written, badly, it merely said: 'Local radio prog. approx. time of death – phone in on AIDS.'

O'Neill's instant reaction hung somewhere between elation and fury. Fury at himself for forgetting to check up on the programme, and fury at the idiot who didn't bring it to his attention. Elation, though, won a surprised Bluey a resounding kiss on her plump cheek.

Fran's arrival at eight a.m. coincided with a call from the desk sergeant to say Mrs De Souza was now wide awake and demanding to see her husband and O'Neill.

"Get her taken to one of the interview rooms, I'll see her there," said O'Neill as he simultaneously flashed the note in front of Fran.

"It could be a red herring," said Fran.

"No," said O'Neill. "This is it."

In the interview room, Anna De Souza still seemed huddled into her coat but she said in a calm voice, "I would like to see my husband, Chief Inspector. He's very depressed and anxious at the moment and whatever he's told you, he can't be trusted."

O'Neill sat down opposite her and said quietly, "Last night your husband confessed to two murders. Depression and anxiety don't lead to murder confessions, in my experience. Perhaps you'd like to tell us all about it."

Anna's lower lip trembled and she clasped her hands tightly in front of her. "I would like to see my husband. Now."

"Why?" asked O'Neill.

"Why?" she echoed. "We have things to discuss."

"I'm sure you discussed the situation quite fully when he came to make his confession last night."

"But I . . . must see him. Please . . ." Her voice trailed off miserably as if fully realising the hopelessness of the situation.

"I think in the circumstances, Anna, we should have a little talk first and then you can see your husband."

There was a long pause as if she were searching her mind for options available to her and, realising she had none, finally said, "What do you want know, Chief Inspector?"

"I'm not going to shilly-shally with you," said O'Neill. "I'll make my questions simple and direct. Are you understanding me?"

She nodded, a faint line of perspiration showing on her upper lip.

"I have reason to believe," said O'Neill, slowly and deliberately, "that you killed both Denise Parks and Marcus. The forensic evidence will undoubtedly prove that you did, so the sooner you tell us why, the sooner you will be able to see your husband."

"I didn't . . . I didn't . . ." She took a deep breath and continued in a voice that barely rose above a whisper. "I didn't mean to kill Denise. I paid Tara with a twenty-pound note I had in my pocket. She was busy at the time; I don't think she noticed I didn't use my purse. I got outside and realised I'd left my handbag behind. I went back through the side door. I didn't see Denise at first, she was behind the curtains. 'I've got your handbag, Mrs De Souza,' she said. She was sitting there in the hot box – like an evil . . . witch. My handbag was at the side of the hot box. 'I've put it there for safe keeping.' I picked it up and was about to leave when she said, 'There's a phone-in on the radio, a subject dear to your heart.' I listened of course, for a few moments. Then I asked her what she meant. 'Well, my dear,' she said, 'surely you realise your husband is a sufferer?' I remember feeling sick and faint. She was still talking, saying that she'd had vague suspicions for some time. That she'd have to change dentists, that most patients would if they had any sense. I looked round for some way to shut her up. There was a pair of plastic gloves in the bin. I put them on. I knew I was going to shut her up. I'd pulled the curtain around her – she was still talking. I tried to calm down but I couldn't . . . all I needed was a weapon. I walked into the staff room – I suppose I wanted to be stopped – there was no one around, so I grabbed a can of mousse from one of the boxes. I went back. The last words she said were, 'You'll be better off with out him, dear – he's got Marcus, after all.' And then I killed her. Afterwards I took her diary from her handbag. There was nothing in it – just appointments. I burnt it."

She relaxed back into her chair as though both relieved and exhausted. She closed her eyes. When she opened them again, O'Neill saw that she was dry-eyed and completely composed. "I'm not sorry I killed her," she said, "but I am sorry I killed Marcus."

"I presume your husband is bisexual and Marcus was his lover."

"You presume wrong about Henri. He's not bisexual, he's homosexual, but you're right about Marcus. He and Marcus were lovers, but on a casual basis. Marcus was also my friend. I used to lunch with him occasionally out of town. He didn't want Dale to know about Henri for obvious reasons. Marcus loved Dale but he could be promiscuous. I arranged to meet him that night at the salon. Marcus was out and I wanted Marcus to tell me that he'd taken an HIV test. He was drunk, he said he wanted me to cut his hair, he said he loved Dale but he felt trapped. Cutting his hair would show Dale he didn't own him. I said I couldn't cut hair but he kept insisting loudly and I was afraid Dale would hear us, so I agreed.

He said that using his best scissors I couldn't go wrong. I chopped off his ponytail and when he saw himself in the mirror he was very upset. I kept asking him if he'd taken the test because I was worried about Henri. He turned nasty – said he always practiced safe sex and what was I worried about, anyway? Was I worried about my precious reputation or was I merely trying to protect my source of income? If I really cared about Henri, as he did, he said I'd let him 'come out' and be his real self."

Anna paused and gazed at O'Neill with bright, almost feverish eyes. "I couldn't let him say such things to me. I starting stabbing . . . he couldn't say I didn't care about Henri. Henri was mere sexual gratification to Marcus. To me . . . he was my whole life. I knew Henri was gay when I married him. He told me he would never sleep with me, that we would never have children . . . but that he would always love and cherish me. And I love him now more then ever, and he loves me and always has." She swallowed hard and rubbed her hands as though she were feeling cold. "I suppose you find that difficult to understand?"

O'Neill nodded. "It seems you sacrificed a great deal in your marriage."

Anna smiled fleetingly. "I had affairs that meant nothing but physical release. Strange, isn't it? All my married life the only person I ever really wanted sexually was the man I couldn't have, the man I loved longest and dearest."

"I'm very sorry," said O'Neill.

"Don't be," said Anna. "We'll both die soon but we'll always be together in death."

She pulled the collar of her coat up. "I'm glad I haven't cried," she said. "Henri wouldn't want me to be upset. I have to be brave for his sake. Appearance is so important, isn't it?"

Thirty-Three

Anna De Souza's confession left both O'Neill and Fran subdued for several days. As they ploughed through the termination paperwork and tried to work out where they had made mistakes, how procedures could be improved and how they could have avoided some of the time-wasting, their eyes would meet in sympathetic recognition. Recognition of what, O'Neill wasn't sure, perhaps it was that this would be their last case together.

O'Neill's offer of a tango and celebratory meal hadn't materialised, partly because neither he nor Fran could manage to feel any jubilation at the course of events. Henri, it seemed, had been HIV positive for some time, acquired not from Marcus but a from an encounter made dangerously casual by the overuse of alcohol and the underuse of condoms.

Dale had been told a minimum about Marcus's liaison with Henri and in true Dale fashion, he offered to help Henri 'at any time, dear heart'. The salon continued as before and O'Neill was gratified to see Dale responding well to being 'mother hen' to Mandy and Tara.

As loose ends went, Janine had remained just that. Although there had been an initial improvement in her condition, now it seemed she was still very disturbed and depressed. O'Neill decided to see for himself, less out of desire to find out information that would now be purely academic, more as a simple excuse for leaving the office for an afternoon.

The sun shone weakly but at least it shone, and their first sight of the hospital was quite cheering: a large country house set amidst green rolling lawns with a wooded area at the back, plus tennis courts, a cricket pitch and a small golf course. "Not crazy golf," said O'Neill. "Rather bad taste in the circumstances." Then they both laughed.

Janine was painting in the art room when they arrived but she left it easily enough. "Come and see my room," she said. "I'm glad you've come."

They followed her to her room. "I've got some new clothes," she said, opening a small wardrobe. Fran noticed that Janine looked more normal. She wore jeans and a red checked blouse, her nails were painted, she wore eye make-up and a bright red lipstick. "The staff take me shopping," she said cheerfully, "which I really like, and this room is lovely and warm."

Fran found the room too warm, but it was pretty and comfortable with pale tangerine walls and matching lampshades, a small bookcase and a bedside table stacked with books. On a cork board Janine had put up postcards and pictures of pop stars.

"You seem to have settled in well," said O'Neill.

"I like it here," said Janine. "Everyone is so kind. It's just like a hotel."

O'Neill looked at her quizzically. She laughed at his expression. "I know it's not a hotel. It's a hospital, I know that. I'm better now, I really am. I'm thinking of training to be a nurse. I've got my own nurse here – Sally. She's wonderful, I tell her all my problems."

"We've come to see you today to let you know that we have found out who killed your sister."

A puzzled look crossed Janine's face and she turned

to stare out of the barred windows at the lawns and the trees.

"They have to have bars on the window to stop people trying to get in." Then she laughed again. "My sister's coming to see me soon. She can't visit often, she's looking after Gran."

"Oh, I see," said O'Neill. He signalled to Fran with a flick of his head towards the door that it was time to leave.

"It was very nice of you to come and see me," said Janine. "I'm so sorry I can't remember who you are, but Sally says I'll remember in time."

They left Janine in her room selecting a book to read and then toured the corridors to find a member of staff. The non-uniformed staff were almost indistinguishable from the patients and it took some time to find Janine's key worker, Sally. She was short and plump with kind blue eyes and a very soft voice.

"Janine is strongly in denial at the moment," she said earnestly. "The art therapist believes a breakthrough is possible at any moment. But at this moment in time she's refusing to accept the past and is quite happily living for the moment."

As they drove away O'Neill said, "Are you living for the moment Fran, or is it something only the mentally ill can do?"

Fran smiled. "Are you trying to be deep and meaningful, Connor?"

"I've been trying to be deep and meaningful with you, Fran, ever since I first met you. You'll have none of it, will you?"

"Perhaps your blarney hasn't been up to scratch. To be honest, I haven't seen you turn on the charm with a woman for ages."

O'Neill's hands tightened on the steering wheel.

"You know full well I've only got one woman on my mind."

"I've been thinking about that," said Fran. "And I think it's time you changed your approach."

"What's that supposed to mean?"

"It means," said Fran, placing a hand on his knee, "less work, more wining and dining, more moonlight and roses."

O'Neill smiled broadly. "At this rate you'll be wanting me to show you how to tango."

"I'll believe that when I see it," laughed Fran. "Any man who'll dance the tango with me has got to be special."

O'Neill stopped the car in a lay-by, held her face in both hands and said, "I'll be showing you now just how special I can be."